MURDER ON PRINCIPLE

Also by Eleanor Kuhns

The Will Rees series

* available from Severn House

MURDER ON PRINCIPLE

Eleanor Kuhns

SEVERN
HOUSE

First world edition published in Great Britain and the USA in 2021
by Severn House, an imprint of Canongate Books Ltd,
14 High Street, Edinburgh EH1 1TE.

Trade paperback edition first published in Great Britain and the USA in 2022
by Severn House, an imprint of Canongate Books Ltd.

severnhouse.com

British Library Cataloguing-in-Publication Data
A CIP catalogue record for this title is available from the British Library.

ISBN-13: 978-0-7278-5007-2 (cased)
ISBN-13: 978-1-78029-797-2 (trade paper)
ISBN-13: 978-1-4483-0536-0 (e-book)

All Severn House titles are printed on acid-free paper.

MIX
Paper from
responsible sources
FSC
www.fsc.org   FSC® C013056

Typeset by Palimpsest Book Production Ltd.,
Falkirk, Stirlingshire, Scotland.
Printed and bound in Great Britain by
TJ Books, Padstow, Cornwall.

ONE

Totally focused on the current state of politics and the coming election between John Quincy Adams and Thomas Jefferson – Will Rees did not care for either candidate – he did not hear the hoofbeats pounding up behind him. He was on the last leg of his journey from town and he could in fact see the turn off to the lane that led to his gate.

'Rees,' Constable Rouge called. 'Will Rees. Stop.'

Rees darted a glance over his shoulder and, spotting the churning legs of Rouge's bay, reluctantly pulled to the side of the road. As the mud-splashed forelegs pulled alongside of the wagon, Rees tipped his head back to look into the face of his pursuer.

Black-haired and black-eyed, and with a scraggly beard, Rouge looked even more unkempt than usual.

'What's the matter?' Rees asked in annoyance. 'I just left town.'

'You didn't stop by the tavern,' Rouge said. A tavern owner by trade, he also served as the town constable. With a sinking feeling, Rees guessed Rouge was not here to discuss ale.

'What happened?' he asked in resignation.

'We have a body,' Rouge said.

'Of course we do,' Rees said. Although not a constable or even a deputy, but with a gift for detection, he had assisted Rouge, and many others besides, in identifying murderers. Still, Rouge's sudden appearance surprised Rees. The constable, who always tried to best Rees, would not ask for help if he could avoid it.

'Where?'

'Here. On your farm.' Rouge grinned, revealing his stained and rotted teeth.

'What?' Rees cried, aghast.

'Yes.' Rouge tipped his flat-brimmed hat back. He had worn that headgear ever since Rees had known him and the brim was ragged from the constant application of Rouge's fingers. He looked at Rees's horrified expression and chuckled. 'But not on the acreage you farm. Where they do it.' He nodded to the fields on Rees's right. The Shakers from the nearby community of Zion tilled this section of the farm that Rees's wife had inherited. The issue of ownership – the Shakers laid claim to the property – still was not resolved.

'Who found the body?' Rees asked. It was already within two weeks of November's end and the furrows between the cut stalks glistened with ice. Few would choose to be out and about now.

'Brother Jonathan,' Rouge said, referring to the senior Elder at Zion. 'He sent a boy into town. Jonathan said he was searching for a lost cow.' He grimaced to illustrate his disbelief.

Rees ignored Rouge's doubt. The relationship between constable and Shaker Brother had been conflicted, Rees would say antagonistic, since their first meeting. But the fact that the body was found on property the Shakers farmed, and Brother Jonathan had found it, would place the suspicion on them.

'He's waiting with the body,' Rouge said. And then, almost diffidently, he added, 'I thought, since it was found on your farm, you might want to join me.'

Rees stared at the other man in surprise. Where was the belligerent and self-confidant man Rees knew? But when he examined the constable's face, he noted the heavy eyes and pale cheeks. 'Are you all right?'

'Just a little tired,' Rouge replied, shrugging off Rees's query. 'Well, will you come?'

'Of course,' Rees said. He did not want his farm to be tarnished with even the suggestion he or any of those he loved could be guilty. And he knew that the more ignorant members of the town would immediately assume one of the Shakers was the murderer. Rees knew that could not be true. They were pacifists and to a large extent a kind and gentle people.

'Where do we go?'

Rouge pointed down the road, toward a dead tree. Now Rees could see a figure wearing black; Brother Jonathan no doubt.

'Go on,' Rees said. 'I'll follow you.'

Rouge dug his heels into the bay's sides and the horse jumped forward. A wave of cold dirty water splashed up, covering Rees's stockings with icy mud. He swore. He had not adopted the new fashion of trousers and his legs were already cold from the chilly fall air. Muttering under his breath, Rees slapped the reins down on Hannibal's back and they slowly started forward.

Brother Jonathan, warmly clad in a heavy coat, scarf and hat, was pacing back and forth. Besides the dead tree, missing its top and half its bark, and pocked with holes left by woodpeckers, there were several other smaller trees. A few rust-colored leaves still clung to their branches; otherwise they appeared as dead as the lightning-struck splintered trunk. Jonathan pointed over his shoulder at the weir behind him. 'This way is quickest.'

Rees climbed down from his wagon and went to examine the small dam. Most of the rocks that made up its construction were dry, although the thin sun glittered from some random bits of ice. 'All right,' he said.

'Isn't there any way to ride there?' Rouge asked unhappily. His lips tightening, Jonathan shook his head. Grumbling, Rouge dismounted. Rees eyed the constable's boots. Riding boots, almost to the knee, and with silver spurs attached at the heels. They did not look appropriate for a hike across the late autumn countryside. As Jonathan turned and started walking, Rouge said, 'Wait. Wait.' He detached the spurs and put them in the saddlebag. Then he tied his horse firmly to one of the trees and pronounced himself ready.

Rees had crossed the weir a few times, always in the summer when the water was low. Then it had been enjoyable. Now, with the wind sweeping across the water, it was quite cold. Rees could hear Rouge swearing as his smooth leather soles slipped on the rocks. They reached the other side and within a few steps crossed the narrow wooden bridge. The new stream ran along the edge of the fields. During dry times the Shakers used it for irrigation.

Now the three men entered forest. Fallen leaves formed a russet surface and crunched underfoot. Everything except the evergreens looked dead. 'How did you happen to find the body?' Rees asked Jonathan as they tramped deeper into the woods.

'You'll see,' Jonathan said.

'The constable said you were searching for a cow?' Rees persisted. Jonathan looked at him sharply. Rees hadn't meant to sound dubious, although the Shakers were so careful with their livestock the loss of a cow did seem a little unbelievable.

'Yes.' And then, spurred by what he thought was Rees's disbelief, Jonathan hurried on. 'She and some others were split from the herd. They are sick and need to be cared for separately. Several ran away. She is the only one still missing.'

'Ah.' Rees guessed one of the boys had been instructed to move these cattle and his inattention had led to the escape.

They walked more deeply into the forest and Rees began to wonder how they would make their way out again. Everything looked the same: the lichen-spotted, gray, leafless trunks all around, the reddish leaves underfoot, and the masses of downed trees tangled in the skeletons of climbing weeds. The green stands of the pines provided welcome relief to the eyes.

It was to one such thicket of pine that Jonathan pointed. 'The body is there. When you circle to the other side, you will see . . .' His voice trailed away.

Rees exchanged a glance with Rouge and they increased their pace. And, just as Jonathan had promised, as they neared the firs, Rees spotted something yellow on the ground ahead. It was not a fallen leaf yellow but a bright lemon. He began to trot, his shoes sliding on the damp leaves. The ground rose a little here but as soon as Rees crested the small incline, he saw the form on the ground; the bright waistcoat a beacon.

'Here,' he called to Rouge, who was struggling to keep his footing. 'He's here.'

Rouge panted up the slope to Rees's side. 'Sacre Bleu,' he muttered as he stared down at the body. 'What is this fashionable gentleman doing in our Maine woods?'

TWO

Rees inspected the body. The man lay on his back, arms and legs flung out as though he'd been dropped here, an unwanted parcel. But he was not a local man. No one, not even the wealthiest among the townsmen, dressed so fashionably. Besides the vivid yellow waistcoat, with another of red beneath it, he wore a frock coat and a white linen cravat. His fawn-colored pantaloons were tucked into Hessians, polished to a gloss. Like the under waistcoat, the turn-down cuffs on the boots were red. Over it all, he wore a long overcoat.

But he was bareheaded, his fair hair nestled in the leaves.

'Where's his hat?' Rees wondered aloud. 'A gentleman of such fashion would hardly be seen without one. And it would probably be of beaver, besides.'

'He had one,' Rouge said.

Rees turned an astonished glance upon the constable. 'You know him?'

'Yes. No. Mr Randolph Gilbert and I played cards a few times. He's been here a little less than a week. He and his man arrived when? Last Wednesday? Thursday?'

Rees nodded. Today was Monday. That would mean Mr Gilbert had been in town for about five days. Rees guessed Mr Gilbert had been dead at least one day, maybe two. The cause of death was not immediately obvious. The only marks Rees saw from this preliminary examination were a scattering of red spots marring the pale forehead.

'He is a Southern gentleman who came looking for some escaped slaves,' Rouge said, looking at Rees with his sharp black eyes. 'A girl and her baby who, he said, appeared white. He said he tracked them all the way up the coast. You wouldn't know anything about that, would you?'

Rees squirmed. Just one month ago he and his wife Lydia had returned from Virginia, where they'd gone at their friend Tobias's request to rescue his wife. But they had returned, not only with Ruth, but also with a young girl and her baby. He had done his best to keep this secret but word had clearly gotten out. 'We must get the body back into town,' he said instead of responding to Rouge. 'But how?'

'And how did he get here?' the constable asked, looking around.

'We are not too far from a lane we use during harvest,' Jonathan said. 'Here. I'll show you.'

He continued walking at an angle from the evergreens. Through the thick growth of the pines and the trunks of oak and maple, the deadfalls and the dead stems of last year's growth, Rees could see a faint lightening. He would not have noticed it at all if Jonathan had not begun walking to it. In the summer, it would be totally invisible.

'Wait here,' Rees said to Rouge as he hurried after Jonathan.

It took close to twenty minutes to reach the lane. They circled around tree roots, ripped from the ground and pointing to the sky, and pushed through the dead stems from last year. Rees paused several times to examine the ground, but the scuffed leaves told him only someone had come through here, and that someone was probably Jonathan.

'What?' Jonathan asked, watching Rees inspect everything around him.

'A strong man could have carried the body into the woods,' Rees said, adding, 'and it wouldn't have taken long.'

The lane, barely more than a track, was narrow and heavily rutted. Rows of apple trees stretched away on the other side as far as Rees could see. When he looked behind him, into the woods, he realized he could not see Rouge at all. The evergreens were clots of green against the ever present gray and brown.

'How did you happen to enter the woods?' Rees asked Jonathan curiously. 'These woods, right here?'

'I heard the lowing of a cow. She must have come this way.' Jonathan's forehead wrinkled anxiously. 'I don't want to lose her in the woods.'

'Whoever hid the body chose well,' Rees said. But for the sick cow, it might have lain there until long past next spring and by then no one would have been able to identify it. 'How far to your village?'

'Maybe twenty minutes, that way, walking,' Jonathan replied. 'By wagon, much less.'

'Hmmm. Good. Thank you. Let me fetch the constable . . .' Rees turned and walked back the way he'd come. If he hadn't had his eyes firmly fixed on the stand of pines, and if Rouge's black hat hadn't become visible, Rees would have soon been lost.

'We'll go through Zion,' Rees said when he reached the other man. He wasn't sure he could find his way through the forest to the weir.

'Are we far away?' Rouge asked. 'My feet are killing me.' He had found a log and was sitting upon it, legs outstretched.

'Not too far,' Rees said, not altogether truthfully. He held out a hand to help Rouge to his feet.

The two men followed the lane out of the forest, across the fields, and past the barns and sheds where the livestock were kept. Once they reached the village, Rouge refused to take another step. Rees realized the constable probably could not continue walking; by then he was limping and groaning with pain. 'Blisters?' Rees asked.

'I could have ridden my horse there,' Rouge replied sullenly, 'if I had known of that lane. Walking through the trees was not necessary.'

'No matter,' Rees replied. 'I'll get my wagon. We'll need it anyway to bring the body into town.' He sighed. This would not be the first time his wagon had been used to transport the dead. 'I'll tie your horse onto the wagon as well. You can wait here.' He started walking, wishing he had some way of letting Lydia know he would be late home. It was early afternoon now but by the time he finished transporting the murder victim into town and then returned home, dusk would be fast approaching. He wanted to be home before dark. He hadn't brought his lanterns; he hadn't thought he would need them.

Although he hurried, the walk to his wagon took longer than he expected. When he glanced at his pocket watch, he saw it was past three. As the sun dropped westward, the bald spots on the tree trunk shone white. Rees tied Rouge's bay to the back of his wagon and started for Zion. It did not help his mood to see Rouge seated comfortably on the steps to the Dwelling House and eating a large slice of bread and a slab of meat. Rees, who'd expected to eat his dinner when he arrived home, and was now quite hungry, scowled at the constable. 'Where did you get that?'

'One of the Sisters—'

'Don't worry, Will,' said Sister Esther as she appeared on the path. 'I made a plate for you too.' Rees could smell the beef and water rushed into his mouth. 'You don't think I would forget you, do you?' she added.

An escaped slave, she had joined the Shakers several years ago and was now one of the two Eldresses. She had become a good friend to both Rees and Lydia.

She handed the plate up to Rees and waited while he flipped aside the napkin and took a bite. 'Constable Rouge said you

found a body in the woods,' she said. Rees, his mouth full of
tender beef, nodded. Esther waited while he chewed and
swallowed.

'Brother Jonathan found him.'

'He went out to search for the sick cows,' Esther said with a
nod. 'I'm guessing you don't know much yet?' Since Esther had
assisted Rees and Lydia in their investigations several times in
the past, he readily replied.

'We don't know anything except he wasn't local. That we
know.'

Esther nodded and with a quick glance at Rouge, she said,
'I'm sure you gentlemen can do with some ale. Let me fetch
some for you.'

She disappeared again, down the path to the kitchen. Rees
concentrated on devouring the remainder of his meal. By the
time she returned, he had finished and after he accepted
the tankard, he returned the plate and napkin. Esther handed an
identical cup to Rouge. He took a large draught and then, staring
at his jug, said, 'I wish I could hire the Shaker's brewer. Their
ale is excellent.'

'Not likely,' Rees said dryly. 'Finish up. We still have to collect
the body and bring it to town.'

'I'll ride as far as I'm able,' Rouge said. He put the tankard
on the step and struggled to his feet. Groaning loudly, he limped
slowly to his horse. 'I think my feet are bleeding.'

'Fashion demands much,' Rees said unsympathetically. He
knew Rouge was proud of those boots. 'You should have guessed
we would need to walk to the body.'

Rouge threw him an angry glance. 'Sometimes you are simply
unlikeable,' he said.

Rees drove his wagon to the lane, and as far in as he could.
Jonathan waited by the entrance. 'I'm glad to see you there,'
Rees said. 'I don't think I could find my way to the body without
your guidance.'

Jonathan nodded. 'Neither horse nor wagon can press
through that underbrush. I took the liberty of bringing a wheelbarrow from the barn.' He gestured to the small wooden vehicle.
Mud and bits of straw still covered the bed. 'I know it's a little
dirty . . .'

'I don't think that deceased gentleman will care,' Rees said.

'I'll wait here,' Rouge said from his perch on the bay.

Rees and Jonathan exchanged a glance. Then, without speaking, they turned toward the woods.

Even the small wheelbarrow had to be manhandled through the underbrush and over the thick layer of wet leaves. Rees didn't complain. How else would they recover the body otherwise, unless he carried it from its current resting place, something he did not want to do. At least he had Jonathan's help. The Brother bent back branches and cleared sticks and branches from the path of the wheel.

Still, despite the cold, Rees was sweating heavily and had discarded his coat, placing it in the wheelbarrow, by the time they reached the body.

THREE

Blowing like a running horse, Rees upended the wheelbarrow and perched on the bottom to rest. He knew the trip back, with the body in the cart, would be even more difficult. For a few seconds, he stared blindly at the figure on the ground. Then he realized what he was staring at and stood up to examine the remains more closely.

The young man was probably mid-twenties. His wavy, dark-blond hair was cut close to the head in one of the newer styles. Rees picked up his hands and looked at them. Although the backs bore several scratches, the palms and fingers themselves were soft and unmarred by calluses. He did not work with his hands then and Rees would venture to say this gentleman did not work at all. Rigor had passed off completely so although the cold temperatures had inhibited corruption, Rees knew his initial estimate was correct. Gilbert had probably died within the last two days.

'What are you looking for?' Jonathan asked.

'The cause of this gentleman's death,' Rees said. He pried open an eyelid. Although the film that covered his blue eyes made anything difficult to observe, Rees thought he could see the red spots characteristic of strangulation.

But the fellow's cravat was scarcely disordered. Rees wondered if someone had retied it; the lacy folds were arranged simply. Rees untied the linen to expose the throat. Mottled bruises were clearly visible.

'This man has been strangled,' Rees said.

Rouge had told Rees that this Mr Gilbert had been hunting for an escaped slave. 'But this fellow does not look like a slave catcher,' Rees murmured to himself. Too well-dressed, for one thing. Still, if Gilbert had come north in search of the young girl Rees had rescued from Virginia, maybe someone connected with the escaped slave Sandy Sechrest had moved to protect her. Rees's thoughts flew to Tobias and Ruth. Although Rees had known Ruth all his life, he had only become attached to her and Tobias during the trip to rescue Ruth from the Great Dismal Swamp. They had returned just last month.

Had Gilbert found Sandy and attempted to re-capture her? Had Tobias tried to save her? Now Rees thought of Tobias's hands. They were not overly large. Would he be strong enough to strangle this man? And why bring the body here?

'We'll have to take him to the doctor,' Jonathan said, breaking into Rees's thoughts.

'We'd better get him into the wheelbarrow and wheel him out of the woods. The light will be going soon.'

Rees looked around. Here, in the forest under the trees, the light was already dimming. He did not want to be caught in this forest after dark. 'Yes,' he agreed.

They lifted the young man, who weighed far more than Rees would have guessed, and maneuvered him into the wheelbarrow. It promptly tipped over and spilled its cargo on the ground. Rees shuddered as the ghostly pale face stared up at him. 'Hold the handles,' Rees said. 'Keep it steady while I lift him . . .' Grunting, Rees bent over and scooped his arms under the body. With a shout, he jerked the body up and into the wheelbarrow. Jonathan staggered but kept the cart level. Rees wiped his sticky hands on his breeches, only realizing when he saw the dark streaks that he had blood on his palms. He stared at them in shock. Had

Mr Gilbert been stabbed and not strangled? But Rees had seen the bruises around the corpse's neck.

He looked up to meet Jonathan's horrified gaze. The Shaker Brother swallowed and said, 'Let's get the body to the doctor.' He did not say, and away from Zion, but Rees heard it nonetheless.

With Rees holding one side to keep the vehicle from tipping, they started back to the lane.

The front wheel caught on unseen roots and tangled in long stems. Jonathan was gasping for breath after only a few feet. Rees took the next turn; and soon found himself so breathless he had to stop. The muscles in his arms were already burning from the weight. His palms and fingers stung; he feared he would see blisters from this.

Jonathan took the next shift but, like Rees, he could not manage for more than a few minutes.

In that manner, they managed to reach the lane. By then, a significant amount of time had passed. When Rees glanced at his pocket watch, it was well past four and shadows had crept among the trees. In these woods it was already almost too dark to see.

Rouge, who had chosen not to dismount, stared down at the two sweaty and panting men and then at the body in the wheelbarrow. He had the good sense to keep silent; Rees would probably have turned on him for any remark at all.

'Can you at least help us shift him into the wagon?' Rees demanded, staring at the constable accusingly. Rouge swallowed and shook his head.

'I can't. My feet.'

Rees turned to Jonathan. 'Do you mind?' In answer, Jonathan took up the body by the ankles. Rees reached in and grabbed the man under the shoulders. 'One, two, three.' Together, they swung the body into the wagon bed. Rees pulled himself up and climbed into the wagon. Grasping the body's shoulders, he pulled the head toward the front, grunting as he straightened out the cadaver. He climbed down from the tail and leaned against the back to rest.

'Thank you,' he said to Jonathan. 'I don't think I could have managed without the wheelbarrow.' Still breathless, Jonathan inclined his head. Rees climbed into the wagon seat. 'Thank you again. Good luck finding your cow.'

'I'll start the search again tomorrow. It's too late today.' He glanced behind him at the dark woods.

Rees knew Lydia must be wondering what had happened to him. Clucking to Hannibal, he turned the wagon around and started for town. Rouge, who'd left, was out of sight. Rees was glad of it; he couldn't be civil to the constable just now.

Dr Smith was not pleased when Rees called him out of the surgery and was even less happy when he saw the body in the wagon. 'The constable warned me you would soon arrive. I don't understand your predilection for murders.'

Rees shrugged, looking over Dr Smith's head at the constable. He'd come through the surgery door and was standing there on thickly bandaged feet. He was quite pale and Rees regretted his ill-temper. Rouge must truly be in pain.

'Bring your wagon to the back,' Dr Smith said in a resigned tone of voice. 'My nephew will help you.'

Rees chirped at Hannibal. They followed the drive to the shed at the back. Rees had been here more than once, frequently with murder victims. A young man with a shock of reddish hair and bright blue eyes stood by the shed door.

'Hello,' he said, raising a hand to shake Rees's. 'I'm Ned.' He was probably close to the age of the victim, but instead of fashionable pantaloons and a silk waistcoat, he was in shirtsleeves and a bloodstained vest.

'You're helping your uncle?' Rees asked, glancing at the dark stains.

'Yes. I'll take over the practice when he retires.' Ned glanced at the body in the wagon bed. 'Hmmm. The constable said you found the victim in the woods?'

'Yes. I don't think he was killed there, though. Where did you go to school?' Rees asked politely.

'Dartmouth. The Geisal School of Medicine. Then I spent a year at the University of Edinburgh.'

'Scotland?' Rees couldn't help but think Durham, a backwater in the District of Maine, was an odd location for Ned to settle. Ned nodded but did not explain.

'Let's get this body into the shed,' he said. 'If you grab the feet, I can carry his shoulders.'

Rees hesitated and then nodded, unsure whether this stripling would be able to lift the upper portion of the body. But as they lifted the inert figure, Ned's arms bulged with muscles that were clearly visible through his soft linen shirt. In fact, as they carried the corpse into the shed, Ned took most of the weight.

They stretched out the body on the large wooden table. Ned opened both doors so the western facing opening would catch as much of the dimming light as possible. 'Help me with the greatcoat,' he said to Rees. As he began unbuttoning it, he turned to Rees. 'Did you do this? Button his coat?' Rees shook his head. Ned grunted and continued. Once the heavy coat lay on the floor, and as Ned leaned over the corpse, Rees said, 'Allow me to fetch the constable. He ought to see this.'

'I'm here,' Rouge said, hobbling through the door that led inside the house. He winced with every step despite the thick wad of bandages.

Ned looked at the faint bruising around the corpse's neck. Then he pried up an eyelid and examined the milky eye.

'He was strangled,' Rees said, discomfited by Ned's silence, 'but I don't think that was the cause of death. When I picked him up, I found blood on my hands . . .'

Ned nodded and unbuttoned both waistcoats. He pushed up the white shirt and inspected the corpse's belly. Finding nothing of note, he said, 'Help me turn him over.' When Rouge did not move, Rees hastened to obey. Once the back was exposed, Ned peeled off the jonquil silk waistcoat. The back of the silk vest was stained a dark brownish red. The red waistcoat was next; it too was stiff with dried blood. 'He was stabbed,' Ned said, gesturing at the white linen shirt. Even with the bloodstains, Rees could see the long rip in the linen. When Ned lifted the fabric to expose the skin, the long and deep gash was obvious. 'Strangled and stabbed. But it was the stabbing that killed him,' Ned said. 'Was there a pool of blood where he was found?'

'No,' Rees said. 'Not on the ground anyway.' He looked at his hands and then up at Rouge who shook his head.

'There was nothing.'

'As I said, I believe he was murdered somewhere else,' Rees
said.

'But I'm confused,' Rouge said, turning to Ned. 'Were there
two murderers?'

Ned shrugged. 'Not necessarily. It could be there was only
one – but he became impatient. Strangling another fellow is
neither easy nor quick. And this poor gentleman here on my
table might have had enough sense remaining to attempt to flee.
The murderer picked up a knife and . . .'

'Stabbed him in the back,' Rees said.

Ned nodded. 'He was dead before the killer hid him in the
woods. And he's been there since . . .' He pointed at the red and
purple mottling on the back. Rees, who was familiar with the
pooling of the blood at the lowest point of the body, nodded.

'How much time passed between his death and the placement
of the body in the woods?' Rees asked.

'Oh, almost none, I would say,' Ned replied as he leaned forward
and peered at the blotchy skin. 'His killer was exceedingly determined. Look here.' Motioning Rees to his side, Ned pointed
to the victim's back. 'Do you see this? The darker bruise underneath the stab wound?' Rees bent forward and peered at the
wound. He could smell the faint odor of decomposition and put
his hand over his nose and mouth. But, as he stared at the wound,
he saw what Ned had noted: a darker squarer bruise underneath
the discoloration left by the pooling blood.

'What do you think?' Rees asked. 'The hilt of a knife?'

'I'd say so,' Ned replied. 'This does not look like an unusual
wound. Made by an ordinary kitchen knife probably.' Picking up
the greatcoat, he spread it out and stroked the inside with his
hands. 'Soaked with blood,' he muttered.

'Wouldn't the blood have gotten on the killer's clothing?'
Rees asked.

'Most likely,' Ned said. Picking up a rag, he began wiping his
hands. 'He would have been covered with it. The victim bled
heavily. You'll know where this man was murdered when you
find a large bloodstain.'

'If the clothing absorbed the blood,' Rouge said, 'why would
there be a bloodstain?'

'Because the greatcoat was put on after. He wasn't wearing it when he was stabbed. After his death, he was re-dressed and discarded in the woods.'

'How do you know that?' Rees asked curiously.

'You have here a dandy, his clothing expensive and the latest fashion. He would not leave any establishment with his coat buttoned improperly.' Rees nodded slowly. That made sense.

'He might if he were in his cups,' Rouge argued belligerently.

'Perhaps. But there is no smell of alcohol. I believe this man was sober.' Ned stared at Rouge.

'And where do you suggest we look?' Rouge asked. Ned lifted his shoulders in a shrug.

'That's your first task, I suppose,' he said, unmoved by Rouge's frustration.

Rouge muttered a curse under his breath.

'One other thing,' Ned said. Rees looked at him. 'The motive for Mr Gilbert's murder was not robbery. He had a significant amount of money on his person. I will put it aside, in case we ever find a relative we can send it to. Otherwise, we will use some of it for his burial.'

FOUR

Night was fast approaching as Rees left town. Everything had taken far longer to do than he'd expected. He knew Lydia would be worried. He'd hoped, moreover, to stop in and visit Tobias and Ruth. Did they know this gentleman? Did Sandy, the young woman who had fled north with them? If they did, and she did, and Mr Gilbert had come north with the sole purpose of recapturing these people, they could be involved in his murder. Rees did not want to think it but the possibility kept running through his mind.

Now his visit would have to wait until tomorrow. But tomorrow Lydia could accompany him. That was the silver lining. She frequently could draw information from women that Rees himself would never have gotten.

He flicked the reins over Hannibal's back, urging him to run faster. The light was fading very quickly, even on the open road. Hannibal seemed eager also to reach his stall in the barn and have his supper; he broke into a rapid trot. The rhythmic clip-clopping of his hooves was curiously soothing, and Rees found his thoughts drifting to the murder.

Randolph Gilbert had come a long way to recapture Sandy. Although slave takers regularly searched the Northern states for escapees, Mr Gilbert was not one of the disreputable men whose livelihood rested on capturing these unfortunates. Besides, the hunt for Sandy seemed oddly specific. What was she to him?

Then there was the murder itself. Mr Gilbert had been both strangled and stabbed. Rees's first thought was that two people, acting in concert, had been involved. Thus far, he had no reason to suspect Tobias or Ruth, but Sandy Sechrest was living with them. Would they murder a man to keep their friend safe?

By the time he reached his farm gates, darkness had fallen and since the waxing moon had not yet risen, the farmyard was black. Rees unhitched Hannibal and released him into the paddock. It was far too dark to put the wagon away, and Rees didn't feel like struggling with his tinder box to light the lantern that hung on the nail by the door. Instead, he ran up the steps. Lydia flung open the door as he reached for the handle.

'Where have you been? I expected you hours ago.'

Rees caught that flicker of uncertainty that she had not lost since last spring. With a pang of guilt, for it had been his attraction to a circus performer that had planted the seed of her insecurity, he wondered if she would ever trust him completely again. He stepped inside and her gaze went immediately to the bloodstains on his breeches. He pulled her into his arms.

'We found a body,' he whispered into her ear. She pulled back and stared at him with wide eyes. 'I'll tell you more later,' he promised. Releasing her, he looked around at his children. 'And what is happening here?'

'Supper is almost ready,' Lydia said. He glanced at the table. He could see where his two youngest had already eaten corn meal mush by the splashes and spills. Sharon, the baby of the family, was almost two. She wouldn't be the baby for much longer. He glanced at his wife. Since the new baby wasn't due until April there were no obvious signs yet.

'I have something to tell you, Father,' said Jerusha proudly. His eldest girl, she had been only nine when he and Lydia had adopted her. Now she was quite the young lady. Her hair was up, her skirts were down, and she was almost Lydia's height.

'After supper, Jerusha,' Lydia said. Jerusha nodded and bent to scrubbing the table.

The only child missing was Simon. He'd elected to live with David, Rees's son by his first marriage. Rees missed both of them every day.

'I'm wicked peckish,' Rees said. 'I was too busy to eat any dinner.' He accounted the meat and bread he'd eaten around midday as more of a snack than a meal.

'Chicken and dumplings,' Lydia said, lifting the cover from the pot simmering over the fire and releasing the fragrance of chicken and sage into the room. 'We'll eat an early supper.' She smiled at her daughter. 'Jerusha won't mind. Wash your hands, Will.'

Rees went to the basin and poured in some cold water from the pitcher. With a smile, Lydia took pity on him and added some hot from the kettle so he had warm water to wash in. Rees scrubbed his hands twice. He'd been mucking about in last year's leaves and touched a dead body.

After drying his hands on a towel – one of the weaving projects where he'd made several mistakes – he joined Jerusha in setting the table. He was looking forward to spending time with his family and not thinking about murder or bodies or the possible guilt of his friends at all.

After supper, and the clearing up that followed, Jerusha usually sat down with her younger siblings and worked with them on their schoolwork. She concentrated on reading but also gave them mathematics and spelling from the blue-backed speller. Rees had become so accustomed to the scratching of chalk on the children's slates he scarcely noticed it anymore.

After finishing with her brother and sister, Jerusha would pull out her own books and study.

But tonight, as soon as Nancy and Judah had completed their

work to Jerusha's satisfaction, and she had put away the materials, she approached Rees where he sat reading the newspaper.

'Father,' she said. He glanced at her. She was twisting her hands nervously together.

'Are you ready to talk now?' he asked. When she nodded, he folded the paper and put it down. He really did not want to continue reading the paper anyway. Both of the presidential candidates and their supporters seemed to vie with one another to make the most inflammatory claims about their opponent. Alexander Hamilton, a supporter of Adams, warned that if Adams won, Jefferson, and his supporters would rise up and use physical force to prevent the Federalists from serving. Meanwhile, the Republicans led by Jefferson, believed, or pretended to believe anyway, that Adams and his party would change the law so he could serve as president for life. A local clergyman predicted that if Jefferson won, he would collect every Bible in the country and burn them.

Rees wanted to strangle the lot of them.

He sat down at the scrubbed table and looked at his daughter. She joined him at the table but did not speak, instead looking over her shoulder at her mother. 'I'm coming,' Lydia said, quickly drying her hands and tossing the towel at the sink. She hurried over and sat down. Jerusha looked at Lydia hopefully. 'This is your story,' Lydia said.

Rees felt his heart sink with dread. The last time Jerusha had been this nervous she had been on the verge of expulsion from school. Surely that could not be the case again; Jerusha and the Widow Francine had appeared to be dealing well together lately. Jerusha's enemy had left school and Rees had heard she'd married.

'Yes?' he said.

'Mrs Francine . . .' Jerusha began. She threw an agonized glance at her mother and when no help came from that quarter burst into rapid speech. 'She wants me to take over the teaching. In the school.'

'What?' Rees felt as if his chair had crashed to the floor with him in it.

'She's getting older,' Jerusha said. 'She can't manage some of the older boys anymore. The Whitehead boys especially.'

'Jerusha has been doing quite a bit of the teaching already,' Lydia interjected.

'I don't understand,' Rees said, mystified.

'She's offering Jerusha a job,' Lydia said. 'Not only will Jerusha be paid but the Widow Francine will waive the school fees for Judah and Nancy.'

Rees's gaze moved to his daughter. 'What about your chores here?'

'Jerusha will still live here,' Lydia said with a smile. 'And Nancy is old enough to take some of them. We will manage.'

'Do you want to do this?' Rees asked Jerusha.

'Oh yes,' she said, clasping her hands together and holding them so tightly her knuckles went white. 'I do. I love it.'

Rees gazed at his daughter for several seconds. Somehow, almost overnight it seemed, she had grown up and become a stranger. For a moment he wanted to grab her and hold her tight and say, 'Don't keep growing. Stay this age.' But of course, even if that was possible, he couldn't do it. She was already set on her own path. He heaved a sigh, guessing she would soon marry and have children of her own, as David had. It was a terrifying thought.

'Of course, you may do this, if you really want,' he said. Teaching in a classroom of loud children would never appeal to him. But Jerusha had her own dreams.

'Thank you,' Jerusha said, jumping to her feet and hurling herself at him.

'You're very welcome,' he said, laughing. He watched her dance away, humming as she picked up the speller and brought it to the fire.

'Not every father would allow his daughter to work,' Lydia said approvingly.

'Oh, she has always been the scholar of the family,' Rees said. At least she would still be home.

'Tell me about the body.' Lydia leaned forward so that Rees could lower his voice.

'Brother Jonathan found the victim,' Rees said, also bending so that they could speak without being overheard. 'In the woods near Zion. But, according to Rouge, on our property.'

'Oh dear,' Lydia said involuntarily.

'Yes. And he was a Southerner,' Rees added.

Lydia's cheeks blanched. 'A slave taker?'

'He was very well-dressed, far more fashionably than a slave catcher would be. The ones I've seen have been shabby and down at the heels. He told Rouge he was searching for a young girl and her baby . . .' As his voice trailed away, he directed a pointed look at his wife. When he and Lydia had rescued Ruth and Tobias from the Great Dismal Swamp, they had also taken Sandy and her baby. The federal law was quite specific. The slave's owner, or his representative, could come north to recover his property. Rees had been worrying about that ever since – and now it looked as though his fears had been realized.

'Maybe it is just a coincidence,' Lydia said. She bit her lip until a bead of blood bloomed. She did not seem to know she'd done that.

'Some coincidence,' Rees said. 'I thought, tomorrow, we should talk to Ruth and Tobias.'

'Surely you don't suspect them?' Lydia said, her voice rising.

'Shh.' Rees leaned closer. 'She is staying with them. Maybe they tried to protect her.'

'They are our friends!' Lydia exclaimed darting a quick glance at her children. 'I won't believe they are involved in murder. That is what you are thinking, isn't it?'

'I agree with you,' Rees said. 'But it is too early to worry. We don't know anything right now and won't until we speak with them.'

'And maybe not then,' Lydia said. But the anxiety did not fade from her eyes. Like her husband, she could draw a line connecting a slave owner and their friends.

FIVE

Annie arrived early the following morning. Rescued from a brothel in Salem, Annie had been brought to the Shakers by Rees and Lydia but had quickly discovered she had no interest in becoming a Shaker. She spent as much time as she could at Rees's farm, and he was dreading the day when his family asked him if she could stay permanently.

This morning, for the first time, he considered it. With Jerusha taking on a teaching post and unavailable to watch her younger siblings, Annie would be needed. He was glad to see her arrive.

After giving Annie some last-minute instructions, Lydia joined Rees outside. Despite wearing her oilcloth rain cape, she cast an anxious glance at the gray sky.

'I suppose now we must buy another horse,' he said as he checked Hannibal's bridle.

'Why do you think so?' Lydia asked, scanning the sky. It was a solid iron gray and although no rain was falling, she put up her hood.

'Jerusha won't want to walk to school,' Rees replied. 'Now that she is so grown up.'

Lydia smiled at him and patted his arm. 'She takes the cart most days now, anyway,' she said.

The ride was a cold one and both were glad to reach Main Street. Rees glanced at Rouge's tavern – where he was no doubt presiding over the customers from his bar – and thought long-ingly of hot coffee. He slowed down as they passed Commerce Street, preparing to make the next right turn into the tavern's yard.

'Look,' Lydia said, nudging him with her elbow. Rees followed her gesture. There, standing in front of the hat shop, was Aaron Johnson. Formerly a Shaker, he had been expelled for disobedi-ence. Rees privately believed that the Elders, as well as many of the other Believers, simply could no longer tolerate Aaron's surly and combative nature.

'I thought he left town,' Rees said. Aaron must be doing well. His clothing looked new and he wore those fashionable trousers as well as a brightly colored waistcoat and a top hat.

'I did as well,' Lydia said. She sounded faintly regretful. A former Shaker herself, she had left the community and Rees sometimes suspected she missed the peace and order, as well as the network of other women.

As the wagon continued moving, and Rees prepared to turn into the tavern's yard, Lydia put a hand on his sleeve. 'We should not stop. It is more important we speak with Ruth and Tobias,' she said.

So Rees pulled on the reins and the wagon swerved back into

the street. The farmer behind them shouted at them angrily. Rees knew he would not have been able to pull that maneuver on a summer Saturday, when the town was busier and the roads congested with traffic.

Tobias, a talented cabinet maker, lived over his small shop. Rees parked his wagon behind Tobias's vehicle. Then he and Lydia went down the steps to the workshop on the lower level.

'Rees,' Tobias said when his visitors stepped through the door. 'What brings you here?' He put aside the mallet and turned the chair upright.

'That is a beautiful piece of work,' Rees said.

'Thank you. Did you come here to put in an order for chairs?'

'No. I wanted to ask you and Ruth a few questions,' Rees replied. 'Brother Jonathan found—'

'A body in the woods,' Tobias supplied, completing Rees's sentence. 'The constable has done nothing but talk about it in the tavern. Why do you want to speak to us?'

'I thought – I hoped – you might know something about him,' Rees replied.

'Why would we?' Tobias said in surprise.

'I'd rather explain to both of you,' Rees said.

'Well, let's go upstairs then, where we can be more comfortable.' Tobias led the way up the interior stairs to the main floor. The fire in the fireplace was burning energetically and both the visitors shed their outer garments. Ruth greeted them with pleasure and offered refreshment: hot drinks and warm bread fresh from the oven.

After Lydia inquired after Ruth's health – her baby was due in less than two months – Rees got to the object of their visit. 'The body,' he said.

'He means the man found in the woods by Zion,' Tobias explained to Ruth.

'Oh yes, I remember you mentioned him,' Ruth said.

'He is from the South,' Rees said.

Both Tobias and Ruth stared at him blankly. 'An escaped slave?' Tobias asked.

'No. He's white.'

'A slave taker,' Ruth said with a gasp. Despite their births as free people, she and Tobias had been abducted by one of the slave catchers and sold in Virginia.

'I don't think so,' Rees said. 'He is well dressed. Very well dressed. I suspect he is – was – a gentleman. Or fancied himself one. His name is Randolph Gilbert.'

Ruth and Tobias exchanged a glance. 'We don't know him,' Ruth said.

'And why do you think we would?' Tobias asked, an edge to his voice. 'Are you implying we murdered that man?'

'I didn't mean to suggest that at all,' Rees said quickly. Not for the first time, he cursed his clumsiness.

'He meant no offense,' Lydia said. 'We just thought that, since we met no one in Virginia but those who lived in the village, and you both lived in the Commonwealth for some time, you might recognize the victim.'

Tobias glanced at Ruth. She had her hand pressed to her bosom. 'Do you believe he came after us?' she asked.

'Not after you,' Rees said.

'"Not after you" what?' Sandy, the young woman they'd taken from the Sechrest plantation, entered the room with her son, Abram. Both were as white as Rees and Lydia and Abram, whose father was the son of the plantation owner, had fair hair. 'What are you talking about?'

'A man was murdered near here,' Tobias said shortly. 'A white man. Rees here thinks we might have something to do with it.'

'That's not true,' Rees said. 'I mean, there was a murder victim found near here.'

'We believe he is from Virginia,' Lydia said, jumping in to rescue her husband.

'He might be a slave hunter,' Ruth put in.

'His name is Randolph Gilbert,' Rees said, turning to look at Sandy. She went pale and the hand holding Abram's tightened so that he whimpered and tried to pull free.

'I don't think . . . I probably don't know him,' she said loudly.

'Why should we help you?' Tobias asked Rees. 'If the victim is a slave catcher, well then, I say thank you to his murderer.' He darted a glance at Sandy's ashen face and said to Rees, 'I beg you, drop this investigation.'

Rees stared at the other man, too surprised by Tobias's sudden animosity to speak. Once again, Lydia came to his rescue.

'If he is a slave taker or, God forbid, someone sent here to look for you, we need to be prepared. To do that, we need to know everything about this man. Likeliest,' she added in a calming voice, 'the victim has nothing to do with any of us. But we can't know that without identifying him. And you are the only ones we know who lived on a plantation in the South and who might be able to help us.'

No one spoke for several seconds and the silence was becoming awkward when Sandy finally spoke. 'Where is he now?'

'With the doctor,' Rees replied.

'Then I suggest we look at him. I will recognize more of the plantation inhabitants than they do,' Sandy went on, gesturing to Ruth and Tobias. 'If we don't know him, that answers your question.'

'But this is no scene for a woman.' Will nodded at Sandy. She was only sixteen and seemed so delicate. Lydia shook her head at him. 'What I meant . . .' he began and then stopped, knowing he was floundering.

'We should all go,' Lydia said. 'Tobias can look at the victim first. But if he doesn't recognize him, then Ruth and Sandy should be invited in.' She turned a jaundiced eye upon her husband. 'And don't give me any of that claptrap about the weak woman. You know better.'

Rees did. Even if he believed that claptrap, he knew better than to say so in Lydia's hearing.

Her proposal being accepted, everyone put on their outdoor wraps and walked across town to Dr Smith's. He was very surprised to see them and not pleased, but Ned, after one glance at Sandy, volunteered to take them through to the shed. As arranged, Tobias – and Rees who wanted to observe – went to examine the body first. Rees could not tell from Tobias's impassive expression whether he knew Gilbert or not.

'Never saw him before in my life,' Tobias said with a shake of his head. He glanced at Rees as if to say 'See, I told you I was innocent', before returning to the surgery and the others.

Huh, Rees thought. If Gilbert threatened Tobias or his family, Rees could easily imagine Tobias lashing out.

Sandy came through next, without Abram, Rees was glad to see. She kept her hands clasped tightly together, steeling herself for this unpleasant experience. She took one quick look at the gray face on the table. Uttering a scream, she fainted dead away on the dirt floor.

SIX

Before Rees could respond, Ned swept Sandy up in his arms and carried her through the door into the surgery. 'What possessed you to permit a gently reared woman to see such a terrible sight,' Ned scolded Rees over his shoulder.

Rees puffed out a breath, amused in spite of himself. If only Ned knew of the challenges Sandy, an escaped slave, had already surmounted.

Rees did not follow Ned and Sandy immediately. Thinking that he might not have another chance to examine the remains, he paused by the body and lowered the sheet. The bruises on the victim's neck had come out in all their purple glory. Gilbert had been throttled by someone with large strong hands. Rees wondered if the victim would have died from strangulation if he had not been stabbed instead. Although it was possible only one person had been involved – Gilbert might have escaped and begun running away – Rees still considered the presence of two murderers not only conceivable but likely. He reminded himself to keep both options in mind.

Rees then pulled the sheet down to the body's waist. He saw a faint line of bruising on the victim's bicep as though he'd been grabbed by the arm. There were few defensive wounds on his palms; he had not feared his murderer. Or murderers. Rees turned the hands over and examined the backs. The knuckles on his right hand were reddened. Had he been involved in a brawl? Southerners, by reputation, were notoriously thin-skinned about perceived insults. But they resolved such conflicts with a duel, or so Rees had heard.

Everything about this man spoke of a life of privilege. Why

had he chosen to journey all the way to the District of Maine in search of escaped slaves? It was puzzling.

Flinging the sheet over the face, Rees followed the others into the surgery.

Choking and gasping as she pushed away the smelling salts, Sandy sat up. She promptly began to weep. Seeing his mother sobbing, Abram began wailing loudly. Dr Smith put up his hand and shook his head. Ruth and Tobias looked at Rees. But he did not want to explain anything while in front of others.

'We should take her home,' he said.

'Yes. Take her home,' Dr Smith agreed. 'Now. I can't have this caterwauling in my surgery.'

'But she is so distressed,' Ned protested, his expression softening as he looked at the beautiful young woman.

'We have patients to see,' Dr Smith said curtly.

'She'll be fine soon,' Rees said at the same moment. He pulled Sandy from the chair to her feet and hurried out the front door. He did not wait for the others to catch up or for Sandy to compose herself. 'All right,' he said as soon as they were in the road outside, 'tell me about that man.' He suspected she would have lied and claimed not to know him if her body had not betrayed her.

'Will, please,' Lydia said, running down the stairs. 'Don't interrogate the poor child on the street.'

'Let's go home,' Tobias said. 'We can sit before the fire and warm ourselves.' He looked at Sandy with concern. 'She can answer your questions there.'

But Rees was not disposed to wait. The walk to Tobias's shop – and Rees's wagon – was at least fifteen minutes away. Maybe twenty with Abram. He looked around for another meeting place and spied the tavern. 'Let's go,' he said, taking Sandy's arm.

'The tavern?' Lydia asked.

'It's closer. And at this time of the morning, it will be nearly empty.'

Within a few minutes, they were seated in one of the smaller rooms by the fire. This location would not have been Rees's choice; they were under Rouge's gaze, but it was empty. The few other customers, mostly folks waiting for the stage to Boston, were in the other room. When Therese, Rouge's cousin, approached, Rees ordered coffee for himself, ale for Tobias, and tea for the others.

'What do you have on the menu?' Lydia asked, eyeing Sandy who was still sniffling and quite pale.

'Fresh scones,' Therese said, smiling. 'One of that lot,' and she tossed her head toward the other room where the coach passengers were loudly conversing, 'insisted on them. We have plenty.'

'Fresh scones with butter and jam then,' Lydia said. 'And thank you.'

Lydia handed Sandy a handkerchief. Rees tried to restrain his impatience as they waited for the refreshments to arrive. He felt like he could not sit still and rose to his feet to stir up the fire although it did not need it. A large pot of tea came first with milk and sugar, then the ale. Perhaps sensing Rees's edginess, Therese hurried. A plate of the scones came next with the accessories on the side. Ruth took one and split it, filling it with both butter and strawberry jam. Then she broke it into pieces for Abram.

'The coffee will be a few minutes,' she said apologetically to Rees. 'I just put the pot on the fire.' Rees nodded, stifling his urge to order her away.

When they were finally alone, he looked at Sandy. 'You said you didn't know the man. Explain yourself.'

'Will,' Lydia said in reproof.

'Do you know Randolph Gilbert?'

Tears filled Sandy's eyes once again. 'Yes, that is the Mr Gilbert I know.' She pronounced the name in the French manner, without the 't'. 'I so hoped it was another gentleman with the same name. I prayed it was not Miss Charlotte's brother.'

'Miss Charlotte,' Rees repeated blankly. Who was Miss Charlotte?

'The new wife of Mr Sechrest?' Lydia asked in astonishment. 'The plantation owner?' Sandy nodded. 'The vile woman who beat you?' Sandy nodded again.

'He told the constable he was searching for an escaped slave,' Rees muttered. 'A young woman and her baby.'

'He was looking for me.' Sandy's voice broke.

'Surely Charlotte Sechrest could have hired some scruffy slave taker to hunt for you,' Lydia said. 'Why did her brother come all this way, to the District of Maine?'

Sandy stared at the window as though something outside had captured her attention. Rees knew that was impossible. Smeared with years of accumulated grime, the glass was far too dirty for her to see through it.

'What's the matter, girl?' Tobias said.

Hot color stained Sandy's cheeks and she clenched Lydia's handkerchief into a tight ball.

But Ruth, understanding something the others did not, reached over and put an arm around Sandy's shoulders. 'He wanted to buy you, is that it?'

'Yes. And Miss Charlotte promised me to him.' Now she looked up. 'When I protested, Miss Charlotte said I was uppity. I had no say in the matter. And she beat me.'

Rees nodded, recalling the desperate flight into the swamp with Sandy after she'd been severely whipped.

'Here comes the coffee,' Lydia said suddenly, in a cautioning tone.

No one spoke as Therese put the mug on the table.

'Leave the pot,' Rees said, as he splashed milk into the black brew. Therese obeyed and, knowing she was not wanted, scuttled away.

'As long as Abram's father was there,' Sandy said in a despairing voice, 'I was safe. But once she sent Gregory away . . .' She gulped and tears began running down her cheeks once again. Rees exchanged a glance with Lydia. They had learned much about the suffering of the enslaved people during their visit to the South; an experience that had prompted Lydia to join the Durham Antislavery Sewing Circle. Now she buttered a scone and put it in Sandy's hand.

'Eat something,' Lydia said sympathetically. 'And drink some tea. You'll feel better.'

Sandy choked down a bit of biscuit and took a sip of the hot beverage. 'That wasn't the worst,' she said. 'Randolph Gilbert is an evil and vicious man. Was so, anyway. Other women gossiped about him. He had depraved appetites, everyone said so. And once he was done with me – and no girl ever kept his interest for very long – he would sell me to a fancy house in New Orleans.'

'Dear God,' Lydia murmured. 'That is appalling.'

'I'm glad he's dead,' Sandy burst out. 'I pray all the devils in Hell torment him.'

There was a loud crash as crockery smashed to the floor. When Rees turned, he saw Therese, staring in dismay at the broken tableware at her feet. She still held a tray in one hand and had evidently been coming over to remove the dirty plates and cups.

She darted a quick horrified glance at Sandy. 'I'll come back later,' she said and fled.

'Oh, my dear,' Lydia said, putting a hand on Sandy's.

Rees glanced at the girl, whose skin was barely a shade darker than Lydia's and nodded. 'But that's not the point,' he said. And when the questioning faces of the others turned to him, he continued. 'Don't you understand? Randolph Gilbert tracked Sandy here. He knew roughly where she was. If someone hadn't killed him, he might have found her.'

'Then I thank the man who killed him,' Sandy said, her gaze going to her son. Since the status of a child rested on that of his mother, this blond toddler would have been dragged back into slavery. Abram smiled at her, his mouth full and his face sticky with red jelly.

Rees shook his head. They still weren't grasping his point. 'Listen. We have to assume that if Gilbert knew Sandy was somewhere here, in Durham, others know it,' Rees said, leaning forward and speaking vehemently. 'There may be other slave catchers still to come.'

Sandy went pale. 'They'll be coming for me,' she said faintly.

SEVEN

When Rees went up to pay the bill, Rouge grasped his arm and leaned so close Rees flinched from the odors of ale, sweat, and tobacco. 'Listen, you,' Rouge said. 'I know you are pursuing this investigation without me. I want to make sure you know you must tell me everything you learn.'

'Why do you think I'll learn something?' Rees asked.

'Because I'm not a fool. And I've known you a long time. And a young girl doesn't scream and cry and consign someone to Hell for nothing.'

Rees grinned, baring his teeth. 'Yes, all right. I planned to anyway.' Pulling his arm from Rouge's sweaty hand, Rees joined Lydia and the others.

They walked to Main Street in silence. As they turned down the lane that led to the cabinetry shop, the ladies, slowing their pace to match Abram's shorter stride, fell behind. Tobias sped up, walking more quickly to catch up to Rees. When they were several feet ahead, he spoke.

'I want you to drop the investigation.'

'What do you mean?' Rees asked. Lost in his own thoughts about Randolph Gilbert, he had not noticed Tobias's angry expression.

'I mean, don't apply yourself to identifying Gilbert's murderer. He was an evil man and of no loss to the world. Let the constable struggle along on his own.'

Rees stared at Tobias in mounting astonishment. 'But it is unlikely Rouge will determine the identity of the murderer without my help,' he said.

'I know.' Tobias threw a quick glance at Rees. 'Everybody experiences some successes and some failures. Let this be one of your failures.' He paused in front of his home and tipped his hat. 'Good day to you, Mr Rees.'

Rees mumbled something, he was too shocked to know what, and watched Tobias and the women disappear into the house. Tobias was a friend, a good friend up to now, and his sudden antagonism stung.

'What's the matter?' Lydia asked, looking up into her husband's face.

Taking her arm, Rees turned her toward the wagon. 'He wants me to let Gilbert's murderer go free.'

'What?' Lydia stopped and stared at her husband. 'That doesn't sound like Tobias.'

'I know.' Rees helped her over the step. 'Perhaps I am not

being fair. Tobias asked that I not investigate. He didn't specifically request that I free the murderer.'

'I perceive he has no confidence in the constable,' Lydia said dryly.

'Exactly,' Rees agreed.

'Do you think Tobias . . .' Lydia's words trailed away and she glanced unhappily at her husband.

'I don't know. His reluctance to see me investigate certainly does not argue for his innocence.'

'I don't want to believe Tobias is involved,' Lydia said.

'I know. But consider this, of every soul in this town, the only people who had any reason to murder Gilbert live in that house. I wondered about Tobias and Ruth when I first thought Gilbert was solely a slave taker. Now, well . . .' He stopped and shook his head.

Lydia remained silent as she settled herself on the wagon seat. Finally, exhaling a deep sigh, she said, 'I wish I could disagree with you. But truly, I can think of no one else in town who might have a reason to murder Mr Gilbert. The vast majority will not even know who he is.' She turned an anxious glance upon her husband. 'Surely it would be impossible for Ruth to take part in anything so physical. She is close to the end of her pregnancy.'

'Perhaps,' Rees said. He paused and added slowly, 'Of course, there is one more member of the household.'

'Sandy.'

'I would swear her swoon at seeing Gilbert was genuine and that she did not know he was in town. But she may be just a very fine actress. She admitted she knew the man. And her reasons for loathing him are understandable. I might be tempted to take a knife to Gilbert myself, if I were in her shoes.'

Lydia nodded. 'I certainly would be. But she is so delicate. Would she possess the required physical strength?'

Rees shrugged. He had seen other female murderers and so did not always subscribe to the theory of womanly frailty. But although he could envision Lydia or Ruth, or several other women of his acquaintance, of exhibiting the necessary determination, his imagination resisted seeing Sandy as anything but weak and helpless. Still, he had been fooled before.

'We can only hope Mr Gilbert ran afoul of someone,' Rees

said. 'Maybe he offered someone a deadly insult? Or cheated at cards? Rouge said he played . . .'

'I pray so,' Lydia agreed. 'I don't believe either Tobias or Ruth could even entertain the thought of murder.' She spoke with assurance, but her worried frown did not ease.

Midday was fast approaching, and Rees was eager to get home. A cold drizzle had begun to fall, each drop like a barely melted ice pellet. And he was hungry, ready for a hot meal. A buttered scone and a cup of coffee could hardly be called a snack and it certainly could not fill him up.

'If this continues,' he said aloud, 'we'll see snow tonight.'

'I hope we won't,' Lydia said. 'I'm not prepared for winter.'

Rees nodded. Although he'd received several weaving commissions, and could keep busy as the days grew short, he too preferred the light and warmth of spring. And that was in spite of the farming chores he did so unwillingly. The green of May was more pleasant to the eye than the grays and browns of November. Once the snow began to fall, the pines would stand out; green against the white. But now their color appeared dull and lifeless, almost invisible against the gray.

They turned into the farm gates. Despite the rain, which was now falling steadily, Annie was in the yard, pulling a cow behind her. Joseph and Sharon were on the porch, jumping up and down and calling out to her.

'What in Heaven's name is happening?' Lydia muttered, climbing down from the wagon as soon as it stopped rolling. 'Get in the house, you two. Immediately.'

Rees jumped down and walked across the muddy yard toward Annie. She had looped a piece of rope around the cow's neck and was guiding it toward the barn. 'You found the cow Jonathan was searching for?' Rees called out to her.

'I think so.' She wiped an arm across her wet face. 'I heard it mooing in the trees back there. She needs to be milked; she's in distress.'

'Jonathan said she was sick,' Rees said.

'Cowpox. It's not serious,' Annie said. 'And I already have it.' She lifted her arms so they could see the blemishes on her forearms. 'There's stew warming over the fire. I'll be in shortly.' She disappeared into the barn. Shaking his head, Rees climbed back into the wagon. Today he would park the vehicle in the shed next to the barn and put Hannibal in his stall. No one, not even a horse, wanted to be out in this weather.

By the time he stepped into the warm kitchen and hung his damp coat on the hook, Lydia had the children seated at the table with bowls of stew in front of them.

'It's too hot,' Joseph complained.

'Blow on it,' Lydia said, taking up the spider. The cornbread had been staying warm in the ashes. She cut several pieces and put them on a plate.

'What was Annie doing with that cow?' Lydia asked.

'It belongs to the Shakers. She's milking it now. After dinner, I'll bring it back to Zion. I wanted to speak to Jonathan again anyway,' Rees said.

Lydia turned, wiping her hands on her apron. 'I suppose you'll be taking Annie home as well,' she said. Although she did not ask, Rees knew she wanted to accompany him.

'Taking me home?' Annie came through the door and put the full milk pail down. 'I don't want to go. Tell them I am needed here, to watch the children.'

'You know, if you continually leave the village, the Elders will expel you,' Lydia said seriously. 'You have chores assigned to you there.' As a former member of the community who had been banished – although for the much more serious crime of falling in love and conceiving a child – Lydia knew that could happen.

Annie shrugged and picked up the pail. No longer the skinny child Rees recalled from Salem, she now overtopped Lydia by two inches. 'I am not suited for that life,' she said.

Rees stared at her, fearing he would be compelled to take her in to live with them.

'Wash your hands, please,' Lydia said to her husband. As Annie brought the milk pail to the pantry, Lydia put out three bowls. She added more cornbread to the plate and put butter and honey on the table. Rees washed his hands as he'd been told and then moved the coffee pot away from the fire. It had been merrily perking for a while; it would be as strong as sailor's tar. Lydia had mentioned purchasing one of the new Franklin stoves and Rees had begun to consider it.

'Well, if you don't mind,' Lydia was saying to Annie. 'I'd very
much enjoy visiting Esther.'

'I don't mind,' Annie said cheerfully, taking a cloth to Sharon's
food-smeared face.

Lydia joined Rees at the table and passed him the cornbread.
'Do you think Jonathan knows anything further about the body?'
she asked her husband, leaning forward and speaking in a low
voice.

'I don't know. Maybe. But I want to ask him if they've seen
any strangers lately. Besides the body, Mr Gilbert, I mean.' He
shot a quick glance at the children. They were paying him no
attention at all. Lowering his voice, he continued, 'This is what
puzzles me; the woods on that side of the fields are not easily
accessible. In fact, the simplest and most direct route to that part
of the forest is through Zion.'

'That's true.' Lydia agreed. 'Anyone passing through the village
would be seen. At the very least, a visitor must pass the barns
to reach the woods. Or pass the still house where the herbs are
handled. Someone would have seen something.'

'Exactly,' Rees said. 'But what if the body was brought to the
forest after dark? Or, more plausibly, what if the murderer walked
across the fields? At this time of year, even the Shakers are not
out and about.'

Lydia stared at her husband for a few seconds. Then she nodded
slowly in agreement.

EIGHT

By the time Rees and Lydia left a few hours later the sky
was beginning to brighten in the southwest. The rain had
stopped but the air was still very damp and cold. They
drove slowly. The cow was tied on back and she mooed pit-
eously the entire distance. One would almost have thought she
knew she was going to certain execution. Rees felt sorrier for
Hannibal who had already been taken from his warm stall once
today.

Zion's main street was empty. The morning service and midday dinner were over and all of the members of this community were back at work. Usually Jonathan was to be found in the workshop making brooms, whip handles and the like, but there was no guarantee. The Brothers and Sisters rotated through the chores necessary to keep the village running so both Jonathan and Esther could be anywhere.

Rees pulled the wagon next to the barn and covered Hannibal with the horse blanket. As Lydia headed for the kitchen, planning to start her search there, Rees walked toward the workshops. Today he was lucky; Jonathan was turning broom handles on the lathe. He stopped when Rees entered. Since curiosity about the World was frowned upon, the Elder waited while Rees closed the door.

'Did you identify the poor soul I found in the woods?' Jonathan asked at last.

'Identified him,' Rees said. After Sandy's description of Randolph Gilbert, he should not be described as a poor soul. But Rees ignored that for now. 'We don't know who might have murdered him, though.'

Jonathan looked at Rees sharply. 'Surely you don't suspect any of us.'

'No. But I have good friends who—' Rees stopped abruptly and shook his head. 'I wonder how the body was brought to that part of the woods. Have you seen any strangers passing through here?'

Jonathan looked startled. 'Strangers? No.' He grimaced. 'I've seen Aaron several times.'

'Aaron?' Rees repeated in surprise.

'Yes. He wants to be accepted back into our Family.' He shook his head and Rees thought Aaron's chances were almost non-existent. Besides, he wondered whether Aaron would want to surrender his fine clothing.

'Anyone else?'

'No one has come through the village that I know of. But then, if someone arrived here from the south, from Surry, he wouldn't necessarily pass through the main part of the village.'

Rees, who knew the village well, visualized Zion's layout. If Gilbert had approached Zion from Surry, and that certainly made sense, he could have pulled in at the southernmost entrance. A wagon or carriage could go no further. A small bridge, far too narrow for most vehicles, spanned the stream. A right turn would bring a visitor to the icehouse and then to the laundry.

Crossing the bridge would put the visitor on the main street. A left exit went to the mill, a rightward path went first to the physic gardens, with the still house at the back, and then to the kitchen. Although the physic garden had been planted at first to minister to the illnesses of the Shaker community, the herbs and the medicines made from them had soon become much in demand. The Shakers sold them on their regular spring and summer trips around the area.

Rees had been to the laundry several times but had never had occasion to visit the still house and he couldn't imagine any reason why Gilbert would either. But it was true that both workshops backed up to the stream. Following that tributary northeast would lead one into the forest.

'And none of the Sisters has mentioned a stranger passing through here?' Rees asked.

Jonathan shook his head. 'No one. Why do you want to know this?'

'I am puzzled by the location of the body,' Rees said. 'How did it get there, so far into the woods?'

'Clearly someone brought him,' Jonathan replied.

Rees frowned at the other man. 'I know. But did the murderer carry the body through the village with no one noticing?' When Jonathan, who seemed much struck by this, said nothing, Rees continued. 'Of course not. He would have been seen. So, the question is, how did the murderer get the body into the forest with not one person seeing him?'

'I will ask around,' Jonathan said.

'Thank you,' Rees said. Since unnecessary speech was forbidden, Jonathan had made a generous offer.

'But I do believe that if one of my Family had noticed something,' Jonathan added, 'he would have told me.' Jonathan returned to his post at the lathe. 'In any event,' he added, 'that man had nothing to do with us.'

Nodding in agreement, Rees took his leave.

He did not have to wait for Lydia for very long. Flushed and smiling, she came down the path from the kitchen. 'You enjoyed your visit?' Rees asked.

'Indeed I did,' Lydia agreed, smiling. 'I told her about the baby.' She rested one hand on her belly. 'And she extracted a promise that I will bring Sharon one day.' Since Sharon had been born while Rees and Lydia were staying here, in Zion, many of the Sisters felt a particular attachment to the child.

Rees helped his wife into the wagon. He removed the blanket from Hannibal's back and climbed into the seat himself. The air had grown much colder and some of the shallower puddles were beginning to freeze over. Lydia folded her hands tightly together underneath her cloak.

'I did learn something of interest, though,' she said.

'What?' Rees asked, hearing his voice lift with excitement.

'Brother Aaron, well, he isn't a Brother now, but he wants to rejoin the Shakers.'

'I know,' Rees said, disappointed. 'Jonathan told me.' He'd hoped she was going to tell him she'd discovered a bloodstain or that one of the Sisters had seen a stranger; something that applied to the murder.

'Yes. Don't you see the humor in that?' Lydia smiled at him, inviting him to share the joke. Rees thought about the irascible man who was as different from most of the Shakers, a gentle and kindly people, as chalk to cheese.

'I do. Why would he want to? He left under such difficult circumstances.' Rees had suspected Aaron of murder, in fact.

'Esther suspects he might be a Winter Shaker and planning to leave again in the Spring.'

Rees nodded. It was not uncommon for drifters and landless men especially to join for the hot meals and the warm bed over the winter. But in the spring, when the season turned and the community's rules began to bind, most of them left once again. 'I am not so certain he will leave,' Rees said slowly. 'Aaron has no one else. And despite his conflicts with the others, he seemed as happy and as contented there as he could be. Annie did not mention that to us.'

'She may not know yet. From what Esther said, Aaron has only approached a few. I daresay he is testing the waters before he jumps in and swims.'

'Aaron is not an easy man.' Rees flicked the reins over
Hannibal's back but, instead of driving to the road, he turned the
wagon toward the southern end of the village.

'Where are you going?' Lydia asked.

'Jonathan told me no one has seen strangers here,' Rees said.
'But I know the Elders are not told everything.'

Lydia nodded in agreement. 'That is so. Some of that might
be considered unnecessary talk.'

'Therefore, I thought I would stop at the herb house and at
the laundry and speak with the Sisters myself.'

'Good idea,' Lydia said approvingly.

'So,' Rees said, returning to the earlier topic, 'how does Esther
feel about Aaron?'

'Oh,' Lydia replied, her voice taking on a note of surprise,
'she is in favor. I didn't think she would be. But she said she
feels he should be given another chance.'

'She is a saint,' Rees said. 'I am not sure I could be so
forgiving.' Aaron engendered mixed feelings within him. An
argumentative, opinionated and irritable fellow, Aaron could also
be loyal and kind. He'd wept at the death of a disabled boy and
to Rees's everlasting admiration had punched the young man's
murderer.

'That's why you could never join the community,' Lydia said
teasingly.

Rees parked the wagon near the little bridge. They did not
cross it – it was too small for the wagon anyway – but followed
the path past the herb gardens to the still house in the back.

The still house was a small white building. Windows on the
upper level indicated a second floor but when Rees and Lydia
entered through the door they saw that most of the activity took
place on the ground floor. The air was aromatic with the spicy
scents of herbs and quite warm. Rees unbuttoned his coat.
Bunches of what looked like dead leaves and stems hung from
the ceiling and racks of other drying plant matter stood to the
left. The rear wall was entirely taken up with a large fireplace.
Over the blaze bubbled a kettle and from it came a pungent
aroma. The scrubbed floor was a crazy quilt of stains where
various liquids had been spilled.

Three Sisters worked in here. While one of the young girls

stirred the concoction boiling over the fire and another youthful adolescent moved through the racks inspecting the drying leaves and flowers, Eldress Agatha chopped vegetation with a long knife. She paused when she saw Rees and Lydia enter but resumed her chopping until she had finished the material in front of her. Then, putting down the knife, she wiped her hands on a towel and said, 'Well?'

Rees knew Sister Agatha did not approve of him. Although she had never voiced her dislike, he felt the censure rolling off her in waves. He glanced at his wife and stepped back. Lydia would be more successful at questioning this Sister than he would.

'You may have heard that a body was found in the woods nearby,' Lydia began. Sister Agatha inclined her head. 'Since it would be difficult to carry the body—'

'Unnecessary speech,' Sister Agatha said. 'Ask your question.'

'Have you, have any of you,' Lydia said, gesturing at the young girls, 'seen any strangers about?'

'No,' said Sister Agatha.

'Not since the summer,' one of the girls began. Agatha turned a look of reproof upon the young woman and she instantly quieted, dropping her gaze to the floor.

'We have seen no one,' Agatha said firmly. 'I have work to do.'

Rees and Lydia found themselves once again outside in the cold.

'Maybe we'll have better luck at the laundry,' Lydia said hopefully.

But the women there also proved unhelpful although the Sister in charge was friendlier. It was quite hot inside the laundry and the warm wet body linen steamed when it was hung on the drying racks outside. The Sister seemed tired and Rees thought that the constant movement from hot to cold and back again must be difficult. But, although the Sisters in the laundry seemed willing to stop work and answer questions, none of them remembered seeing any stranger about.

'Well, that was futile,' Rees said as they walked back to the wagon.

'You wouldn't have been happy if you hadn't questioned the Sisters yourself,' Lydia said.

'So, if no strangers passed through Zion, how did Gilbert's body end up in those woods?' Rees wondered aloud.

'My guess?' Lydia said. 'They brought the remains to the dam by wagon at night and crossed the water by the bridge to the north.'

'But that would take several hours,' Rees objected.

'But there would be no risk of being seen,' Lydia pointed out. 'They could carry lanterns; no one would see the lights. And the body could be hidden anywhere they chose.'

Rees nodded unhappily. Lydia's suggestion was a feasible one. If true, it would make the identification of the murderer even more difficult.

As they climbed into the wagon, the first thin flakes of snow began to fall. It was almost past five and already dark. Rees lit the lanterns on the wagon so they would have light on their way home. As a lifelong resident of the district, he knew that by January, sunset would begin by mid-afternoon. Ah, winter in Maine.

Speaking to Constable Rouge must be left for tomorrow.

NINE

Both Jerusha and Lydia were already awake by the time Rees went downstairs. Jerusha was eating bread and Lydia's honey for breakfast. Rees thought Lydia was cooking porridge for breakfast but when he peered over her shoulder the contents of the pot was a peculiar grayish green and emitted a powerful and familiar smell.

'Umm, delicious?' Rees said. 'What's that?'

'Tonic,' Lydia said, crumbling another piece of the dark green brick into the water. 'For the children. Esther gave it to me. This is one of the many herb preparations they sell.' Rees nodded; he recognized the odor now. She folded the paper wrapper over the remainder of the dried herbs and put it on the mantel over the fire. As she swung the pot away from the fire, she added, 'When it cools, I'll give it to the children to drink. Esther assures me this will keep them in good health through the winter.'

'That was nice of Esther,' Rees began.

'Goodbye, Father.' Jerusha kissed him on the cheek and swung her cloak over her shoulders. With her arms full of books, she hurried through the door. Rees went to the window and watched her hitch the donkey to the cart – the cart Rees had purchased for Lydia – and drive away.

'What else were you going to say?' Lydia asked him.

'I've forgotten. And anyway, the kids are awake.'

Lydia quickly mixed up a bowl of eggs and put the yellow mess in the spider. While she changed Sharon and dressed her, the older children went to the table. Rees stirred the eggs, moving them from the heat when cooked through. He divided the scrambled eggs between the plates.

Lydia brought Sharon to the table and for a few seconds all was quiet as everyone ate. In this small space of time, Rees quickly put together the coffee pot and moved it to the fire. Once breakfast was done, Lydia checked faces and hands for cleanliness. Then all but Joseph and Sharon put on their outer clothing and rushed out to walk to school. Suddenly, all was quiet.

Rees drank a mug of coffee and began donning his greatcoat. 'You're not going to eat breakfast?' Lydia asked.

'I want to talk to Rouge,' Rees said explained. 'Don't worry. I'll return early. But I gave my word I would keep him informed.'

'You aren't going to tell him you suspect Tobias and Ruth, are you?' Lydia straightened up and fixed her husband with a glare.

'No, of course not. I'll share what I know, not what I guess.' He knew better than to confide his thoughts to the constable; he was likely to hare off half-cocked.

'Very well,' Lydia said as Rees started for the door. 'And do discover Ned's surname please. It is poor manners to refer to him so informally.'

'Huh,' Rees said with a grin. 'That from a former Shaker Sister who referred to everyone by his first name.'

Rees went directly to the tavern. Besides being breakfastless and therefore a bit hungry, he knew his best chance of finding the constable was at the ordinary he owned. Rouge left it when forced, but now – especially with his blistered feet – he would want to stay home. And sure enough, when Rees arrived, Rouge was on a stool up at the bar. When he saw Rees, he called out to his cousin Therese to mind the bar. Wearing moccasins over grubby bandages, he shuffled over to the table.

'So, what did Tobias and his wife have to say? Did they know Mr Gilbert?'

'They don't know him,' Rees said.

'They *claim* they don't know him,' Rouge said.

'Huh,' Rees said. 'They probably don't. They weren't down south very long. And Tobias and Ruth were both born free, right here in the District of Maine.'

'I know you like Tobias. That doesn't mean he didn't lie to you. Sometimes the simplest answer is best,' Rouge said. He smiled at Rees's thunderous expression. 'What does your wife say?'

When he had first met Lydia, Rouge had treated her as some sort of talking animal but since then she had earned his grudging respect.

'She doesn't believe they are lying,' Rees said. He thought a moment and then added honestly, 'At least not yet, anyway.' He paused for a few seconds and continued. 'What do you know about Mr Gilbert?'

'He stopped here only a few days,' Rouge said. 'What could I possibly know?'

'Did he have gambling debts? Cheat at cards? Flirt with someone's wife?'

'He did play cards, played pretty deep, but lost and paid up right away.' Rouge grinned. 'I won a couple of dollars from him myself.'

'Whom did he play with, besides you?' Rees asked.

Rouge paused a moment, thinking. 'Different gentlemen. He played every night.'

'Were those men local?'

Rouge shook his head. 'Only one. Solomon Whitehead. Do you know him?' Rees shook his head. 'He owns a farm to the south of town. He's in here pretty regular.'

'And the others?'

'They were all travelers. I know one of them fairly well. He goes back and forth to Boston on a regular basis. Always breaks his journey here. The others? They all played with him one night and left the next morning for their various destinations.'

'Did any of them quarrel with Mr Gilbert?'

'He won a significant amount of money the first night he was here,' Rouge replied. 'But he lost the second and third nights. Lost quite a bit. So, no joy there. Anyway,' he added, after a pause, 'none of those men were here long enough to murder Mr Gilbert.'

Rees, who'd been hoping one of those strangers might be the guilty party, sighed. 'All right. So, Mr Gilbert arrived here when? Wednesday?'

Rouge stared into space for a few seconds, thinking. 'Yes. Wednesday.'

'And he played cards Wednesday, Thursday, Friday and Saturday?'

'Not Saturday. He did not turn up at the inn that night.' Rouge looked at Rees. 'He was probably already dead, but I assumed he'd found some female companionship. So, Wednesday through Friday nights. I played with him once. Whitehead was in here twice.' Rouge grinned. 'He came in Saturday looking for Gilbert. I guess Whitehead thought he would win another pot of money.'

'I will speak with Mr Whitehead then,' Rees said.

'He's not the only one,' Rouge said.

'What do you mean?' Rees asked.

'I'm partial to the theory of an escaped slave myself. Let's consider the possibility you are correct, and your friends are not guilty. There are others living in town who have escaped bondage. There's a blacksmith, I know. In fact, gossip has it that there's someone in town who takes these black folks from the safe houses and spirits them to Canada. And no, I don't know who it is,' he said, holding up a hand. 'I've heard rumors, is all. It's something most people don't talk about. But I'll bet you this tavern, yes, and the rooms above it, that Tobias knows who it is.'

Throwing a few coins onto the table, Rees leaped to his feet. 'I'll go ask him now,' he said.

'I wouldn't be surprised if he won't tell you,' Rouge said warningly. 'But good luck.'

Rees pulled on his coat. As he slid out from behind the table, Rouge added, 'Oh, I almost forgot. Dr Smith was in last night. Said his nephew wanted to see you about something.'

'Thank you.' The words floated back on the gust of cold air as Rees hurried through the door. Leaving his wagon and horse in the inn yard, he took off at a rapid walk. Since the surgery was across the street, he would stop there first. Then he would visit Tobias once again.

But Dr Smith was not in. 'A wagon fell on a farmer,' his daughter informed Rees. 'My father had to go tend to him.'

'Well, it's Ned I've come to see, anyway,' Rees said.

'I do not know if he will want to see you,' she said.

'The constable said Ned left a message for me,' Rees said. 'I'm certain he will want to see me.'

'He's out back in the shed,' she said with a moue of distaste.

Rees went through the back door and into the shed. The air was just marginally warmer than outside and Ned's breath floated in the air. Today, he did not wear only a shirt but was instead swaddled in layers of shirts and sweaters with a large coverall over them. The body on the table had been opened so that the chest and belly cavity were exposed, and blood and other fluids spattered Ned's large canvas apron.

'Oh good,' he said, looking up. 'You received the message.'

'What are you doing?' Rees asked in horror.

'Examining the body; more fully than I am usually able to,' Ned said as though that should be obvious to the meanest intelligence.

'I see.' Rees averted his eyes from the grisly scene on the table. Thank God he was a weaver and not a doctor. 'There's something you wanted to show me?' He hoped Ned did not want him to examine Gilbert's entrails.

'Come here.' Ned gestured with one crimson hand. With the other, to Rees's great relief, he pulled up the sheet over the mutilated body.

Rees shook his head. Besides the macabre scene on the table, he could now smell the sickening smell of corruption. Although the air was cold here, the murder had occurred a few days ago and decomposition was progressing.

Turning, Ned washed his hands in a basin of already bloody water and dried them on a stained towel. 'Come here, please. You need to see this. And you can't from that distance.'

Reluctantly, Rees approached the table. Ned turned back the

corpse's lip. 'I found this when I examined Mr Gilbert more closely. Do you see them?'

'See what?' Rees asked. In truth, he was trying hard not to look.

'Those red spots. Maybe they will be more visible to you inside the cheek.' Ned pulled the flesh back to expose the grayish inside of the mouth.

Rees looked. 'Yes, I see them. Are they important?'

Ned allowed the flesh to return to its normal position. 'I should say so. This man was within hours of exhibiting the characteristic lesions.'

'Lesions? A rash? What are you talking about?'

Ned turned and looked Rees straight in the eye. 'This man had smallpox.'

TEN

Rees took a big step backward. Ned looked at him in surprise. 'You haven't had smallpox? It comes around so regularly, I just assumed . . .'

'I had it as a four-year-old, at least according to my mother. I don't remember it.' He touched the pockmark on his forehead, the one reminder of the illness.

'Then you are immune.' Ned looked back at the body on table.

'You've had smallpox?' Rees asked.

'No. But I was inoculated when I was in Scotland.'

Rees nodded. He had heard of the attempt to stimulate immunity by taking some of the fluid from a smallpox pustule and injecting someone with it. 'You are fortunate you survived the variolation. Some of the less lucky come down with a virulent case of the disease and die.'

Ned smiled. 'That's not what it was. Edward Jenner found a new way. He's begun inoculations with cowpox. We are not quite sure why but that confers immunity to smallpox.' Ned's gaze sharpened. 'Do you have children?' Rees nodded. 'I suggest you inoculate them as soon as possible. Mr Gilbert here spent almost

a week in this town and there is no telling how many have been
exposed.'

'How do you do that?' Rees asked, recalling the sick cow
from the Shakers. He wondered if she had communicated the
disease to Rees's own cow Daisy. Although he wasn't sure about
Jerusha and her brothers and sister – they may have come down
with the disease before he adopted them – he knew Sharon had
no immunity.

'Scratch their arms and put some of the fluid from a cowpox
lesion on it.' Ned threw a glance over his shoulder at Rees. 'I'll
do it if you feel too squeamish.'

'I had help bringing the body to you,' Rees said, his thoughts
going to Jonathan and Constable Rouge. 'Are Brother Jonathan
and the constable at risk?'

'Probably not,' Ned said. 'Usually the disease travels from
person to person once the rash comes out. But I would warn
them, just in case.' He paused and then added, 'If they are willing
to consider inoculations, you can share what I told you.' His
hesitation and his sudden bitter expression told Rees there was
more to that story.

'Why would they not choose inoculation?' he asked, not
troubling to keep the surprise from his voice.

'There are many who refuse,' Ned said. 'The reasons are
varied. Some are frightened. Some claim illness is God's will.
And some believe they will never fall ill.'

Rees regarded the young man thoughtfully. 'Is that why you
are no longer in Scotland?'

'Change comes slowly,' Ned said. Again, that sour twist of
his lips.

'But it does come,' Rees said.

Ned shrugged. 'Sometimes too slowly.'

'I must go now.' Rees circled the table and went around to
the outside door. 'I want to warn the others . . .' When he looked
back over his shoulder, Ned was already bending over the body
once again. 'Ned. What's your last name?'

'Burke. Why?'

'My wife wanted to know.'

With a wave, Rees went out the door and down past the surgery
to the main road. He hesitated for a moment, considering who

he should speak with first. Rouge? He had been beside Rees at the discovery of the body. But, because of his blistered feet, he had done nothing to assist with the body.

If Tobias or one of the women, though, had interacted with Gilbert prior to his death and had been involved in the placement of the body, he or they could have been exposed to the illness. Rees opted to speak to them first. When he crossed the street, he went right to the corner and turned onto Broad Street.

When he entered the cabinetry shop, he made sure to stand by the door. 'Yes, Mr Rees?' Tobias said. From the formality of his address, Rees knew Tobias was still angry with him. 'More questions?'

'Do you know of anyone here in town who takes those who have fled from the slave states to Canada?'

Tobias finished applying varnish to the tabletop and turned to face Rees. 'Why should I tell you? Are you planning to accuse someone else of murder?'

Rees paused a moment, startled by the hostility in Tobias's voice. 'Someone murdered Randolph Gilbert,' he said. 'He may have been an evil man but neither of us is judge or jury. But I have a more important reason for identifying the man – the people – who killed him. He was infected with smallpox. Anyone who came in contact with him has therefore been exposed.'

Tobias gaped at Rees. 'Smallpox? Are you certain?'

'I just came from speaking with Ned. Uh, Dr Burke.'

Tobias stared at Rees for another few seconds. Then, tossing down his brush, he turned and sprinted for the stairs, shouting for his wife. As he ran up the steps, Rees followed slowly behind him.

'Smallpox,' Ruth was saying. 'Is he sure?' Then, as she saw Rees's red head rise above the bannister, she asked, 'Are you sure?'

'Ned is.'

'I had smallpox,' Ruth said. 'When it came through at the beginning of the war. I was about five or six then.' Rees nodded. The disease had infected many revolutionary soldiers then.

'But we haven't had it,' Sandy said, rising from her sewing. 'Abram and I. Oh no. My baby.' Wringing her hands, she began pacing back and forth. 'What shall I do?' She began circling the room. 'We must leave this town and go somewhere safe.'

'There may be another way,' Rees said. 'Speak to Dr Burke.'

As Ruth moved to comfort the young mother, Rees turned to Tobias. 'If you know someone, tell me now. Otherwise, those people who have fled from one horror may be forced to endure another. Or worse, they may be spreading the contagion as they go.'

'Promise me, this is not some ploy to discover the identity of a brave man who guides people like Sandy here to freedom?'

'Tobias,' Rees said, hurt. 'I've known you ten years and more; your wife longer than that. I was the man you approached to help you bring Ruth back from the Great Dismal in Virginia. We fled together. How could you even say that to me?'

'You know why. I believe you should walk away from Gilbert's murder. He was an evil man and if there was justice in this world he would have already been dealt with. Because he was born white and rich, he does what he pleases with no penalty.'

Rees could not disagree. In fact, he thought Tobias was probably correct. 'Benjamin Rush, the doctor who served in the yellow fever epidemic of 1793, once said, "Two wrongs don't make a right. Two wrongs won't right a wrong." The murder of Gilbert, whether he be evil or not, is still a wrongful act. And anyway, that has little to do with my need to warn everyone who might have come into contact with Gilbert about this illness.'

Tobias sighed. 'That is the only reason I will surrender the name of this man.' Lowering his voice as though anyone might be listening at the keyhole, he said, 'John Washington.'

'Washington?' Rees repeated.

'He was named something else once. Probably Scipio or Prospero or one of the other preferred slave names. He put that past behind him and chose a new name.'

Rees understood why someone might want to reject the degradations of enslavement. And how tragic he had to.

'And where might I find this gentleman?'

'He is a blacksmith down on River Road.'

'A blacksmith,' Rees repeated. Rouge had mentioned a blacksmith. Tobias nodded. 'Thank you.'

ELEVEN

A cold wind laced with rain had kicked up while Rees was inside. Gentlemen's hats were flying down the street and Rees saw more than one woman with her hands pressing her skirts down, striving for modesty despite the gusts. Rees, who had the squall at his back, sped down the lane that connected Broad Street with River Road.

As soon as he stepped inside and saw the burly and muscular black individual working at the forge, Rees knew he had found his quarry. 'Mr Washington?' he said.

'Yes.' Instead of the giant pounding the horseshoe, the reply came from a slimmer man standing to one side. He had Rees's height; they were eye to eye, but he was far thinner. And, unlike the giant wielding the hammer, this man was light-skinned. He stared at Rees.

'Tobias suggested I speak to you,' Rees said, lowering his voice.

'And what would that be about?' Washington asked. His husky voice still maintained a suggestion of a drawl.

'A man, a southerner, was found murdered,' Rees said.

'I heard.' Washington's entire body tightened, taut as a bowstring.

'He had smallpox,' Rees said, lowering his voice further still. 'Have you, by chance, met anyone from the South lately?'

Washington's face went carefully blank. 'Why, I don't believe I have,' he said. 'Did he stay in town long?'

'Few days.'

'I don't frequent the tavern and I don't believe I met that gentleman.' Washington made as if to turn away.

Realizing that stronger measures were called for, Rees caught Washington's arm. Although the man appeared a mere stripling, his forearm was solid with corded muscle. 'Have you guided anyone north lately?' Rees asked.

'I don't know what you mean.'

Rees inhaled in frustration. 'I brought Tobias and Ruth as well as Sandy and her baby from Virginia last month. I am as guilty of breaking that infernal law as you are.'

Washington said nothing, his lips tightening. Rees struggled with the urge to press the other fellow up against the wall and make him talk. Finally, stepping back, he said, 'If you or anyone you know came into contact with Mr Gilbert, please warn them. They might be sick.'

Rees turned and started for the door. He would have to make another attempt at Washington. Although he understood the smith's fear, he felt like shouting, 'But this is me. I won't hurt you.' But of course Washington did not know him.

He was almost outside when Washington called after him. 'Rees. Only one I know that had smallpox recent is Gabriel here. That was before he started working for me; three or four weeks ago. He still got the scars to prove it. But neither one of us met that Virginian you was talking about.'

Rees nodded and continued on. He had walked a block when he realized exactly what Washington had been hinting. Gabriel, the man hammering at the horseshoes for all he was worth, was Washington's most recent rescue. But was his claim Gabriel had been in town almost a month true or not? Rees stopped and almost returned to the smithy to continue the discussion. Washington had raised more questions than answers. After a moment's cogitation, Rees continued on his way. Washington would say no more, at least not right now. He might later, after speaking to Tobias about Rees. And Tobias would certainly know how many weeks Gabriel had spent in town. Rees trusted him not to lie.

Rouge, tavern keeper as well as constable, could confirm whether Washington was a regular patron of the tavern or not. Moreover, Rouge might have heard gossip relating to Tobias, Washington, or Gabriel. Rees quickened his pace.

Since it was drawing on to dinnertime, the tavern was more crowded than it had been during Rees's earlier visit. He could hear the clamor of voices from outside the door and when he stepped inside it was to a loud and smoky interior. Therese was flying around from table to table, her expression harried. Rouge also was waiting on his customers, although his gait was more of a slow hobble. Rees grinned at him and, as soon as one of the farmers vacated his place, Rees slid into it.

'What do you want?' Rouge growled.

'I need to speak to you in private.'

'Can't you see we're busy.' Rouge gestured around at the throng.

'Two minutes,' Rees said. 'It relates to' – he glanced around quickly and lowered his voice – 'the Southerner.'

Grumbling, Rouge shouted through the kitchen door at Therese's brother Thomas. 'My office,' he said, gesturing Rees forward.

Rees, who'd been inside the office many times, went ahead. Then he had to stop and cool his heels in front of the locked door until Rouge caught up and brought out the large iron key. The office was messy, as usual.

'Don't make yourself comfortable,' Rouge said. 'You won't be in here for very long.'

'I have a few questions,' Rees said.

Rouge nodded impatiently. 'Get on with it.'

'First,' Rees said, preparing to discuss his morning in chronological order, 'I spoke to Ned. He examined the body more closely and ascertained that Mr Gilbert was suffering from smallpox.'

'Smallpox!' Rouge went white.

'Haven't you had it yet?'

'No. My father was a trapper. We only rarely even made it to Mass. I mostly saw my mother, my brothers and sisters.'

That explains a lot, Rees thought. Aloud, he said soothingly, 'You don't need to worry. You didn't touch the body; Jonathan and I took care of that.'

'I didn't touch him then,' Rouge said, his voice rising. 'But he stayed in one of the rooms here. He ate here.' He swept his arm around to encompass not only this room but the entire tavern. 'And he played cards here with a number of other gentlemen, every night during his stay. I played with him; I told you that. That's how I knew who he was and where he came from.'

Rees glanced around at the untidy office. As was customary, the only chair not heaped with ledgers and documents was the one Rouge usually sat in. Rees took Rouge's arm and urged him toward the seat. Rouge collapsed into the seat and put his head in his hands. Picking up a stack of correspondence from creditors, Rees moved them to the nearby table and sat on the barrel. 'Calm down,' he said. 'Likeliest, you will be fine.' He hoped so. Smallpox was a dreadful disease with a high mortality rate.

'Let's see,' Rouge said in a shaky voice. 'That Shaker found the body on Monday and it is Wednesday now. Mr Gilbert arrived the previous Wednesday afternoon. I played whist with him that evening. So, it has been seven days since he first arrived in town.'

'Eight,' Rees corrected him. 'Counting today.'

'How soon will I know if I caught smallpox?' Rouge asked in a small voice. Rees suddenly felt very sorry for the other man. Sometimes helpful, more often an impediment, Rouge tended to drive straight at life's challenges as though he could surmount them with sheer force of will. This was one time when one needed more than bluster and determination to win.

He was not a friend, nor an enemy either, but he had become a fixture in Rees's life. He jumped off the barrel and went to Rouge's side.

'I don't know,' he said, putting a hand on Rouge's shoulder. 'You'll have to ask Dr Ned. He seems to be something of an expert on the disease.'

Rouge nodded and with an effort pulled himself together. 'What else do you want to know?'

'Do you know John Washington?'

'The blacksmith?' Rouge looked up in surprise. And then, with a knowing expression, he added, 'Did you talk to him?'

'Yes. Does he frequent this tavern?'

'No. I've seen him stop in once or twice.' Rouge shook his head again. 'I suspect the colored folks have another place they go but I don't know that for certain. He told me he works too hard for his money to spend it on drink.'

Rees smiled. He could visualize Washington saying that. And he'd told the truth, at least about frequenting the tavern.

'Why do you want to know?' Rouge asked suspiciously.

'I wondered if he had been introduced to Mr Gilbert,' Rees said carefully. He did not want to confirm that Washington was the man who smuggled people into Canada, even though Rouge had heard the rumors. As constable, he might feel he had to obey the letter of the law and arrest him.

'Huh,' Rouge said. 'Washington is smart enough to steer clear of a man like Gilbert. That Virginian would have had the blacksmith trussed up like a turkey and shipped back south. Anyway, I suspect Washington is on the other end of that trade.' He looked hard at Rees to see if he understood. 'He seems to organize a rotating supply of helpers who remain for a little while and then disappear.'

'You mean like Gabriel?' Rees said with a nod.

'Exactly like Gabriel,' Rouge said. 'Now, there's someone I can see putting his hands around Mr Gilbert's neck and strangling him.'

'How long has he been with Washington?' Rees asked.

'Longer than usual; almost a month. Probably because Gabriel is also a blacksmith. Some of the others didn't know which end of the hammer to use.' Rouge grinned, forgetting for the moment his own concerns.

Rees considered the large muscular blacksmith. Had Gilbert attempted to re-capture Gabriel? 'Does he have a wife?'

'Not that I know of.' Rouge paused. 'I did hear gossip that Washington is sweet on Tobias's houseguest.'

'Sandy?'

'Is that her name? White girl with a baby? Who appeared out of nowhere when you returned to town with Tobias and Ruth?' Rouge grinned knowingly.

Now that, Rees thought, put an entirely different perspective on the matter. What if Randolph Gilbert had seen Sandy with Washington and had attempted to abduct her? Washington would have defended her. Why, he might have attempted to strangle Gilbert. But now Rees's imagination failed him. He could not imagine Sandy stabbing anyone, not even to save herself.

TWELVE

I t was past midmorning when Rees left, and the gray sky had cleared. The thin sunshine did little to warm the air. Rees drove to Broad Street and turned left to go south, toward the

Whitehead farm. He passed Tobias's cabinetry shop and, shortly thereafter, Broad Street narrowed and soon after, as Rees left the town's limits, it became a narrow dirt road. Rouge had assured him that he would have no trouble finding the Whitehead farm, and Rees found that to be true. He turned right on a narrow track and followed it between stands of firs and a few stony and unkempt fields. The dry cornstalks and the withered buckwheat, uncut to stubble as they should have been, rustled in the cool air. Whitehead, it appeared, was an indifferent farmer.

Rees pulled to a stop in front of the ramshackle farmhouse. He climbed down from the wagon but before he'd taken more than a few steps the front door opened, and a tall man stepped onto the porch. Untidy brown hair and a bushy beard disguised his features.

'Who are you?' he asked.

'Will Rees.'

'Oh. I've heard about you. You're the weaver. Rouge's lackey.'

'Hardly,' Rees said, suppressing his flare of annoyance.

'What do you want?'

'I understand you played cards with Mr Gilbert at Rouge's tavern?'

'Yes. So?'

Rees hesitated a moment but decided the gentle approach would not be necessary with this fellow. 'I was not certain you'd heard. Mr Gilbert was found murdered.'

'And you came here to accuse me?' Whitehead took several steps toward Rees.

'No,' he said, although he had intended to question the man. 'I thought you might not know. And—' But before he could continue, Whitehead interrupted.

'I won more 'n twenty dollars from him. And that was the first time I played.' He grinned. 'He is one of the worst card players I've ever seen. So you see, I had no reason to kill him.'

'What happened the second time you played?' Rees asked. From the condition of this farm compared to the elegant Mr Gilbert, Rees suspected Whitehead was being drawn into a net from which he could not escape.

'I lost a few bucks,' Whitehead admitted. 'Sometimes the cards don't go your way. But I would've won it back on Saturday. I know it.'

Rees nodded, reflecting that Solomon Whitehead had had a lucky escape. Rees had no doubt Gilbert would have won everything Whitehead owned, including this farm. 'Did Mr Gilbert talk at all with you?'

Whitehead shook his head. 'No. Not really. He said only he was looking for someone.' He shrugged. 'I didn't care anyway. I was there to play cards.'

Rees nodded. At the moment, he could see no reason for Whitehead to murder his fellow gambler. 'One other thing,' he said. 'Mr Gilbert had contracted smallpox.' Whitehead's eyes widened. 'I thought I should warn you.'

Without even a goodbye, Whitehead turned and went inside, slamming the door behind him.

Shaking his head, Rees climbed into his wagon.

As Rees passed the turn-off to Zion on his way home, he decided he would stop and warn Jonathan. He didn't want to; he dreaded seeing the same fear on Jonathan's face that he had witnessed on both Rouge and Whitehead. But it was the right thing to do. He turned Hannibal to the right and drove down the lane that led to the village.

The entire community was in the street, walking to the Meeting House. Rees glanced up at the sky, realizing he had spent more time in town than he'd realized. Before the midday dinner, the Believers participated in prayer. Rees hoped he could find Jonathan before he went inside.

His eyes roamed over the crowd, searching for the Elder. All the men were garbed in black coats and white shirts with black hats. The women wore navy blue, purple and black with the berthas, the shawl they draped around the shoulders for modesty. The similarity in the clothing meant finding one individual was difficult. Then Rees saw him. Instead of his usual unhurried pace, he was walking very quickly as he threaded his way through the crowd.

'Jonathan,' Rees shouted, waving his arm. Jonathan did not respond. Either he couldn't hear, or he was pretending he couldn't. 'Brother Jonathan.'

Unable to ignore the shouts which were attracting increasing attention, Jonathan turned. He acknowledged Rees with a nod and began to make his way through the crowd. 'What is this wild noise,' he reproved Rees as he approached the wagon.

'I need to speak to you,' Rees said. And when Jonathan hesitated, as though he wished to refuse, Rees added, 'It's important.'

With a sigh, Jonathan gestured to the space beside the Dwelling House. 'What is so important you insist on speaking to me as I go to worship?' Jonathan asked, his tone stiff.

'The doctor in town performed another examination on the victim,' Rees said, leaning over so he did not have to shout. Jonathan nodded impatiently. 'Mr Gilbert was suffering from smallpox,' Rees said. 'You helped me with the body. I was worried . . .'

'I had the smallpox years ago,' Jonathan said tersely.

'Ned has a method for inoculation. There may be folks among your Family who are susceptible—'

'I will refer this suggestion to Mount Lebanon,' Jonathan said briskly. 'Since I was the only one to help you, we can rest assured none of my Family will come down with the contagion. Farewell Rees.' He sounded as though he were bidding Rees goodbye forever. Somewhat annoyed, Rees turned his wagon around and started back for the road. Now he could go home to his wife and family with the pleasant certainty he had done his duty. Even if Jonathan did not appreciate it.

Lydia had just put dinner on the table when Rees came through the door. Chicken pot pie, with the leftover chicken from the previous day. 'Wash your hands,' she said, sounding beleaguered. He looked around.

'Where's Annie?'

'She didn't come this morning, I'm not sure why.' She turned and called the two youngest children.

'She has cowpox. Maybe she is ill,' Rees suggested.

'It is more likely she is being punished for leaving Zion as often as she does,' Lydia said.

'I just visited Zion,' Rees said.

Lydia glanced at Rees as she lifted Sharon into her chair. 'Why?'

'Ned – Dr Burke – continued his examination of Randolph Gilbert and discovered he was infected with smallpox.'

'Smallpox!' Lydia's gaze went to the two children and she blanched. 'Oh no.' She sounded terrified. 'Perhaps I should keep the children home from school.'

'And then what? There will be another wave of smallpox. You know that. Besides, it is too late. That Mr Gilbert stayed at Rouge's inn for several days. He ate there. He played cards with several other men. Rouge never had the illness, was in close contact with Gilbert, and has been serving customers. Jerusha, Nancy and Judah have been going to school. And I . . . I handled the body, Lydia.'

'Will you become ill?' Lydia asked, her voice shaky.

Rees shook his head. 'I came down with smallpox as a child. But others in our town have never suffered the disease. We need to consider the children.'

Lydia bit her lip. 'Variolation? My parents had me variolated as a young child. Once I suffered a light case, I was fine. But another child, a boy I knew, died.' She looked at Rees, her expression one of anguish.

'Ned says he has a cure. Not variolation. He says if we inoculate the children with cowpox, it will confer an immunity upon them.'

'Is he sure?' Lydia shook her head. 'Or will he be giving them another dangerous disease?'

'The cowpox is never fatal,' Rees said, hoping that was true.

'Where would we find a cow with cowpox?'

'That is what the cow at Zion is sick with,' Rees said, going to the sink to wash his hands. 'In fact, Annie has cowpox. She displayed her sores to me.' He took his hands out of the water and dried them.

'Annie did not even appear ill.' Lydia took a deep breath. 'Then that is what we should do; inoculate the children with cowpox.'

'You're sure?' Rees said, turning to his wife. She nodded although she was pale with fright.

'That cow was in the barn with Daisy,' Rees said. 'She may have contracted cowpox. I'll check.' He started for the door.

'Wait, please, Will,' Lydia said. 'After dinner is soon enough.' Rees halted and meekly went to his seat at the table.

Nevertheless, after eating, Rees went outside to examine Daisy.

Although he had a few other cattle, and Daisy's calf, now a bullock, Daisy had been the only cow still in the barn when Annie put the sick cow next to her. He examined Daisy carefully but saw none of the identifiable lesions. Deciding to be cautious, Rees released her into the meadow by herself. He leaned against the fence as he watched her trot into the enclosed pasture. To his eyes, she appeared sluggish, without her usual energy, but that, he decided, could be his own anxiety. She ate the frosty grass with some appetite so she could not be terribly sick.

Growing cold despite his coat, he turned to the house.

Someone was galloping up the road. The bay horse resembled Rouge's mount, but the rider was not Rouge. Rees began walking to the gate, only identifying Rouge's cousin Thomas when he rode through the gate.

'Thomas,' Rees said in surprise.

'Hello, Rees.' Dismounting, Thomas began to walk the horse around the yard.

'What are you doing here?' Rees fell into step with Thomas.

'I have a message from my cousin.'

'Why didn't Rouge come himself?' Rees asked.

Thomas turned with a grin. 'I don't know what you said to him, but he is afraid to leave his office. Merde, but he is frightened.'

'Oh dear,' Rees said. 'Did he visit Ned – Dr Burke?'

'No.' Thomas frowned. 'I believe he sent someone to ask the doctor to come to the tavern. But that is not why I came. My cousin wanted you to know Randolph's sister has arrived in town.'

'His sister?' Rees turned a blank look on Thomas. 'Why should I care about that?'

'He assured me you would know what that meant.'

'How would I know his sister?' Rees said as they made another circuit of the yard. 'I just learned about Gilbert the day before yesterday, and he was already dead then.' Suddenly recollecting the conversation with Sandy, Rees said, 'Charlotte Sechrest?'

'Gentlemen.' Lydia stood on the small porch outside the kitchen door and called to them. 'Please come in for a hot drink and some refreshments.'

'I believe he is cool now,' Rees said, laying his hand on the bay's neck.

'I'll just give him some water,' Thomas said.

While Thomas saw to Rouge's horse, Rees joined Lydia on the landing. 'Thomas came with a message from Rouge,' Rees said. 'Gilbert's sister has arrived.'

'Already?' Lydia turned to Rees in dismay. 'I didn't expect to see her for another week or more.'

'So, that is the woman Sandy mentioned?' Rees said.

'Yes. Charlotte Sechrest, the woman who had beat Sandy bloody and left her scarred for life.'

'She can't possibly know Sandy is here, in town,' Rees said. 'It's too soon.' Even riding flat out, a trip from Virginia would take several days.

'Nonetheless, we must warn Sandy as well as Tobias and Ruth.'

THIRTEEN

Rees, believing he would have just enough time to drive to Tobias's shop before dark, planned to go as soon as Thomas left. But Thomas didn't leave. He ate cake and drank ale and, when he was done, he lingered at the table chatting. By the time he finally went out to collect the bay and leave for home, it was almost four and shadows were obscuring the road. Rees suspected Thomas only departed then because the children – and Jerusha – had come home from school and the farmhouse was suddenly crowded and noisy.

Rees and Lydia followed Thomas out to the porch and watched him mount Rouge's horse. 'Why did he stay so long?' Lydia asked, her tone sharp with impatience. 'I have a meeting with the sewing circle tonight and chores to finish before then.' She watched Thomas trot down the road outside the gates before she turned and went inside. Rees chuckled, guessing she had followed their visitor out just to make sure he was really leaving.

The air was already quite cold and snow was beginning to sift down from the sky. Shivering, he turned and followed his wife into the warm kitchen.

'I never expected him to linger here for most of the afternoon,' Lydia said when Rees shut the door behind him. She clattered the dishes together and put them in the wash basin. 'Surely he has work of his own that needs doing.'

Rees thought about it. 'Most certainly,' he agreed. 'No doubt Rouge keeps Thomas on a short rein. I'll wager Thomas rarely escapes the kitchen and almost never sets foot outside the tavern. This was his chance at freedom.'

'I wish he'd chosen another farm for his day of rest,' Lydia said, snapping her towel in annoyance. 'Oh dear, I hope that terrible woman does not find Sandy before we can alert her.'

'Sandy rarely leaves the protection of Tobias's house during the day,' Rees said soothingly. 'I am certain she will not venture out after dark.'

'I hope you're right,' Lydia said. But she sounded less alarmed.

'I suppose we could have asked Thomas to leave,' Rees said. 'Of course, that would be an affront to civil behavior.'

'Indeed. And then we might have explained why we were asking him to leave,' Lydia pointed out. Since neither she nor Rees knew how Thomas felt on the matter of slavery, it was best to be cautious.

'Are your friends coming here?' Rees asked.

Lydia shook her head. 'Mrs Perkins is hosting. We take turns.'

'Will Ruth attend?'

'Maybe. I don't believe she enjoys the group.' Lydia's brow puckered. 'She is the only one among us who has been enslaved yet few of the other women want to allow her to speak. It is puzzling.'

Rees nodded. He'd met some of the women and suspected they felt too superior to listen. 'When are you leaving?'

'Soon. Jerusha will put supper on the table and clear up.'

'Be careful,' Rees said anxiously. 'Bring the lanterns.'

'Will,' Lydia said with a smile, 'I have driven in the dark many times. I'll be fine.'

'It's beginning to snow,' he said.

'Just flurries. If it gets bad, I'll come home.'

Snow showers continued through the night. When Rees arose next morning, several inches shrouded the world in white. But it was already melting in the warming air, and he knew the thin coating would be gone by noon. Anything that fell from the solid gray sky today would be rain but it would not be long now before they saw heavy snow. Winter was on its way.

He was quite surprised to see Annie plodding toward the farm in the early morning light.

'What are you doing here?' he asked as he met her by the gate.

'I have no chores today,' she said, her eyes sliding away from his.

'Are you sure?' he asked, eyeing her suspiciously. One of the Shaker adages was 'Hearts to God, hands to work'. He could not believe Annie would be spared the daily toil.

She nodded. Reaching up to brush back her hair, she said, 'I was not needed.' The fall of her sleeve revealed the cowpox blisters on her wrist. She began walking toward the house. Rees followed, certain she had just lied to him. In all the years he had known the Shakers in general and the members of Zion in particular, he had never seen them refrain from setting each person to work. But she was here, and he knew Lydia would be happy to see her. Annie's presence meant Lydia could join Rees on his trip into Durham.

Another surprise: Annie had not eaten breakfast. Since the Believers always supplied large and hearty meals, Annie must have left the village prior to serving. But Lydia did not question Annie's availability. While the girl sat down with the children, Rees and Lydia ate hurried bowls of mush and departed.

Lydia was smiling, glad for this unexpected outing, but a knot of worry furrowed her forehead. 'I won't rest easy until I know Sandy is safe,' she said as she climbed up to the wagon seat beside her husband.

'We'll drive straight there,' he promised. 'Then we will call on Constable Rouge. He feared he might become ill with the smallpox.'

'Tobias and Ruth are somewhat at risk of recapture,' Lydia said, continuing her train of thought, 'but at least we all know them and know they were born free.'

Rees darted her a quick look. 'True enough. Do you think . . . Sandy certainly has a good reason to wish Gilbert dead,' he said.

'She might have been involved somehow,' Lydia agreed. 'Although I cannot imagine her planning his murder. But that does not mean she deserves to be dragged back into servitude. Or into whatever hell Mr Gilbert had planned for her.'

'My imagination fails at envisioning her wielding a knife. Or tramping through the forest to conceal the body,' Rees said, smiling at his wife.

Lydia darted an anxious glance at him. 'I can easily conceive of her stabbing Randolph Gilbert.' Rees shook his head in disagreement. 'Perhaps she might have hesitated if the danger posed only affected her,' Lydia explained. 'But she will do anything to protect Abram. Almost any mother would, to safeguard their child, and Sandy is no different. Mr Gilbert might have promised Abram a terrible future, not just enslavement but something worse. In that case, I can easily see Sandy attacking that man.' She paused and then added unhappily, 'But she would have had to solicit help in moving the body. That means Tobias and probably Ruth would be involved as well.'

'Not necessarily,' Rees said, although that exact thought worried him as well. 'The blacksmith, that John Washington, is sweet on her. He is certainly strong enough to grab Gilbert by the neck. And he's smart. He could figure out a way to move the body. He might have had help too,' he said, recalling Gabriel and the powerful arms pounding the hammer down. 'But why put the body there, why in those woods so far to the east of town?'

'If Washington is as smart as you say,' Lydia said, 'then he would be clever enough to hide that murder victim as far away from him as possible.' Rees nodded slowly. The explanation was a plausible one although it did not sit right with him. Woods clothed the hills to the western side of town as well. Surely the body could have been deposited in the wilderness there. And not on his land!

When they arrived at Tobias's shop, they found him loading a newly finished table into his wagon. He was in his shirt and vest only, and clearly had not expected to linger in the cold.

When Rees's wagon pulled up, Tobias stared at him incredulously. 'What is this? Three days running. I don't know whether to be flattered or insulted.'

'It is imperative we speak to Sandy,' Lydia said.

'We are not here to see you,' Rees said at that exact moment.

Tobias stared at them, his gaze moving from one to another. Finally, it was Lydia's anxious expression that persuaded him. 'Very well,' he said. 'Come this way.'

They went through the back door and into the kitchen of the living quarters. Ruth, making tea, turned with a gasp. The teacup in her hand smashed to the floor.

'Abram, no,' Sandy cried as the little boy started forward to investigate.

'What now?' Ruth asked, sounding a little irritated. 'Do you truly think we had something to do with that slaveholder's murder?'

'We are here to see Sandy,' Rees said. As Ruth swept the child into her arms, Lydia sat down at the table and put her hand on Sandy's arm.

'I am very sorry to tell you this . . .' she said. When she paused, unsure of her next words, Sandy began to weep.

'I did not murder that man, I swear it.'

'It isn't that,' Lydia said.

'Charlotte Sechrest arrived in town yesterday,' Rees said.

'No,' Sandy cried out. 'No.' As Sandy began to sob in noisy earnest, Lydia turned a reproachful look upon her husband.

'What are you thinking,' Ruth scolded Rees. 'Telling her like that.'

'We've got to run,' Sandy said, jumping up from the chair with such suddenness it fell over. 'She can't find us. Maybe John can take me to Canada.'

'That would take some days to arrange,' Tobias said.

Turning, Sandy clutched at Lydia's hands. 'You've got to find a hiding place for me. Miss Charlotte can't find us.'

Rees's thoughts went immediately to Zion. He'd brought others there, not always with the best results. But Sandy and Abram might be safe for a short time at least.

'She only just arrived,' Tobias said comfortingly. 'We'll sort out something soon.' He stared at Rees.

'Of course,' Rees said. 'She won't find you, I promise.'

'We won't allow Mrs Sechrest, or anyone else, to take you,' Lydia said, reaching forward to clasp the girl in her arms.

FOURTEEN

On the silent drive to the tavern, Lydia spoke only once. 'I will be very interested to see what Mrs Charlotte Sechrest is like to cause such fear,' she said. Rees easily found a space for his wagon near the tavern. He could not fathom why this was so until he and Lydia went inside. Most of the tables were empty and Thomas was manning the bar. When Rees asked about Therese, Thomas replied angrily.

'Upstairs with Herself.'

'Herself?' Rees asked. Thomas flung a hand at the window. Rees and Lydia turned to look. Almost the sole vehicle in the tavern yard was a magnificent equipage with four matched white geldings.

'Mrs Charlotte Sechrest,' Thomas said. 'She has two maids with her plus a coachman, a driver and some other men whose purpose I cannot ascertain. You would think that would be sufficient to cater to her whims. But no. Nothing is to her liking and Therese is upstairs trying to satisfy the lady's caprices.'

'Particular, is she?' Lydia asked.

'Particular?' Thomas snorted. 'The sheets are rough, the bedchamber, which she has taken by herself, is drafty, the fire too scanty. And don't even ask me about her supper last night and breakfast this morning. Tea and coffee would not do. She must have hot chocolate.' Thomas shook his head, aggrieved. 'I had to send a boy to the coffee house.'

'She sounds charming,' Lydia said, her voice signifying exactly the opposite.

'What does Rouge think?' Rees asked. The constable would put a flea in Mrs Sechrest's ear. Thomas smiled bitterly.

'He hasn't met her. After Dr Smith's nephew came yesterday, my esteemed cousin has not set foot outside his office.'

'I'll talk to him,' Rees said. He and Lydia went down the long hall. He knocked on the door.

'Go away,' Rouge said from within.

'It's Will Rees,' he said, opening the door.

The office was in even more disarray than before. A pallet made up of blankets and a ragged pillow had been laid over the carpet, with all the stacks of paper and books moved to the sides. It looked as though he was sleeping in a small library. Rouge was seated on his chair, evidently trying to review invoices. Unshaven and with his hair uncombed, he looked more like a landless man traveling the roads than the owner of a successful business.

'What did Ned say?' Rees already suspected with a sinking of his heart what the reply would be.

Rouge turned hollow eyes upon Rees. 'That I have the contagion. He saw the bumps in my mouth.'

'How do you feel?' Lydia asked as she crowded in behind her husband.

'Terrible. Feverish and I have a headache.' He forced a bitter smile. 'Ned says I'll feel worse when the rash comes out. He estimated that might happen as early as tomorrow or as late as Sunday.'

'Oh my,' Lydia said, raising a hand to her mouth.

'And, to make this even more unbearable, I have the Queen of Sheba upstairs.'

'We heard she was difficult,' Rees said.

'Wait until you meet her. She seems as sweet as honey, like butter won't melt in her mouth. Then the claws come out. So, when you meet her, don't be fooled. And you will meet her,' Rouge added, throwing a warning glance at Rees. 'She asked for you.'

'Asked for me? I've never met her.'

'Thomas said she didn't use your name, but she described a tall red-haired man.'

Rees felt his heart sink to his boots. While down south in Virginia, he had participated in a raid on the Sechrest plantation. Wanted posters with a reward for the capture of a big redheaded man had soon gone up all around the Great Dismal Swamp.

But there must be hundreds of redheads, Rees thought. He would have to brazen this out.

'That doesn't mean my husband,' Lydia said. When she looked at Rees, her eyes were pinched with worry. Knowing that she was remembering the raid just as he was, he nodded encouragingly.

'I'll be happy to meet Mrs Sechrest,' Rees said. 'But I don't believe I am the man for whom she searches.'

Rouge nodded. 'To be honest, I don't believe she came north to find you. Not entirely, anyway. She had a letter from her brother.'

'Go on,' Rees said, holding his sudden dread in check.

'I didn't read it. But in it he claims to have found evidence of an escaped slave in this town. And he described you as a local troublemaker.' He grinned. 'I could only agree with her on that score.'

'Troublemaker!' Rees exclaimed. 'I'm a solid and upstanding citizen.'

'That's a matter of opinion.' Rouge chuckled, evidently finding this very humorous.

'No doubt they are searching for an entirely different man,' Lydia said.

'No doubt,' Rouge said derisively.

'I shall see if she'll meet with me now,' Rees said. 'There's no time like the present.' He ushered Lydia from the room and followed.

As he prepared to shut the door behind him, Rouge spoke. 'Be careful, Rees. This is a case where the law is on her side. She has come north, accompanied by several slave takers, to reclaim what the law recognizes as her property. Behave wisely lest I am forced to arrest you.'

Rees did not acknowledge Rouge's warning with so much as an eyeblink as he shut the door behind him. 'That is a bad law,' he muttered to himself. 'I will not surrender that girl and her baby.'

'The constable did not tell you to obey the law,' Lydia said with a smile. 'He said to behave wisely. We just won't get caught.'

Rees grinned. 'That's right, he did.'

He had planned to ask Thomas to request a meeting with Mrs Sechrest but when he and Lydia reached the bar a young woman stood in front of it. Since she spoke with a soft southern drawl, and was as elegantly clothed as Randolph Gilbert had been, Rees guessed this was his quarry.

'Here is Mr Rees and Mrs Rees now,' Thomas said in relief.

Charlotte Sechrest turned. She was quite young, probably no more than early twenties, and clad in a soft gauzy gown of light pink. It was far too thin for mid-November in the District of Maine. Although Rees was not familiar with current fashions, as a weaver he did know fabric and this handkerchief fine cotton was very expensive. An embroidered ribbon framed the low neckline and high waist. Over her shoulders, she wore a shawl woven with a geometric design that was both ornate and exotic.

Two clusters of blond curls hung over her ears, but the remainder of her hair was drawn back into a bun decorated with enameled flowers. She was very pretty. Worse, in Rees's estimation, she knew it.

She looked at Lydia, taking in the plain dark blue dress and simple hairstyle at a glance. Turning back to Rees, Mrs Sechrest smiled. 'Mr Rees. I am Charlotte Sechrest. I understand you found my brother's body.' Although her voice was sweet and calm, Rees had the impression of some strong emotion simmering underneath.

'No, I did not,' Rees said. 'Another man found the body. The constable enlisted my assistance in bringing your brother's remains back to town.'

She nodded, raising a handkerchief to her eyes. Despite that gesture, Rees saw no sign of grief: no tears or reddened eyes. Of course, he did not know the relationship between brother and sister. She may have disliked him, for all he knew.

'Perhaps we should sit down,' he said. He swung his arm in invitation toward a nearby table. This was not the tavern's primary room, nor the most comfortable. Armed with Rouge's warning, Rees did not want to even suggest the impression he and Mrs Sechrest were friends. He was very glad of Lydia's presence.

Mrs Sechrest nodded and preceded them both to the table. She held her clothing away from the table as she sat although the surface had been scrubbed almost to bare wood. Thomas hurried over with a coffee pot, a teapot and three cups. Rees would not have asked for them, he hoped this conversation would be short, but since Thomas had brought them, he nodded his thanks. 'Sugar and milk, if you please,' he said.

Lydia poured a cup of tea and offered it to Mrs Sechrest. 'No thank you. I prefer coffee.' Her tone made it clear she accepted coffee only when it was paired with tea. 'Although I do find the coffee here poorly made.'

'I enjoy it,' Rees said. He drank coffee regularly and did not find the beverage here any worse than at any other establishment. Thomas brought sugar and cream and a plate of beignets fresh from the kitchen.

Lydia took the cup of tea without comment and sipped. As Rees added a lump of sugar and enough cream to lighten the coffee to ecru, Mrs Sechrest helped herself to a beignet and nibbled at it delicately. 'Since the constable is indisposed, would you please tell me the circumstances of my brother's death?' She looked at Rees and applied the handkerchief to her dry eyes once again.

'We know very little,' Rees said. 'We know he suffered some violence prior to his death.'

Mrs Sechrest gasped. 'I heard that and hoped it was not so. Who? Who would mistreat Randolph so?'

'I am sorry to say we have no idea,' Rees said cautiously. 'He was found in the forest, far from any house or farm. Anyone could have put him there.' He hesitated. Should he tell her about the illness from which her brother was suffering. While he vacillated, Lydia spoke.

'Did you know your brother was ill? With smallpox?'

'No.' Mrs Sechrest took a small sip of her coffee. 'I believe there was some sickness in the quarters. He may have contracted the disease there. And of course, he traveled north, stopping at inns and other ordinaries along the way. Who among us could guess who he might have met?' She smiled slightly. 'I am afraid my brother demonstrated an unfortunate partiality for slaves and other riff-raff.'

Lydia put her cup down with a click. Astonishment warred with indignation. 'Surely you do not believe everyone—'

But Mrs Sechrest, ignoring Lydia as though she had not spoken, interrupted. Turning her attention solely to Rees, she said, 'Where is my property, Mr Rees? Where is the slave girl and her brat you brought north?'

FIFTEEN

The stunned silence lasted several seconds. Rees broke it by saying, 'I don't know what you are talking about.'

'Most certainly you do.'

'No, I don't. I just met you.' Rees looked at the young woman sitting across the table. She was completely convinced of the justice of her request. Rees guessed she had never been denied anything she wanted. Despite that, her mouth was pursed in discontent. 'I've had no opportunity to take your property, even if I wished to,' he said. Lydia took a beignet from the plate and nervously began breaking pieces from it.

'Oh, Mr Rees,' Mrs Sechrest said in her sweet voice, 'meeting me was not necessary. We have not met socially, oh my no. You stole two valuable slaves.' She opened her reticule and extracted a thin piece of paper. Rees glanced at it, recognizing the wanted poster with dismay.

'What is that?' he asked. She slid it across the table. He stared at it, trying to pretend he had never seen it before.

'It says a red-headed man,' he said. 'There must be hundreds of red-headed men. Why, many of my relatives sport red hair.'

'How many of them recently spent time in Virginia?' she asked. 'And don't pretend you did not visit Virginia. Thomas already admitted you are a great traveler.'

'I am a weaver,' Rees said shortly. 'I have no need of traveling to Virginia. My services are not required in that state.'

'From Virginia to Maine?' Lydia said, jumping into the conversation. 'That seems a long distance to travel.'

'Indeed it is. I sent several slave takers after the wench, but they quickly lost the trail. I probably would have abandoned the search then. But Randolph?' She laughed softly. 'He refused to capitulate. When he sets his mind on something, he cannot be turned aside. He was able to describe Sandy and some of the innkeepers along the way identified the red-headed man with her. And when he arrived in this small hamlet' – she might just as easily have said this God-forsaken wilderness – 'he found reports of both the red-headed man and my slave.' She extracted another piece of paper. 'He wrote me this missive informing me of the imminent capture of both.'

Rees stared at the letter as though it were a snake about to strike.

'You say you are hunting for my brother's murderer? I propose that you and that murderer are one and the same.' Charlotte Sechrest smiled, as though she had succeeded in landing a blow.

'That's ridiculous,' Lydia said. 'Of course he isn't a murderer.'

'But you admit he is a thief?'

'Of course not. You are making this up from whole cloth, pretending something that isn't true,' Lydia said fiercely.

'The loyal wife. How charming.' Mrs Sechrest smiled at Lydia. 'The wench stolen from me is very attractive. Why, my own stepson was captivated by her. It was a great tragedy. I would wonder about your husband's motivation, if I were you.'

'That's disgusting,' Lydia said hotly.

Of course, Rees thought, Miss Charlotte could not know Lydia, garbed in boy's clothing, had participated in the raid.

'I brought, besides several slaves, some experienced slave takers. They will find the girl, I promise you that.' Smiling, she gathered up her papers. 'It has been such a pleasure meeting you.' She waited for a moment and when Rees did not jump to his feet to pull out her chair, she pushed herself back from the table. 'Good day.'

Dumbfounded, Rees and Lydia sat in a mute silence while Thomas returned to the table. As he began gathering the cups and plates, Rees reached into his pocket. Thomas held up a hand. 'Don't worry,' he said. 'I'll put it on her tab.' He grinned. 'It's the least she can do.'

Rees nodded. 'Based on her dress, she can well afford it.'

Rees and Lydia refrained from speaking until they were crossing the street, away from the tavern and out of earshot of all other people. Then Rees said, 'We must warn Tobias and Ruth and John Washington, everyone we know.'

'Yes,' Lydia agreed.

'And Sandy and Abram have to be taken out of town. Spirited away to somewhere safe.'

'To somewhere safe,' Lydia agreed. 'But not to the farm. That woman already suspects you. Our home is the first place she and her toadies will look.'

'Where then?'

Exchanging a glance, they said in unison, 'To Zion.'

Rees drove out of town as quickly as he dared. As they left the last house behind, Lydia asked Rees, 'Do you believe in evil?'

'Evil?' Rees repeated in surprise.

'Yes.' She turned to look at him, her blue eyes troubled. 'You focus most of your energy on identifying murderers. Do you believe they are evil?'

'You mean, possessed by the devil?' Rees did not believe in the devil. Some days he wasn't sure he believed in God.

'Yes. No. I don't know.' Lydia bit her lip.

Rees gave some serious thought to her question. Usually he left such philosophical questions to others, preferring to go straight ahead to the solution without side trips. Mostly, if he reflected upon his role as a hunter of the villainous, he thought of himself as speaking for the victim.

'Why do you work so hard to attain justice for the victim if you don't believe in evil?' Lydia persisted. 'The victim doesn't care anymore.'

'Everyone else does,' Rees said. Of that he was certain. 'And the victim has lost his own chance of speaking.' He halted, recalling the murderers he'd known. When he tried to explain once again, his words were slow and spoken with difficulty. 'I do believe there are evil people although I strongly doubt the devil has anything to do with it. I mean, some murders are an act of selfishness, aren't they? Me above all else. But some of the murderers, although they have done terrible things, are not evil. They're just people who are broken inside. I feel sorriest for them. The action they take to solve their problem becomes a bigger problem.' He turned to look at his wife. 'Why? Do you believe in evil?' He would be surprised if Lydia, a former Shaker, said no.

'I do. I sometimes think evil is all around us. I agree with you though. It is selfishness, isn't it? A monstrous selfishness that does not recognize the value in another person. By ignoring the . . . the humanity of someone else, a person is absolved from feeling compassion, mercy, or benevolence.'

'What brought this on?' Rees asked. Usually Lydia did not
engage in such theoretical discussions either. 'Mrs Sechrest?'

'Maybe. She is selfish. Moreover, she is completely certain
she is in the right. No hesitation about the moral righteousness
of her opinion. She sat there in her expensive clothes discussing
Sandy as though she were a clot of mud, never even raising her
voice.'

'You disliked her,' Rees said. He'd felt the same. That soft
feminine exterior cloaked a core of ice.

'Yes. I certainly did. Did you find her agreeable?' Lydia turned
a serious look upon Rees.

'No.' He did not need to ponder that question. Like Lydia, he
found Mrs Sechrest's absolute certainty worrisome. He often found
himself regretting a casual comment that hurt another's feelings,
a word of comfort unspoken, and especially some impulsive
behavior that caused harm. He knew he was far from perfect. He
suspected Mrs Sechrest never experienced a moment of doubt
about herself. 'But maybe referring to her as evil is overstating
it a bit,' he said with a grin.

Lydia smiled back. 'Maybe it is, a bit,' she agreed. 'Still, I
can't resist hoping she murdered her brother. That would solve
everything in the best way possible.' She was only half-joking.

Chuckling, Rees shook his head.

SIXTEEN

Rees turned off into the lane that went to Zion and they
drove into the village. The main street was still empty as
all of the community were engaged in their daily activities, but within the hour all of the Shakers would flood into the
streets, on their way to the Meeting House for morning prayers.

He pulled to a stop in front of the barn and turned to his
wife. 'What do you think?' he asked. As a former Shaker herself,
Lydia would know the best way to handle the request.

'We will apply to Elder Jonathan first,' she said. 'He will have
to bring our request to the other Elders anyway.'

'Very well,' Rees agreed. Although he did not say so aloud, he wondered if Jonathan would be disposed to help. In the past few years, Rees had appealed to Jonathan for several favors. Thus far, the Elder had always granted them, for several reasons. Lydia had once been a member of this group and Rees himself had a long history with them. Also, the question of the ownership of the farm on which Rees's family now lived continued to be an on-going legal issue. But Rees sensed that Brother Jonathan was growing weary of these all too frequent entreaties. In fact, he'd seemed a trifle brusque the last time they'd spoken.

Rees and Lydia crossed the street and went around the Dwelling House. They walked in silence to the yellow building on the left, the woodworking workshop. But when they stepped inside, there was no sign of Jonathan. Instead, Aaron was delicately tapping on the bottom of a chair leg with a mallet.

'Brother Jonathan?' Rees asked. Although Aaron had surrendered his fancy beaver hat and colorful vest, he still wore the trousers Rees had seen him wearing in town.

'Not here,' Aaron said tersely. 'And, before you ask, I don't know where he is.'

Rees hesitated. He wanted to ask the other man if he had been accepted back into the community. But, in the end, he couldn't quite muster the courage to inquire. With a muttered thank you, he turned and ushered Lydia from the shop.

'I suspect he is on probation,' Lydia told Rees as they walked back the way they'd come. When he glanced at her, she smiled. 'I could see you wondering,' she said.

'Now what?' he asked.

'Why don't we speak to Sister Esther? She may be willing to apply to him on our behalf.'

'That sounds like a good plan,' Rees agreed.

'She is working in the kitchen this week.'

They walked to the path that led to the kitchen. Rees paused and allowed Lydia to go on alone. But she returned within only a few minutes. 'Sister Agatha is ill so Esther is working in the still house today,' she said.

'Ill?' Rees asked. 'With smallpox?'

'They didn't say.' Lydia glanced at her husband in concern. 'Do you think the disease has reached Zion?'

Rees shook his head; he couldn't guess. But he too wondered.

They climbed the slope to the still house. The air inside was as fragrant as Rees remembered. Esther presided over the table, today now crammed with bottles waiting to be filled with the tonic. As one of the young Sisters stirred the tonic bubbling in a kettle over the fire, the other roamed through the drying racks inspecting the flowers, leaves and stems spread out upon them.

'Busy day?' Lydia murmured as she moved toward the table. Rees, feeling both big and clumsy in the midst of this feminine workplace, remained by the door.

'I hope you don't mind if I fill these bottles with the elixir while we talk,' Esther said. 'We must finish by morning prayers.'

'Of course,' Lydia replied. 'Are these all for the Family here?'

'No, not all. One of the Brothers carried a few packets of medicinal herbs and a few bottles of tonic with him on the last selling trip. They proved so popular we decided to prepare add-itional supplies for sale.' As Esther spoke, one of the younger Sisters pushed the kettle away from the fire and began stirring to cool it. Esther nodded at a second Sister. She collected her cloak and left, without a word spoken. For a moment all was silent but for the scrape of the ladle on the sides of the kettle. Then Lydia spoke.

'The murder victim's sister, a Mrs Sechrest, has arrived in town.'

'Has she come to claim her brother's body?' Esther looked up in confusion. 'How did she make that long journey so quickly?'

'Mr Gilbert sent her a letter,' Lydia said.

'A letter?' Dismay and sudden apprehension crossed Esther's face. 'I don't understand.' She glanced at the other Sister who handed Esther the ladle with its hot contents. She poured it very carefully into one of the jars. With a loud snap, the glass shat-tered and the hot elixir ran over the table and spattered the floor. 'Oh dear,' Esther said. 'The tonic is still too hot.'

As Esther gingerly began picking up the broken glass, the young girl found a rag and began mopping up the floor. These spills must happen frequently. Rees saw that, despite much rigorous cleaning that had left the floor rough and splintery, it was still deeply stained. The wood would require sanding to recover its smoothness again.

'Go on to prayers,' Esther told the girl. 'If I am late, I'll explain to Elder Jonathan.' While the young girl left, Esther took up a position by the kettle and began stirring. 'So, the victim's sister has arrived in town?'

'Yes,' Lydia said. 'Mrs Sechrest wants to take Sandy and Abram home to Virginia and into slavery again.'

Esther's arm slowed. 'Does she know for certain they are here, in Durham?'

'She's sure,' Lydia said.

'In fact, she accused me of rescuing the young woman and her baby,' Rees added as he stepped forward.

'How did she know?' Esther asked.

'Her brother's letter.'

'We have to hide Sandy,' Lydia said. Esther turned a look of consternation upon the other woman. 'At least for a short while,' Lydia said quickly.

'We were hoping you would speak to the Elders and the other Eldress for us,' Rees said.

'You know Sister Agatha will say no,' Esther said with a grimace. 'Brothers Jonathan and Daniel? They might say yes. But . . .' She hesitated.

Rees stared at her in surprise. An escaped slave herself, he would have expected her to be enthusiastic about helping another. 'I know this would be a violation of the law,' he said.

Esther nodded. 'And a terrible law it is. As you know, we Believers are in the main opposed to slavery.'

'In the main?' Rees seized on that phrase, his heart sinking.

'Yes.' Esther sighed. 'There are some . . .' Her voice trailed away once again.

Rees immediately thought of Sister Agatha who seemed to feel she alone could protect the ideals of this Shaker community. She was determined to keep the World, and the World's problems, far away.

'I will gladly propose this to the others, if that is what you wish,' Esther continued. 'But I must admit I am concerned. I fear that young woman and her child will not be safe here.'

'Do you mean you believe someone will betray Sandy to Mrs Sechrest?' Lydia asked in horror.

'Not if that meant traveling to town and expending the effort to find her,' Esther said with a grim smile. 'But if she, or one of her tame slave takers, comes to Zion and asks, well, I could not promise you someone here would not reveal Sandy's whereabouts.' Her voice was shaky.

Lydia and Rees exchanged a glance. Neither one wanted to risk even the slightest chance Sandy and her baby would be recaptured. 'I'm already worried about Tobias and Ruth,' Rees said.

'I know,' Lydia said in agreement.

'They at least are already members of the community in Durham,' Esther said. 'If one of the slave takers tries to take them off the street in public, I must believe someone would intercede.'

Both Lydia and Rees nodded.

'We've already warned them not to leave their house after dark,' Rees said. Although he did not say so, he was concerned for Esther too. He did not like to witness her poorly concealed fear. She was usually so tough, opinionated and strong.

Lydia put a hand over Esther's. 'You take care as well,' she said.

Esther nodded. 'It's been many years since I walked north from Georgia and I've lived among the Shakers for most of them,' she said. 'I don't know if I have the strength and the courage to run again.'

'We won't let them take you,' Rees promised rashly.

Esther's eyes filled and she turned her face away. 'The elixir must be cool enough now,' she said in a husky voice. 'I ought to finish this batch. I'm already late for prayers.'

Very quietly, Rees and Lydia left the workshop.

SEVENTEEN

Lydia did not permit her tears to fall until they were some distance from the still house. Rees put a hand on her shoulder. 'I know,' he said. 'I don't like seeing her so afraid either.'

'I am just so angry,' Lydia said, wiping away her tears with her fingers. 'This village, Zion, is her home now. And it has been for many years. How dare they threaten her now. How dare they!'

'Don't worry,' Rees said reassuringly. 'We'll check on her regularly. And if someone tries to take her, we'll go after them and rescue her.'

Lydia sniffed and smiled. 'Of course, we will. Besides, I'm certain if someone came into Zion for her, the rest of the community would rise up to defend her.'

'Yes,' Rees agreed even though he felt any help the Shaker Brothers could provide would prove ineffective. They owned no weapons and were pacifists besides. But he did not say that aloud.

Smiling, and looking somewhat more cheerful, Lydia tucked her hand in the crook of Rees's elbow. 'Oh dear, I forgot to ask Esther about Annie. I know she would not have been released from her duties unless it was for a very good reason.'

Rees recalled the blisters around Annie's wrist. Could a bout of cowpox explain her sudden freedom? He doubted it. Annie wasn't sick.

Since the farm lay only a short distance away from Zion, it took them only fifteen or twenty minutes to reach the lane to it. By then they could both hear shouting and Sharon's piercing wails. Lydia and Rees exchanged an anxious glance. He slapped the reins down hard and Hannibal broke into a gallop. The distance along the lane from the main road to their gate was not long; when they reached it the wagon careened around the turn, skidding across the wet ground and almost slamming into the fence post.

The yard was full. Mrs Sechrest's elegant and very large carriage and the matched four that pulled it occupied most of the space, but several other unfamiliar horses were tied up by the barn. Sharon, Joseph and Annie stood on the front porch. None of them wore their outer clothing and both Sharon and Joseph were sobbing. Both Rees and Lydia jumped down from the wagon and ran to them.

As Lydia knelt beside the children, Rees said to Annie, 'What happened?'

'These people came.' Annie was weeping as well but Rees thought her tears were inspired as much by fury as fear. 'I don't know who they are. They have guns, Mr Rees. There's a woman with them—'

Rees was already moving. He ran through the kitchen door and into the house. The remains of the children's meals lay scattered on the table, half-eaten. In the center of the main room stood Mrs Sechrest. So enraged he could hardly force the words out, Rees shouted, 'What are you doing in my house?'

Mrs Sechrest turned. 'Why, Mr Rees, such an unmannerly greeting.'

Lydia, with the two children and Annie, came up behind her husband. 'How dare you!' Lydia said furiously to Mrs Sechrest.

Even over the screams of his children, Rees could hear the thud of heavy footsteps overhead.

'Get out.' He gestured to the ceiling. 'And take your lackeys with you.'

'Oh, not until we've finished searching.' Mrs Sechrest smiled. 'The law gives me the right to search for my property . . .' she began.

'It does not give you the right to put my children outside,' Lydia said, sounding as though her teeth were locked together. 'In the cold. Without their cloaks.'

'I'm so sorry. But your youngest began screaming. I could not hear myself think.' Mrs Sechrest glanced at the children and added indifferently, 'They're fine.'

Rees glanced at his wife. Her face was pale with rage. 'You endangered my children.' Lydia stopped, so angry she could barely speak.

'I did not suggest they go out without their cloaks,' Charlotte Sechrest said defensively.

'Those men pushed us out,' Annie said, braver now that Lydia and Rees flanked her. 'They did not give me time to get the cloaks . . .'

'What exactly are you looking for, Charlotte,' Rees said rudely.

'You may not speak to me with such disrespect,' Mrs Sechrest responded.

'I'll speak to you any way I choose,' Rees snapped. For a moment they locked stares. Mrs Sechrest's eyes dropped first.

'Anyway, I told you. The wench and her baby that you stole from me.'

'And I told you I did not know what you were talking about.' Rees was angrier now than he had been for a very long time. He wanted to throw this young woman who was smirking at him in his own kitchen through the wall. Instead, although his hands were clenched into fists, he was determined not to allow her to bait him into something he would later regret. But he would be as obstructive as possible.

Two men, clad in shabby imitations of Randolph Sechrest's finery, thumped down the stairs. Neither was shaven and their vests and frock coats were grubby. The lead fellow shook his head at Mrs Sechrest before turning his gaze upon Rees and his family. He had the coldest eyes Rees had ever seen; the color of slate or old ice. He would kill Rees – or anyone including Sharon – without a moment's hesitation. Of that, Rees had no doubt.

'Maybe he put them in the barn?' Mrs Sechrest suggested.

'Get out,' Rees repeated. The two men looked at Mrs Sechrest for permission. She eyed Rees appraisingly, as though trying to determine how far he would go to defend his family from her men. He could not prevent his involuntary step toward her. She inclined her head in assent.

'Very well, Mr Rees. We will leave. For now. Cole, search the barn.'

The gray-eyed man nodded. He gestured to his mistress, indicating she should go first.

None of the three hurried. Mrs Sechrest, in fact, strolled past Rees and Lydia as though they were but shadows, unworthy of her notice. She was so young. Rees couldn't decide if she truly believed in her own superiority or wore her arrogance like a suit of armor to protect a softer inner core. If pressed, he would choose the former. Cole sneered at Rees from under his moth-eaten rabbit fur hat, his hair an untidy black fringe beneath it.

Of the three, only the final man, little more than a boy really, kept his eyes lowered in embarrassment. His cheeks were scarlet.

Rees followed them to the porch and watched as Cole went to the barn. When he exited after a few minutes he shook his head at Mrs Sechrest. 'I told you,' Rees said. 'I don't have anything of yours.'

'I am so sorry we intruded on your family,' Mrs Sechrest said, drawing her mouth down in mock sadness. 'I hope your children do not take a chill.' Rees felt Lydia move past him with her hand upraised. He caught her arm before she could run down the stairs and attack the other woman. 'I will find the girl. I promise you that. All this obstruction is for nothing.'

Rees took two steps forward. 'And I'm warning you,' he said. 'If I see you here again, I will not be so polite.'

Mrs Sechrest opened her mouth but Rees's expression, and another step forward, extinguished her desire to argue. She climbed into her carriage and within a few minutes the yard was empty.

'We must smuggle Sandy and Abram out of town immediately,' Lydia said, turning toward Rees.

'I agree,' he said. 'I'd do it now but Mrs Sechrest is probably just waiting for me to do something foolish.'

'We can't allow that woman to take them.'

'Not even to safeguard your own children,' Rees teased.

'Don't joke,' Lydia said, turning her white face with the two scarlet circles on her cheeks to Rees. 'What would Mrs Sechrest do to Abram?' She raised teary eyes to Rees. 'I don't want to imagine.'

'Some women would abandon Sandy and Abram immediately to protect her own family,' Rees pointed out.

'And what kind of example for our children would that be?' Lydia said vehemently. 'Oh, that woman makes me forget my Christian principles. I want to strike her.'

'I know,' Rees said with a grin. 'That's why I love you.'

'Be serious, Will. This isn't funny. What can we do?'

'I may have an idea,' Rees said.

EIGHTEEN

That night, Rees left his house well after dark. He hitched the donkey to the cart – he and Lydia thought his horse and wagon were too identifiable – and drove to town. Since it was well after the time when most decent folk were abed and asleep, he was cautiously optimistic that he would not be seen. And indeed, the windows of most of the houses he passed were dark. The only lights and activity came from the tavern and Rees turned down a side street, taking a round-about way, to avoid it.

There were no lights at Tobias's. Rees knocked on the door. When he heard nothing, he knocked again. Still nothing. Rees was preparing to throw stones at the windows when candlelight, swiftly masked, gleamed briefly under the door. It opened a crack and Tobias peered through it. 'Rees?'

'Let me in, Tobias.'

'What the Hell are you doing here at this time of night? You scared me out of ten years' growth.' Although he sounded angry, his voice was shaking.

'I'm sorry if I frightened you,' Rees said. 'But this is important.'

Grumbling, Tobias opened the door a bit wider. 'Hurry up, then.' Rees hurriedly squeezed inside. 'Now what is so important?' Tobias demanded. If the situation had not been so desperate, Rees might have had a good chuckle at Tobias's expense. He was wearing a nightshirt that left his brown ankles bare and a nightcap over his hair.

'That Charlotte Sechrest is determined to recapture Sandy and Abram,' Rees said. 'We need to get them to some place safe.' Quickly he sketched in his homecoming and finding his children on the porch. 'It is clear she suspects me—'

'With good reason,' Tobias interrupted.

'Yes. But we can't let her know she is correct. And we need to get Sandy and Abram out of town immediately.'

'And that's why you're here now.'

'Yes. I think I know a place. Better you not know either. That way you can tell the truth when you say you have no idea where she is.'

Tobias mulled that over for a few seconds, finally nodded. 'Very well. I'll get them.' He padded to the stairs, turning only once to invite Rees to sit down. But he couldn't. He was far too nervous. He began to pace.

The few minutes that passed seemed like an hour. Rees kept expecting Charlotte Sechrest to arrive and demand her property. But each time he peeked through the window he saw nothing but a quiet darkness outside.

Finally Sandy, yawning but dressed and carrying Abram, came downstairs. Tobias followed with a sack containing Sandy's few possessions. Ruth, who'd awakened as well, leaned over the bannister and looked at Rees intently. 'Don't worry,' Rees promised her. 'Sandy and Abram will be safe.' Ruth nodded slightly.

Tobias carried the sack to the cart and put it beside Sandy. Rees covered her and her child with a blanket. 'Thank you,' he said to Tobias. 'I'll let you know how she fares.'

With a nod, Tobias withdrew to his door. As he prepared to shut it, Rees said, 'Be careful, you and Ruth. Mrs Sechrest has several men with her. They won't stick at taking you if they find you, free or not.'

'Thank you,' Tobias said as he closed the door.

Rees climbed into the seat. He knew this journey would take most of the night. The distance was great and the night was dark. But this had to be done.

They drove through town. Even the tavern was quieter now, but he saw a candle burning on the second floor. Although he could not be sure Charlotte Sechrest was still awake, he shivered. He urged the donkey to speed up so that they might hurry past the tavern. They turned onto North Road but, instead of going straight, Rees turned right onto the twisty and narrow track that led up Gray Mountain.

He had met Granny Rose, a midwife for the mountain folk, the previous winter. She had helped him then and he hoped, he prayed, she would be willing to assist a young mother and her child now. If Granny Rose refused, Rees did not know what he would do.

He had lit one of the lanterns for the passage through town. Now he stopped and lit the second one. Even with two, the light was dim. Tree trunks seemed to appear like magic from the darkness and then quickly disappear again. At least he was not traveling through a blizzard and the surface of the track, although rutted and full of holes, was not coated with a slippery sheet of ice. Last winter, after he had found the midwife's daughter wandering shoeless and without a cloak in the midst of the storm, he had made the journey into the mountains often, including during a terrible blizzard.

Rees could only hope the donkey kept his footing on the steep grade.

They came to the plateau and Rees stopped to rest in front of the store. The millwheel was shut down for the winter; it was much colder here. And very dark. When Rees looked up at the sky, he could see the faint brightness of the moon behind the thin clouds. He hoped the sky would clear so that the moon would shine down upon the road.

He was already tired. He'd been clutching the reins so tightly his hands ached and the tension ran all the way up to his shoulders. He forced himself to stop clenching his teeth. He knew the last part of the route would be the most difficult. And dangerous. The steep incline was one hairpin turn after another, many with drop-offs on the other side. If he wasn't careful, he and the cart could fly off to land somewhere far below.

He stiffly climbed down from the seat and walked around for a few seconds. Then he twitched the blanket away from Sandy. Abram was fast asleep in his mother's arms, but Sandy was still awake. She looked at him in fear.

'Not far now,' Rees said, his voice rusty with disuse.

'Thank you,' she whispered.

Rees climbed back into the seat. For a moment he just sat there, holding the reins as he steeled himself for the final leg of this journey. Then he called to the donkey and they started off again.

This part of the journey was every bit as difficult as he'd remembered. Even with the lanterns, he could see only a few feet in front of him. And the donkey was struggling with the weight on this steep incline. Rees finally jumped down and walked beside the animal. He did not lead; he couldn't see and anyway he trusted the donkey's instincts far more than his own.

The snow that had fallen in town had melted, but here, where the air was colder, it had formed a thin film over the frozen ground. Recalling his experiences of the previous winter, Rees could almost imagine he heard wolves in the distance.

They turned at the second lane. The path was not so steep here and the donkey speeded up a little. Rees could see light ahead, firelight. He wondered if Granny Rose had already lit the bonfire she kept burning all winter, to keep the wolves away she said, but it also welcomed the weary traveler.

He staggered up the final slope, his hand on the donkey's neck. Inside Granny Rose's cabin, a candle burned, the light seeping around the window curtain in a pale orange line. Rees went to the door and lifted his hand to knock. But before his knuckles touched the wood, the door opened.

'Rees,' said Granny Rose in surprise.

'I need help,' Rees said. He handed her the pound of coffee Lydia had insisted he bring as a gift. 'No, not me.' He was so exhausted he barely knew what he was saying. 'I have someone who needs your help.' He gestured to the cart and to Sandy who had climbed out. She held Abram tightly to her and stared at Granny Rose over his head. The old woman stared at them both.

'I see,' she said at last. 'Well, I suppose you'd better come inside.'

NINETEEN

While Rees unhitched the donkey and put him in the barn next to Granny Rose's animal, the midwife took Sandy and Abram into the cabin. The child stirred but did not fully wake and, by the time Rees went inside, Abram was once again fast asleep on Granny's bed. She had stirred up the fire and put some of her chicory coffee over the flames. Rees hated that counterfeit coffee but he would be glad of a hot drink tonight.

'You must be hungry,' Granny Rose said as she put out a plate of apple fritters. 'You, girl, eat something. You're too thin. Why, your arm is no bigger than my little finger.'

Sandy obediently took a fritter and bit into it.

'What happened?' Granny asked Rees.

He hesitated. He did not know her stand on abolition. But he was far too weary to make up a convincing lie and anyway, if she were to disobey the law and put herself into danger, she deserved nothing less than the truth.

'A month ago, few weeks more than that now, Lydia and I went to Virginia. To the Great Dismal Swamp. We were asked by a friend to help him rescue his wife.' Rees considered telling the entire tale, as well as mentioning the names, but elected to keep that part of the story to himself. He did not want to put Ruth and Tobias into any more danger than they were already. 'While we were in the swamp, we met Sandy and her little boy.' Granny's gaze went to the fair-skinned young woman in surprise.

'She was a slave?'

'Yes,' Rees said with a nod. 'And her baby as well. The woman who lawfully owns Sandy and Abram is now in Durham.'

'Lawfully but not morally,' Granny Rose said.

'Exactly,' Rees agreed, feeling himself relax. 'And "that woman", as Lydia calls her, Mrs Charlotte Sechrest, is not someone to whom I would ever surrender Sandy.'

'Is there anyone you would relinquish this girl to?' Granny Rose asked with a smile. She rose to her feet and moved the coffee pot to one side.

'No,' Rees admitted. 'And Lydia has joined the local chapter of the Abolitionist group so I wouldn't dare even if I wished to. But that Mrs Sechrest more than most. She is . . .' He ran out of words.

'Why has Mrs Sechrest traveled so far to re-capture Sandy?' Granny Rose asked.

'I am not sure,' Rees admitted. 'I know Mrs Sechrest's brother was searching for Sandy. He tracked her all the way from Virginia to Maine.' He glanced at Granny Rose to see if she understood. She nodded, her glance going to the pretty young woman drowsing in her chair.

'Then he was murdered, here, in town,' Rees added.

'And of course you are involved,' Granny said in amusement. 'I ain't never seen a man so eager to put himself into trouble.'

'It is odd, though,' Rees said. 'Mrs Sechrest does not seem to be grieving for her brother.'

Granny picked up the coffee pot. She poured out the dark brew into a large pewter cup and handed it to Rees. While he took a cautious sip, Granny brought out a small loaf of sugar and stepped outside to collect the milk.

When Granny returned, she picked up the conversation where they'd left it. 'Grief takes people different ways,' she said as

Rees put a lump of sugar into his mug and added milk. 'It's likely she blames this girl here for her brother's death.'

'Probably,' Rees said. 'She blames Sandy for everything else.' He thought back to his conversation with Mrs Sechrest and the anger simmering just below the surface. 'She was furious,' he said now, realizing with a shock how true that was. 'So enraged she could scarcely speak to me.'

'You do sometimes have that effect on people,' Granny Rose commented drily. Rees grinned.

'But she'd never met me before,' he said. 'She doesn't even know, she can't be certain anyway, that I had anything to do with Sandy's escape. I don't think she was angry with me. At least,' he amended, 'not at first.'

'Hmm. Perhaps the girl is exceptionally valuable,' Granny suggested, shooting a quick glance at the drowsing girl.

'Possibly. But Mrs Sechrest was going to give Sandy to her brother. From what I understood no money would change hands.'

'Then this is personal.' Granny passed the plate of fritters to Rees. 'Sounds to me like Mrs Sechrest wants to punish this girl for something. What do you know about their past connection?'

'Not very much,' Rees admitted. 'Just that Sandy was favored by Mr Sechrest's first wife. And her son Gregory is Abram's father.'

'Sounds like jealousy to me,' Granny said.

'She's mean,' Sandy put in, surprising Rees who'd thought she was asleep. 'She's just mean.' Granny passed her the plate. Although Sandy took a fritter she did not eat it. Her hands, with the fritter in them, dropped to her lap. She was too tired to eat.

Feeling that they had gone rather far off-topic, Rees changed the subject. 'I hope you are willing to hide her here. At least for a little while.'

'I've been looking for an assistant,' Granny said as she looked at the girl.

'I'm a dressmaker,' Sandy said. 'That's what I do. Not taking care of babies.'

'You'll learn,' Granny said cheerfully.

'I hope this will not be for long,' Rees said, glancing from one woman to the other.

'You can leave her here, as long as you need,' Granny Rose said. 'If the mountain don't discourage that Sechrest woman, the wolves will.'

She pressed Rees to stay the night but he refused. 'I know Mrs Sechrest and her pet slave takers are watching me,' he said. 'I want to be home, just as if I had nothing to do with Sandy's disappearance. I have to keep my family safe as well.'

'You be careful,' she said, fixing him with her sharp eyes. 'You're tired. I don't want you heading off a cliff.'

With a nod, he went outside to hitch the donkey to the cart. The animal was not happy and resisted. Already tired, Rees began cursing the animal and threatening him with a beating. Finally, Granny came out and, speaking in a soothing voice to the donkey, she took the bridle from Rees's hands. Within a few minutes, she had successfully hitched the donkey to the cart. 'Be careful,' she said again.

'I will,' Rees said. Feeling somewhat foolish, he climbed into the cart and started forward. Granny walked him to her gate and when he looked behind him before he made the first turn, he saw her still there watching.

He felt unexpectedly bereft when he could no longer see her bonfire, glowing with its promise of help, behind him.

They went down this part of the mountain much more quickly than they'd climbed up. The steepness assisted the descent but Rees held the reins firmly to slow the donkey if he should be disposed to run.

They paused once again at the plateau where the store was located. Now, when Rees looked up at the sky, he saw the half-moon floating high above in the blackness. The clouds were parting, by morning the skies would clear. But an icy winter wind swept down from the summit of Gray Mountain and cut through his greatcoat like a knife. With a crack, a branch broke off somewhere in the surrounding woods and fell with a thud to the ground.

'Come on,' Rees said to the donkey. 'Time to go.'

The remaining distance to the valley below was neither as twisty nor as steep as the climb to Granny Rose's cabin. Rees began to relax. His mule kept his footing without difficulty and

walked easily, albeit slowly, over the furrowed dirt. The sway of
the cart from side to side as it lurched over the potholes began
to feel as restful as a cradle. Rees's eyes drooped and then closed
before he knew it.

A sharp gust of wind keened through the trees, jerking him
awake. The reins had slipped through his hands and his donkey
and cart stood immobile in the center of the road. In the darkness, surrounded by tall evergreens on every side, this piece of
road looked like every other. He could not tell where he was.

Rees called to the mule and they started forward again. He
struggled to keep his eyes open, but it proved close to impossible. Finally, he climbed down and walked beside the animal,
forcing his body to wake up. He set little goals for himself: I
will make it to that dead tree, the one with its shattered trunk
pointing to the sky. I will make it to the thick-trunked pine. I
will make it to the turn-off to the Benton cabin. And, at last,
I will make it to North Road.

By the time he turned into his own gate, the eastern sky was
beginning to lighten. Lydia was awake and waiting for him. She
opened the kitchen door, the candlelight behind her spilling out
onto the porch, and held it ajar for him as he staggered inside.

TWENTY

The bright morning sun woke Rees. Rubbing his eyes, he
sat up. Although he had slept longer than he'd intended,
he was still tired from his late-night adventure. Yawning,
he slid out of bed and went to the ewer in the corner to splash
cold water on his face. He had chores to finish. Anyway, the goal
was to make his activities seem perfectly normal to anyone who
might be watching.

Lydia had coffee waiting for him. Rees took it to the table.
For once, the house was relatively silent; both Sharon and Joseph
played quietly by the fire.

'Did Jerusha experience any trouble with the donkey?' Rees
asked.

Lydia turned with a smile. 'She did. She couldn't understand why he was so difficult this morning.'

Rees chuckled. He hadn't told Jerusha of his plans and didn't mean to now that they were successfully accomplished. The less she knew, the safer she would be.

'Annie did not come today?' Rees asked.

Lydia shook her head. 'I suspect she is in trouble now for abandoning her chores yesterday. I've already milked Daisy and Hannibal is in the paddock.'

Rees nodded his thanks. 'It was a terrible journey,' he said. 'In the dark and so cold.'

'It's cold now as well, for all that it is sunny,' Lydia said. And then: 'Who can that be riding into the yard. Why, it's Thomas.'

'Oh no,' Rees said, his heart sinking. Although he and Thomas were friendly, they were more acquaintances than friends. They certainly did not enjoy the closeness necessary for regular visits and yet this was the second time this week that Thomas had come by. His presence here could only mean more bad news. Swearing under his breath, Rees rose to open the door. 'Thomas. Welcome. What is it?'

'Rouge sent me. He is . . .' Thomas's face twisted and he fought for composure. Rees drew the young man inside and threw a quick look at Lydia. She poured a cup of coffee and put it on the table in front of Thomas. He took a hasty sip. 'My cousin is not doing well,' Thomas said. 'In fact he . . .' He stopped and swallowed. 'He is very ill. Although he is not as feverish as he was yesterday and the day before, he is developing a rash.'

Rees nodded and looked at Lydia. 'He caught smallpox from Randolph Gilbert. I feared this result. I hope it is not too late to inoculate the children.' Turning to Thomas, he asked sharply, 'Have you had the disease?'

'Yes. Both Therese and I had it as children.' He gulped.

'Sometimes it is worse for adults,' Rees said. 'Rouge will not recover for a week or more.' The words 'if he lives' hung in the air.

'He can't perform his duties as constable,' Thomas said. 'He wants you to take over for him.'

'Why my husband?' Lydia asked.

'Doesn't he have deputies who can perform that service for him?' Rees objected.

'Most of them are the tavern regulars,' Thomas said dismissively. 'Drinkers and the like. Some are farmers who don't even live in town. Besides . . .' He paused.

'Besides what?' Rees asked suspiciously.

'We have another murder,' Thomas admitted. 'Rouge wants you to handle it.'

'Of course he does,' Lydia said tartly.

'Who is the victim?' Rees asked in a resigned voice.

'One of Mrs Sechrest's slave hunters,' Thomas said. He brushed his dark hair back from his face. 'It happened sometime last night.'

'Let me put on my coat,' Rees said. He turned to look at Lydia, attempting to convey without words that he would return home with all of the information. Then he followed Thomas from the house.

They did not get to the body immediately. Hitching Hannibal to the wagon took some time and then, once in town, Rees insisted on visiting Rouge. 'After all,' he told Thomas, 'the dead man will keep.'

Thomas seemed relieved to sit down in the tavern and drink a flagon of ale.

Rees walked along the hallway to Rouge's office and scratched at the door. 'Go away,' Rouge shouted. His voice sounded so raspy that, if Rees did not know to whom he was speaking, he would not have guessed it was Simon Rouge. Rees opened the door and went inside.

The office stank like the den of an animal: close air, vomit and feces. Rouge lay on his pallet. Someone had come in and given him water and a bowl of soup, but he had not drunk or eaten any of it. His red-rimmed eyes stared at Rees from a face so covered with raised lesions he scarcely appeared human.

'My God!' Rees exclaimed involuntarily.

'Told you not to come in,' Rouge said.

'Have you had anything to eat?' Rees asked.

'No.'

Rees knelt and although he didn't want to touch the other man he held up Rouge's head and tipped a few sips of water into his mouth. A few spoonfuls of soup followed but Rouge refused anything more. 'Mouth hurts,' he mumbled.

Rees had seen enough of this disease to know the lesions would grow larger and eventually fill with a fluid. If Rouge survived, those pustules would harden and eventually scab over and fall off, probably leaving behind scarring. Rouge's unhandsome face would be even less lovely.

'From here, I'm going to look at the murder victim,' Rees said. He did not know what to say to Rouge so he took refuge in the practical. 'Thomas did not know very much about the murder. Do you know anything else?'

'Hidden in the woods,' Rouge said.

'Not on my property again?' Rees asked.

'No. Other side of town.' Rouge slumped back, exhausted by even that little effort.

Rees nodded. 'I will let you know what I find out,' he promised. Under normal circumstances, Rees would have reached out and clapped Rouge on the shoulder. But now he couldn't.

Rouge tried to nod.

Rees hastily quit the room and then felt guilty for his obvious eagerness to leave Rouge's company. Once in the hall, Rees shuddered all over, like a dog shaking off the wet, and had to stand there and pull himself together before returning to the public room and Thomas.

'Do you see?' Thomas asked, his voice trembling.

'He'll be fine,' Rees promised the other man. 'Rouge is strong. He'll survive.' His effort at comfort fell flat. Even he did not believe his assurances.

Thomas nodded and drank the last of his ale in one long swallow. 'I'll show you where the body is,' he said.

'How was he found?' Rees asked as they walked to his wagon. No sick cow this time, of that he was sure.

'Mrs Sechrest claimed he was missing this morning and insisted on a search. I looked in his room; his bed had not been slept in.' Thomas glanced at Rees and added, 'She will probably be there.'

'Of course she will,' Rees said, unable to keep the animosity from his voice. Not only would she be there but he knew she would be accusing everyone in sight. He did not doubt he would come in for a large portion of her vitriol.

TWENTY-ONE

'Have you seen the body?' Rees asked Thomas as they climbed into the wagon.

'Yes. No.' Thomas shrugged when Rees looked at him. 'Rouge sent me out to confirm there was a body so I know roughly where it is. But I did not look at it except to be sure it was there.'

'How far out of town is it?'

'Not far.' Thomas shook his head. 'In fact, now that I think of it, it is almost too close. I would have taken the victim much further away.'

'Yes,' Rees agreed. 'So far away the body would never be discovered. The question is, why didn't he? And why leave the corpse there, on the opposite side of town from Randolph Gilbert?' Thomas nodded in agreement but offered no answer.

They drove along Main Street only until River Road, then Thomas directed Rees to turn left. They were driving on the same street where most of the livery stables, the wheelwright, the wagon builder and two of the three blacksmiths had shops. In fact, they passed Washington's smithy. They turned right and then a quick left to cross the bridge over the river. Once on the other side, there were only a few buildings, a lumber mill and another smaller tavern, before they reached the forest.

Rees heard the sound of conversation before he saw anyone. Mrs Sechrest's carriage, with only the driver to guard it, was parked on the verge. Rees pulled to the front of it and climbed out. 'Come on,' he said when Thomas did not move. Reluctantly the younger man jumped down to Rees's side. Together they followed the voices into the trees. Although the snarl of last year's bushes and wild plants had once formed a barrier, the passage of the others had opened it up and the path was easy to follow. They were heading toward a bend in the river; Rees could see the sun shining through an opening in the trees beyond. A few more steps, and Mrs Sechrest's bright blue cloak became visible.

Rees turned and glanced behind him. Although it felt as though they were in the wilderness, they were not more than ten or fifteen minutes outside of town. He walked forward to join the group clustered together.

They stood on the riverbank, some six or eight feet above the rush of the water below. 'Where's the body?' Rees asked as he approached the knot of people.

'Down below,' said one of the men. Since he was a tavern regular, Rees knew him by sight.

Walking to the edge, Rees peered over it. The body was sprawled on the mud below. No doubt the murderer had hoped the river would take the victim away, but the water level was low just now. If he had been thrown over during the spring melt, the body would have been swept away, downstream, and they never would have located it.

Although the victim had landed mostly on the shore, he lay face first in the water. One leg moved gently in the current.

'We have to get him up,' Rees said. 'Who found him?'

'I did,' said the man who'd spoken before. 'I used to play around here . . .' His words trailed off.

'All right,' Rees said. 'As most of you know, Rouge is ill. Quite ill,' he added, recalling the blistered face. 'He asked me to look into this while he is indisposed.'

'Why you?' Mrs Sechrest asked.

'I work with the constable on a regular basis,' Rees replied.

'While I'm sure you are very competent,' Mrs Sechrest said, in a tone that implied the opposite, 'I do wonder if you are the man who should be handling this tragedy? I mean, you know him.'

'I do?'

'You do.' She gestured at the river. 'That is almost certainly Cole. We were at your house just yesterday.'

Rees glanced at the body lying below. He could not see the face and the grimy frock coat could belong to anyone. 'Maybe so,' he said. 'There were several of you there.' He took several breaths, trying to control the anger he still felt at seeing his children thrust outside on the porch.

'You were furious with us. Me, in particular. How can I be certain you will search for Cole's killer?'

'Murder is murder,' Rees said, his face flushing as his temper rose. He understood her implication; that he would not bother to search for the man's killer because of the antagonistic history between them. 'I will always do my best.' He paused. 'Are we even certain this is murder?'

'I climbed down to look at him,' said the initial speaker, pointing to his muddy boots. 'The side of his head is all stove in.'

'Maybe he got drunk and fell,' Rees suggested. 'Hit his head on a rock.'

'Of course that is not what happened!' Mrs Sechrest snapped. 'Some villain murdered him and threw his body into the river, no doubt hoping it would never be discovered. And it was, I'll be bound, someone who already knew him.' She looked very hard at Rees. 'Where were you last night?'

He returned her gaze, staring at her until she dropped her angry accusing eyes. How he wished Lydia had come with him. He did not possess his wife's ability to say something that sounded perfectly innocuous while delivering a body blow. He certainly could never admit to Mrs Sechrest where he had been; doing so would reveal Sandy's hiding place and leave her exposed to recapture. 'Once we bring the victim up here, we will know more,' he said. 'And while you may believe me unable to investigate fully, I am the one available.' Turning, he addressed the men. 'I'll need a few of you to climb down with me so we can carry the remains up. I'll need to bring the corpse to Dr Smith or his nephew.'

'I've already been down there so I'll go,' said the gentleman with the muddy boots.

'Thomas. If you would.' Rees glanced at Rouge's cousin. Although he scowled, he did not protest. 'The rest of you, stay here and grab him when we lift him up to you.' Several men nodded. Rees looked at Mrs Sechrest. She was not looking at the river or at any of the people, although her gaze seemed fixed on the black maid standing to one side. Instead, Mrs Sechrest was staring blindly into the trees.

She was so young, Rees thought. Barely out of her teens. Without her anger to sustain her, she seemed delicate and vulnerable.

'Mrs Sechrest,' Rees said gently. 'Why don't you go back to the inn.'

'No,' she said, her face tightening. 'I must see him.'

'This is no sight for a lady,' one of the other men said. Mulishly, she shook her head.

With a sigh, he couldn't protect someone who refused his protection, Rees shed his greatcoat and prepared to descend the bank to the river. Even wearing his jacket and waistcoat he immediately felt much colder. 'Let's finish this,' he said, eyeing the drop to the river below. It was too far to jump, even with his long legs. He scrambled down in an avalanche of half-frozen dirt clods, landing on the rocky shore with a thump. The other two men joined him and for a few seconds they regarded the body at their feet. Then Rees grabbed the corpse by the shoulder and pulled. Since some of the clothing was saturated with water, the dead body was far heavier than he would have believed, and he could barely shift it. Thomas grabbed hold of the arm, hauling at it with all his might. The body flipped over and the leg that had been immersed in the water emerged.

Rees looked down into the face of the murdered man. It was Cole, the older of the slave takers, his gray eyes now staring sightlessly at the sky. The damage to the left side of his head, only slightly visible before, was now obvious. He had been hit with some force and the wound had bled copiously. Rees stared at the bruise and then looked away, admonishing his stomach to settle.

'Mon Dieu,' Thomas muttered.

'Could he have been hit with a branch?' The other man asked with what Rees felt was inappropriate relish.

'Possibly,' Rees replied, looking around him. He saw nothing that would match the wound. 'Or maybe a rock. Let's get him to the upper bank.'

Rees took the shoulders, closing those awful staring eyes first, while Thomas and their helper lifted the feet. The body was heavy and unwieldy and if one of the men hadn't reached down and grabbed the front of the grubby waistcoat, they might never have lifted the body to higher ground. As the men on the upper bank dragged Cole's body upward, Thomas leaned down and picked up Cole's shabby hat.

Once the corpse lay securely on the upper bluff, one of the men leaned over and held his hand out. Rees needed that assistance too; the eroded surface of the slope was too steep and slippery to climb.

He quickly donned his coat as the others were hauled up to level ground. 'That's him,' Mrs Sechrest said, staring at the body. Although her face was white, she held herself to rigid attention, willing herself to keep her emotions at bay.

'Where's the boy?' Rees asked her. 'The other slave taker?'

'Gone.' She glared at Rees. 'Do not think you can accuse him. He ran away after we left your house. Cole was the one who told me. You embarrassed that poor boy.'

'That was your doing,' Rees said, remembering the young man's scarlet cheeks. 'I have no doubt he found your behavior too much to stomach.'

'Cole was murdered by someone here.' Her voice rose into a screech. 'Someone here in this town. I want justice. I demand justice.'

TWENTY-TWO

Rees drove his wagon as far into the trees as he could, but he still had to leave it a significant distance from the body. Fortunately, the men gathered on the riverbank were willing to help. The body was stiffening and it was heavy, but with the seven of them they managed to transport it to the wagon. Mrs Sechrest remained for a little while but finally returned to her carriage and left.

As the men dispersed, Rees and Thomas climbed into the wagon. Both of them were muddy and tired. Thomas looked at Rees and said, only half-joking, 'The next time you need help, I shall be far too busy.'

Rees grinned. 'I hope Rouge is better by then.' Then his grin faded as he remembered the constable's blistered cheeks. He could not dally and allow his children to remain at risk; he must inoculate them today.

He reached the tavern in less than twenty minutes. After depositing Thomas by the door, Rees continued on to the doctor's office. This time, he drove the wagon up the narrow drive to the shed at the back. Ned came out as soon as he heard the rumble of the wagon wheels. 'What is this?'

'A body,' Rees said. 'Another murder victim.'

Ned approached the wagon and glanced inside. 'There is no doubt about the cause of death,' he said. 'I can see the wound from here. Who is he?'

'One of Mrs Sechrest's southerners,' Rees said. 'A slave taker name of Cole.'

'Let's get him inside then.'

The two men wrestled the body into the shed and struggled to lift him onto the table. 'Where was he?' Ned asked, staring at the sodden clothing.

'In the river. How long do you think he's been dead?'

'Hard to tell. The cold affects rigor mortis. But I would say maybe six to ten hours.'

Rees nodded. The estimate agreed with his own. That meant Cole had died late last night or in the early hours of the morning.

Ned bent over and opened the corpse's mouth. 'Do you know if he had any contact with Mr Gilbert.'

'I don't know,' Rees said. 'Probably. Why, is he suffering from smallpox too?'

'No. That doesn't mean anything, though. He could have come down with the illness as a child and survived.'

'The constable is ill,' Rees said, his voice breaking. He was surprised by the flood of emotion; he had never considered Rouge a close friend but found the danger he was now in shattering. He did not want Rouge to die.

Ned nodded. 'A bad case.' As his forehead creased with worry, he passed his hand through his hair. 'And there's nothing I can do for him.'

Rees did not ask if the illness might be fatal. He'd known others who'd died of this disease. 'Explain to me again how to inoculate my children,' he said.

Ned nodded. 'It's safest if you can find someone with a case of cowpox,' he said.

Rees thought of Annie. 'I know someone,' he said.

'It is simple then, if it is an active case. Take some of the fluid from one of her sores and put it into a scratch on your child's arm. A deepish scratch that bleeds,' he emphasized. 'That's all. You will probably see some of the pustules appear in a week or so.'

'Thank you. I'll do it today.' He just hoped it was soon enough to prevent the more serious illness.

Lydia was not very enthusiastic about inoculating her children with a disease but when Rees described Rouge she reluctantly agreed to do it that day. 'But where are we going to find cowpox?' she asked. Born and raised in Boston, she had not experienced farming life for as long or in as much depth as Rees. 'Annie?'

'At least a few of the Zion herd is infected,' Rees said. 'And yes, Annie. She didn't come today?'

'No. They are probably keeping a close eye upon her,' Lydia said with a smile. 'Seeing as how she is so prone to running off.'

'Either that or she is in the Infirmary. After dinner, I'll drive to Zion. If Annie still has the blisters, I will bring her back here with me.'

'The children may be more amenable to it if they see Annie,' Lydia said. 'It will be a little more familiar . . .' Her voice trailed off and Rees knew she was worrying about her babies.

Rees touched her shoulder. 'It will be all right,' he said.

'How can God allow such terrible things to happen?' Lydia said. Since this was an age-old question with no answer, Rees said nothing.

Lydia pulled herself together. 'And the body?' She forced herself to change the subject.

'One of Charlotte Sechrest's slave hunters,' Rees said. 'You would recognize him; he came here yesterday. Somebody hit him in the head and then tried to dispose of the body in the river. If this had been spring, and the river running fast with snow melt, we would never have found him.'

Lydia, who was setting the table, said, 'God forgive me, I can't be too sorry. Of course it is connected to Randolph Gilbert's murder. And they probably knew one another.'

Rees stared at his wife. 'That's true. Especially since Cole worked with Gilbert's sister, Charlotte Sechrest.' He paused, thinking. 'Rouge did mention Gilbert brought one of the slave takers with him. Perhaps Cole worked for both siblings. I'll ask Mrs Sechrest when I am next in town. That may be tomorrow,' he added. 'It is Saturday and I will need to take Rouge's place as constable. I'll probably be there all day.' Although the market that was usually held on Saturday had ended, farmers and their wives still usually came to town. And some of them, and a good chunk of single men as well, congregated at the tavern. Without Rouge, Rees would be needed to break up fights and put some of the worst offenders in jail.

'I'd like to accompany you when you speak to Mrs Sechrest,' Lydia said hesitantly, unsure of Rees's response. 'It's Saturday so Jerusha will be home. She can watch her brothers and sisters.'

'I think that would be for the best,' Rees replied gratefully. 'I got off on the wrong foot with Mrs Sechrest.' His mother had always told her children to be civil if that was the best one could do.

'That woman,' Lydia said acerbically, 'makes it impossible to do anything else.'

Rees nodded. 'She is difficult,' he said. 'But you are more tactful than I am,' he said. 'Even when you dislike someone. You might have more success obtaining answers.'

Lydia smiled. 'Thank you,' she said and changed the subject. 'I don't understand why the two bodies were deposited on opposite sides of the town. It's almost as if two murderers are involved.'

'Or if the guilty man is trying to throw us off the scent.' Rees thought that was more likely.

'Or if he was in a hurry and didn't have the time to carry the body to the other side of the weir.' She paused, twisting her hands anxiously in her apron. 'Tobias's shop is within walking distance of that bridge. And he owns a wagon. He could have . . .' Her voice trailed off.

Rees had to swallow his surge of worry before he could respond. 'That's true but I don't believe it,' he agreed, more vehemently than necessary. 'I saw Tobias. I pulled him out of bed. He was home, I'd swear to it.'

'He could have done it after you collected Sandy,' Lydia pointed out. 'It was just going on ten when you left here. You must have been gone from Tobias's by midnight. He would have had plenty of time.'

Rees was silent for a few seconds. What Lydia said was true, but he didn't want to believe it. 'John Washington's blacksmith shop lies even closer to the bridge,' he said. As he recalled Gabriel's swing with the heavy hammer, he added, 'And he has the mighty Gabriel working for him. A blacksmith's hammer could easily be the murder weapon. Next time I'm in town I'll speak to them both.'

TWENTY-THREE

As soon as he'd finished his dinner, Rees left for Zion. The Shakers enjoyed a regular schedule and he knew that by the time he arrived they would have just finished their meal and would be returning to their afternoon tasks. He was hoping to happen upon either Jonathan or Esther and as he pulled to a stop in front of the barn he spotted the Shaker Brother exiting the dining hall.

'Jonathan,' he called, jumping down from the wagon seat. He landed badly and twisted his ankle. Although Rees doubted the injury was serious, it hurt now. Limping a little, he threaded his way through the people emerging into the street. Jonathan was too polite to say anything but his expression, when he regarded Rees, was not welcoming.

'Rees. We see you so often I wonder if I should prepare a copy of the Covenant for you to sign.'

'No, thank you,' Rees said. The Covenant was a contract by another name. The signer gave all his worldly goods to the community as well as promising obedience to the Elders and lifelong celibacy. 'I am looking for Annie.'

'She is in the Nurse Shop,' Jonathan said.

'The Infirmary?'

'Yes. Follow me, please.'

'I know the way,' Rees said to Jonathan's back. He hurried to catch up, his aching ankle preventing him from matching the Elder's long-legged stride.

The Infirmary was located a short distance east of the wood-working shop. Rees expected Jonathan to veer off and attend to his afternoon responsibilities and he did. Rees went on alone to the Infirmary and knocked on the door. The Nursing Sister, a short woman whom Rees had spoken to before, stepped out.

'I wish to speak with Sister Annie,' Rees said. The woman pursed her mouth and inspected Rees. She did not favor him. In a previous case, he had insisted on speaking to a dying woman in the Infirmary and would not be put off. This Sister had never forgiven him for it.

'What is your business with her?' she asked now.

'I believe she is suffering from cowpox,' Rees said.

The Sister nodded. 'That is so.'

'I'd like to take her home.' The Nursing Sister stared at him. 'There is smallpox in town,' Rees hastened to explain. 'Dr Smith's nephew has recently arrived from England with a new treatment. I need an active case of cowpox for that.'

'I never heard anything so ridiculous in my life,' the Sister said with a sniff. 'Does Annie know of this plan?'

Rees shook his head. 'Not yet. I hope she will agree.'

The Nursing Sister regarded Rees for several seconds. Finally, she said, 'I will have to ask the Elder.'

Rees followed her across the lane separating the two buildings and into the workshop. Jonathan had just picked up a scarred and deeply stained mallet when they entered. He looked up in surprise. Rees hastily explained why he needed to remove Annie from the village. Jonathan put down the mallet. When he didn't respond immediately, the Nursing Sister spoke.

'You aren't seriously considering allowing this?' she murmured, shooting the Elder an appalled glance.

'She runs to Rees and his family every chance she sees,' Jonathan said. 'I say, let her go.'

When the Sister shook her head in disbelief, he continued, 'And she's been uncooperative as well.'

'Talkative and disobedient,' the Sister agreed with a nod. 'I know if I take my eye away from her for one second, she will run away. It is upsetting. Very well. Follow me, Mr Rees.'

Rees and Jonathan followed the Sister to the Infirmary. The Nursing Sister opened the door and gestured them inside.

Annie was not in bed. Instead, she was staring out of the window on the opposite side of the room. Rees couldn't help thinking of an animal desperate to escape. The adult cradle was pushed to one side; empty for now. And, at the opposite end of the room, Aaron lay in the last bed.

'Has he been accepted as a full member?' Rees asked, still surprised. He had never thought Jonathan would permit Aaron to return.

'Esther spoke for him,' Jonathan said. Rees nodded; he knew. 'She persuaded me to give Brother Aaron another chance. I suspect he may be a Winter Shaker,' Jonathan added, referring to the people who joined for only a few months. 'Esther feels he has turned over a new leaf.'

'Hmmm,' Rees said dubiously. 'What's wrong with him?'

'Fever, headache, general malaise,' the Sister replied.

'Rash?' Rees asked.

'No rash,' she replied. 'Why would you ask that?'

'There is smallpox in town,' Rees repeated. Turning to Jonathan, he added, 'Rouge has come down with it.'

'I am sorry to hear that,' Jonathan said. Although his relationship with Rouge was conflicted, he sounded genuinely sorry.

'I think you should be careful too . . .'

'I've had it already,' Jonathan said without concern.

'Rees?' Unable to restrain her curiosity any longer, Annie burst into the conversation. 'Are we going? Why did you come for me?'

Rees turned to her, his gaze focusing on her bandaged arms. 'I'd like to see the rash, if I may,' Rees said.

'I'm not sick,' Annie said.

'Don't be impudent,' the Sister said with a sharp note in her voice. Rees guessed Annie had tried the nurse's patience to the breaking point. Annie held out her arm. The Sister carefully began to unwind the linen. The blisters on her wrists, although still looking red and angry, had begun to scab over. They did look quite similar to the eruption poor Rouge suffered from.

'Dr Ned suggested a new treatment for the disease,' Rees said. 'It is now being used in England and Scotland, I believe. Using matter from cowpox and inoculating the person confers an immunity to smallpox. I desperately . . .' His voice broke. He stopped talking and took a breath. 'I don't want my children to catch smallpox so, would you come home with me? Dr Ned explained the process.'

'Of course,' Annie agreed, almost before he'd finished speaking. Rees suspected she would have come even if there was smallpox in his house and she might be at risk. 'I'll fetch my cloak.'

'That young doctor is certain this inoculation is effective?' the Nursing Sister asked.

'He is. He claims there is no danger of death with this method, not even the much lower threat that occurs with variolation.'

'Interesting,' the Nursing Sister said. And she looked quite thoughtful.

Annie followed Rees from the Nurse Shop with alacrity. 'I'm not sick,' she repeated. 'I swear it. I feel fine, except for the sores. They itch something awful.'

'I believe you,' Rees said untruthfully, holding the door open for her.

'Brother Aaron is really ill,' she confided, yawning as she passed through. 'He came in this morning, complaining of vomiting.'

'You are absolutely certain you are willing to do this?' Rees said.

'Of course,' Annie said with a wide smile.

How old was she now? Rees wondered. Sixteen? Seventeen? The Zion community would soon expect her to choose her future. She must sign the Covenant and remain in Zion as a Sister or leave to seek her future elsewhere. He sighed. He knew she would resist signing the Covenant and such a life wouldn't suit her anyway. If he and Lydia did not take her in, where would she go?

'Are you all right?' Annie's voice broke into his thoughts.

'Of course,' he said. Annie's future was something he would have to discuss with Lydia. And sooner rather than later.

TWENTY-FOUR

All three adults were required to inoculate the children. While Lydia held a child on her lap, Rees made the scratch. Annie pinned the legs of the thrashing child as Rees transferred the fluid from Annie's blisters. When Sharon was released, she regarded her father from tear-filled eyes, her lower lip trembling. He felt like a monster.

'It's for your own good,' he said. She turned her back on him and refused to look at him.

Lydia, her own eyes filled with tears, bandaged the scratches, finishing just as the cart rattled into the yard. Rees exchanged a glance with his wife. Both of them were dreading the second round.

A few minutes later, after unhitching the donkey and putting him in the barn, Jerusha, Judah and Nancy came into the house. 'What's the matter?' Judah asked, eyeing his distressed younger siblings.

'We have to inoculate you against a disease,' Rees said.

'Inoculate? What does that mean?' Judah asked, his gaze settling on the bandaged arms.

'We make a tiny scratch on your arm,' Lydia said. 'Then we scratch Annie's arm and put the . . . the liquid on your arm.'

'Like blood brothers,' Judah said, his expression clearing.

Relieved that Judah saw this in a way that made sense to him, Rees said, 'Do you want to go first? You can show your sisters how it's done.'

Judah nodded. He kept himself rigid as Lydia rolled up his sleeve and he winced when Rees made the cut. But he didn't cry.

Nancy ran away, through the kitchen and into the front parlor. When Rees pursued her, he found her crouched under the horse-hair sofa. 'Now Nancy,' Rees said, bending over so he could see her face, 'we are inoculating everyone. It will keep you from coming down with smallpox.'

This explanation washed over her with no effect.

'You're a big girl. Sharon and Joseph have already been inoculated.'

Nancy buried her face in her hands and tried to pretend he wasn't there. Out of patience, Rees reached under the settee and grabbed her arm. She resisted him but he finally dragged her from her refuge. He marched her back into the kitchen. Jerusha was just rolling down her sleeve. Nancy began to wail.

'Oh, don't be a baby,' Jerusha said without sympathy as Lydia gathered the eight-year-old into her arms. 'Some of the parents,' Jerusha continued, looking up at her own parents, 'have taken their children from the school. They heard about the smallpox . . .' Her voice trailed away.

'We hope this will safeguard you,' Lydia said, trying to smile. Jerusha nodded.

Rees worked as rapidly as he could with Nancy sobbing the entire time. In less than a minute, Nancy had been inoculated as well.

Lydia put out a plate of doughnuts. Although she poured glasses of milk for the children, she offered tea to Annie. She was at the center of a ring of children who were crowding around her to see her rash. They seemed both repelled and fascinated by it.

'Kids,' Rees said as Judah reached out a tentative finger to touch one of the scabs. The more disgusting, the better.

Annie accepted tea so Lydia pushed the kettle over the fire. She poured Rees's leftover coffee into a pan and put it by the flames.

'I'll have tea as well,' Jerusha said. She spoke with an assurance that did not quite mask her uncertain expression.

Lydia hid a smile. 'Of course,' she said. 'You are a young lady now.'

Having succeeded in making her claim for adulthood, Jerusha sat down at the table next to Rees. She helped herself to a doughnut and bit into it with the same eagerness as her younger siblings.

Rees took a doughnut as well. He didn't care for reheated coffee but knew better than to complain. Wasting food was a sin, and that certainly applied to a luxury like coffee. 'How are you enjoying your new job?' he asked Jerusha.

She put down her doughnut. 'Mostly I like it. I love working
with the younger children. But as they get older . . .' She shook
her head. 'Many of the parents take the girls out when they are
nine or ten. Some even earlier.' She looked at her father. Rees
nodded. He knew many people believed girls only needed to
know how to read, nothing else. And some men felt women
should not even know that. 'So, most of my older students are
boys and some of them are older than I am. They don't respect
me. I spend a lot of time disciplining them.'

'Maybe you should speak to their parents,' Rees suggested.

'That won't work with some of them. And I don't want to
with the Whitehead boys. Their father already beats them . . .'
Her voice trailed off.

'Will it help if I talk to them?' Rees asked. Lydia put a cup
of coffee in front of him and poured tea for Jerusha.

'Don't, please. I want to try and solve the problem myself
first.' Jerusha pressed her lips together and Rees saw her determination. She had a backbone of iron; those boys wouldn't break
her.

'I am so proud of you,' he said. She smiled and ducked her
head in embarrassment.

If they continued causing trouble for her, though, Rees would
intervene.

'What do the boys do?' Rees asked. He could remember his
behavior as a young boy only too well.

'They bother the girls. Typical stuff. Tying their pigtails
together or putting something on the chairs. Today one of the
boys caught two chipmunks and raced them up the aisle.' As he
visualized the scene, Rees bit back his grin. After a moment,
Jerusha began to giggle. For a few seconds they both roared with
laughter. Then, wiping her eyes, she continued. 'It was pande-
monium. I could barely attract anyone's attention after.'

'I don't doubt every classroom in the country experiences
similar problems,' he said. 'Boys will be boys.'

'The other problem . . .' Jerusha's voice trailed off and she
began breaking pieces from her doughnut.

'Yes?'

'Some children, their parents struggle to afford the rate fees,
so they don't have slates and they arrive at school without lunch.'

Although the school was public and open to all, there were fees attached. Not all families could afford the modest sum.

Rees looked at his daughter sharply. 'You're giving those children your lunch, aren't you?'

She nodded and lowered her eyes to the table. 'I know what it is to be hungry,' she said.

Rees felt his eyes moisten. When he'd met Jerusha and her younger sister and brothers, they were living alone and neglected in an unheated shack.

'Maybe your mother . . .' he paused and cleared his throat. 'Maybe we can donate extra food, bread or something, so that you don't have to go without eating.'

Jerusha looked up, smiling widely. 'That would help,' she said gratefully.

'The slates are another problem,' Rees said. 'I'm not sure what to suggest for that. What are you doing now?'

'Right now?' Jerusha bit her lip. 'The children have to share the few copies the school owns of the blue-backed speller anyway. So, while half the class is working with that text, I work with the other half and the kids who don't own slates share with those who have them. But I need a better solution.'

Rees covered her hand with his. 'You'll figure it out. I have no doubt of it.'

'It is no wonder—' Jerusha began but whatever she would have said was lost in a staccato round of knocking on the door.

Rising to his feet, Rees opened it. Thomas stood on the porch.

Rees eyed him with dismay.

'What do you want?'

'A coach load of passengers on their way to Boston arrived at the tavern,' Thomas said as he stepped inside. 'Rouge says you need to come to town, just in case there's trouble tonight.' He nodded at Jerusha. 'Ma'am,' he said to Lydia.

'Now? I'm with my family,' Rees objected.

'When you agreed to help the constable, this became part of it,' Thomas said.

'I didn't expect it to consume my life,' Rees said.

'Please allow my husband to finish his coffee,' Lydia said. 'I need to put together some clean clothing and other things.'

Although she couched her words politely, it was not a request. Thomas nodded, his gaze fixing on Annie. Rees realized they had not met; Annie had been living at Zion and except for her visits to Rees's farm, had never been outside of the village. He introduced them. Annie smiled shyly and Thomas took a few more steps into the kitchen.

'I'm glad to meet you,' Thomas said, his ears turning red.

'Yes,' she murmured.

'Perhaps I'll see you in town,' he said.

Rees smiled. He did not need to worry about Annie's future. She would marry, if not Thomas, some other fellow, and set up her own household.

Rees drank the last of his coffee. As Lydia handed him the parcel, he kissed her. 'I'll return tomorrow and collect you before I speak with Mrs Sechrest,' he promised. He waved goodbye to his children and went to fetch his coat.

TWENTY-FIVE

Rees checked in with Rouge. If possible, the constable looked even worse today. The rash had spread to his eyelids and his eyes were swollen and red. He nodded when he saw Rees standing in the doorway. Rees nodded in response and shut the door. He did not linger. Rouge was far too ill and besides, dusk was fast approaching, and Rees wanted to speak with the blacksmith before dark. All was quiet at the tavern. Since Hannibal was happy in his stall in the stable, Rees set out, walking through the gathering shadows.

Despite his long legs, he took twenty minutes to reach Tobias's shop. But only ten more to make the next turn off. Rees walked past the right for River Road, continuing on until he stood on the weathered boards of the bridge. Yes, Tobias could have succeeded in reaching the forest on the other side of the bridge in twenty or so minutes. And that was by shank's mare. Driving a wagon would have lessened the time even further.

But John Washington's smithy was even closer. When Rees

turned onto River Road, he estimated Washington could have reached the bridge in less than fifteen.

All the shops on this street – the harness makers, the wainwright, the livery – were preparing to close for the evening. The smithy's yard was empty and when Rees walked into the shop, he saw the fire was banked and the tools put away for the evening. It was much warmer inside and Rees took his hands from his pockets.

'Mr Rees,' Washington said. Rees glanced from him to Gabriel who was staring at him in wide-eyed fear. 'I suppose you're here to ask about the body in the river?'

'You heard about it, I wager.'

'It's the talk of the town.'

'Did you hear who it was?'

'Some Southern boy up from Virginia,' Washington said.

'Did either of you know who he was?'

'Pretty hard to say if we don't know who it was,' Washington replied as he glanced at Gabriel.

'Name of Cole,' Rees said. Neither of the other men spoke. 'Did you hear he was murdered?'

'Head stove in,' Washington said.

'You don't think we done it?' Gabriel blurted.

'No,' Rees said. Right now, he had no idea who the murderer might be. 'Did you fellows see or hear anything?' Both men shook their heads. 'No wagon wheels?' Rees added, although he did not expect either to say yes. They shook their heads again.

'We live next door,' Washington said, gesturing vaguely left. 'And after a day listening to the hammering I don't hear nothing.'

'Supper's ready.' A young woman with her black hair arranged in braids opened an almost invisible door at the back. A small child clutched at her skirts. Rees guessed this was Gabriel's family. He nodded at her politely. She stepped back with a gasp. Rees did not have to guess why. After his time in the Great Dismal Swamp the previous month, he knew the conditions from which many of the enslaved desperately tried to escape.

'If you hear anything, would you let me know?' Rees said to the men. He did not expect them to voluntarily approach him but thought it worth a try. 'Good night.' He turned and left the smithy. As he walked back to the tavern, he reviewed the conversation. Would they have informed on one of their own? Probably not, especially since both Randolph Gilbert and Cole were connected to the slave trade.

Was it possible one of them was a murderer? Or both? Yes, especially if either Gilbert or Cole threatened the ones they loved. Both Washington and Gabriel had access to the other side of the bridge. And Washington owned a wagon, Rees had seen it, so transporting a body to the other side of the town and Rees's property would not be so difficult.

Unfortunately, the same could be said of Tobias.

Rees shook his head, finding himself unwilling to judge any of these men. If it had been Lydia and his children under this threat, he would have been tempted to remove those who menaced them by any means necessary.

By the time Rees reached the tavern, the sky was almost dark. A punishing wind from the north had sprung up, bringing with it arctic air and the taste of snow. But all the lanterns inside the tavern were lit and the golden light spilling through the windows beckoned, warm and welcoming. Rees entered gladly. He could hear from the uproar in the taproom that the coach passengers had already imbibed and were tuning up to a fierce argument. Rees listened. Politics, of course. A follower of John Quincy Adams was shouting his opinion of Jefferson as an atheist and a slaveholder who would destroy the country in three months. His opponent, who was equally as passionate an admirer of Thomas Jefferson, claimed Adams would reestablish the monarchy with himself on the throne.

Rees decided he could probably eat his supper before he had to intervene. He sat down and before he had time to ask for coffee Thomas appeared with turkey, potatoes and pickled beets. Rees ate quickly, knowing his spell of peace would not continue. Mrs Sechrest did not appear, electing to take her meal in her room. But before he had quite finished his supper, he heard the loud arguing in the other room rise a notch and the unmistakable sound of someone's open palm hitting flesh. Rising to his feet, he moved to break up the fight before it grew totally out of hand.

After that, the excitement did not settle until past midnight when the combatants finally went to bed. That was in addition to a young man, a farmer's helper, who had come to town on his night off. He could not hold his liquor and ultimately Rees had to put him in the jail to sleep it off. When everything quieted at last, Rees decided he'd had enough excitement for awhile. He searched out the cot that had been allotted to him. As soon as he dropped into it, he fell instantly asleep.

TWENTY-SIX

When Rees awoke, he did not know at first where he was. The room was still dark although he could see muted daylight through the single grimy window. And where was Lydia? Groaning, he sat up and looked around. Oh yes, now he remembered. He was at the tavern. The cot, with its thin mattress, was probably no more comfortable than the pallet Rouge had made up downstairs. He sat on the edge of the bed for a moment, rubbing his hand over the stubble on his chin. Then he searched for his shoes under the bed, deciding that, no matter how much the town fathers paid Rouge to serve as the constable, it was not enough.

He washed his face and hands in the basin. Although Lydia had packed his shaving kit, he decided not to use his razor. He wanted to spend as little time as possible here in this cramped dark closet.

Bag in hand, Rees went down the stairs. It was just past dawn but several of the coach passengers were already in the taproom. A young girl was distributing plates of steak and eggs for their breakfasts. He was glad Thomas had that piece of running the tavern well in hand; Rees did not believe he could handle that as well.

He opted to seat himself in the back room rather than the main room with the coach passengers. The argument from the previous night had not run its course. He could hear snide comments from one of the passengers to another. How did Rouge bear it? He must greet every departure of the coach with relief.

Therese was scrubbing the tables. She smiled at Rees. 'Would you like some breakfast?'

'I thought I'd drive home and collect Lydia,' he said.

'Ah, but you must eat first,' she coaxed. 'It's the least we can do.'

Rees allowed himself to be persuaded. He sat down close to the kitchen door. From there, he could stare down into the main room – just in case he needed to leap to his feet and rush in to break up another fight.

Therese brought a plate of steak, eggs and fried potatoes. A pot of coffee soon followed. Rees, whose eyes felt as though someone had thrown sand into them, poured out the fragrant brew with enthusiasm. He might be able to survive the day after all.

The coach arrived at seven and all but one of the passengers embarked. Rees stepped out to the curb to watch the coach rattle away. As the dust from the wheels faded, he was overwhelmed with a sense of reprieve. Thank the Lord, the coach was gone. When he stepped inside the tavern, the first thing he noticed was the wonderful silence.

'What now?' he asked Therese as he returned to his breakfast.

'We have a spell of quiet. During spring and summer, with the market, we are busy from nine a.m. onward. This time of the year, the first customers will arrive around noon.'

'And Mrs Sechrest?'

'She usually takes her breakfast in the main room. Now that the carriage passengers have left . . .' Her words trailed away as Mrs Sechrest, trailed by her maid, stepped lightly down the stairs. Rees took his final bite, drank his coffee, and stood up. He did not want to engage in a conversation with Mrs Sechrest now, without Lydia. Pulling on his coat, he went out the back door and into the inn yard.

Lydia was dressed and waiting for him. The two older girls, giggling as they cleared away the dirty breakfast plates and cups, were rapidly cleaning the table. Nancy made faces for Sharon who shrieked with delight. Rees looked around and decided he preferred staying home with his family. But Lydia, arranging her cloak around her neck, was ready to go.

'I want you girls to insure everyone finishes his chores,' she said to both Jerusha and Annie.

'We will,' they chorused.

Rees sighed and held open the door. Maybe the demands of the tavern and his position as constable had kept Rouge from marrying, Rees thought.

'After we speak with Mrs Sechrest,' Lydia said as they climbed into the wagon, 'I'd like to see the area where the slave taker's body was found.'

'It is a walk through the forest,' Rees warned.

'Well, if Mrs Sechrest and her maid managed it,' Lydia replied tartly, 'I'm certain I can as well.'

'Maybe you will see something I did not,' Rees allowed. He was always surprised at how differently she viewed the world. As a consequence, she often understood something that escaped him.

'How was last night?' Lydia asked.

'Terrible.' He described the argument that came to blows between the coach passengers and made her laugh. 'And they were still arguing this morning.'

'You can't blame them,' Lydia said. 'This is an important election. It will chart the future course of this new country. Do you know to whom you will give your vote?'

'No. I don't care for either one of them.' Rees turned to look at his wife. 'Who would you vote for if you could vote?'

'I don't know. I agree with many of Mr Jefferson's principles, but I cannot ignore the fact that he is a slaveholder.'

'Exactly,' Rees agreed. 'There are rumors as well about his relationship with one of his female slaves.' Lydia, who had not heard that bit of salacious gossip, looked shocked.

'But Mr Adams has been quoted as saying he approves of electing a President for Life,' Lydia said. 'We just fought a war barely twenty-five years ago to shed a monarch. Why would we elect another? It is a conundrum, for sure.'

'Indeed,' Rees agreed glumly. He had fought in that war as a very young man and did not care to fight again. 'Of course, General Washington also kept slaves and he was an estimable president.'

'He freed most of them upon his death last year,' Lydia pointed out. 'So he must have reconsidered the morality of owning another human being.'

Rees nodded. Was it possible Thomas Jefferson would do the same? Doubtful. Rees decided that if he could not make a reasoned decision beforehand, he would cast his vote on the spur of the moment. No matter who he chose he would regret it later.

When Rees and Lydia reached the tavern, they found Mrs Sechrest still lingering over breakfast. Rees and Lydia exchanged a glance and approached. Although she did not appear happy to see them, she politely invited them to join her. Lydia accepted a cup of tea and a small cake but Rees, still feeling the effects of his heavy breakfast, took only coffee.

'I don't suppose you've discovered the miscreant who is roaming this town and murdering at will,' Mrs Sechrest said with a hint of censure.

'I think I need more information about the victim,' Rees replied. 'Besides, it has not even been an entire day since Cole's body was discovered.'

'Was Cole the gentleman's first name?' Lydia asked. 'Or his last?'

'It was his surname,' said Mrs Sechrest. 'Robert Cole, that was his full name. My brother always called him Cole.'

'They knew one another—' Rees began at the exact moment Lydia spoke.

'So, they were friends, your brother and Mr Cole,' she murmured.

'I suppose they were. Of a sort,' Mrs Sechrest agreed in astonishment. 'They knew each other all their lives. Cole grew up nearby.'

'He grew up on another plantation?' Rees asked, unable to keep the surprise from his voice. If Cole's shabby garb was any indication, he had certainly come down in the world.

'Oh my no. His father was a small farmer. They didn't grow much though. Their soil was poor, exhausted by years of farming. I think Cole's father fed those children by hunting and probably thieving.'

'I'm surprised they knew one another then,' Lydia said, resuming the questioning.

'They were of an age,' Mrs Sechrest said indifferently. 'They spent time together, especially as they grew older. And

when Cole took up the profession of slave taker, Randolph
had occasion to use his services several times. Why is this
important?'

'Had Cole visited Durham previously?' Rees asked, evading
the question.

'He may have antagonized someone here,' Lydia put in
diplomatically.

'Perhaps,' Mrs Sechrest said. 'But if Cole spent any time in
this town, it could not have been for more than a day or two.
My brother sent Cole after my missing slave as soon as he heard
what happened. Cole tracked her through New York and into
Massachusetts. He wrote to Randolph who joined him there, then
they traveled together into the District of Maine.' Her lips parted
in a wintery smile. 'I daresay her trail was easy to follow then.
She must have imagined herself completely safe.'

Rees felt guilt sweep over him. It was true; he had not taken
precautions once they were near home.

'And he wrote you when?' Lydia asked.

'He was already in Maine. Portland, I think. Anyway, he knew
he was close to recapturing her, so he wrote and asked me to
meet him. I started out almost immediately, knowing that my
journey would take several days. At some point, Randolph also
sent Cole south to join me and accompany me north. By the time
we met, I was just outside of Boston. So you see, if Cole stayed
in this town, it was only for a short time. A day or two at the
most.'

'That sounds like a great deal of effort to capture one girl,'
Lydia said. 'And why was it necessary for you to come? I don't
understand.'

'As a young and fertile woman, she has considerable value,'
Mrs Sechrest said stiffly. 'Besides, that wench had the temerity
to seduce my stepson.' Anger vibrated through her voice. 'He
was captivated by her. I wanted to guarantee he was safe from
her forever. Giving her to my brother would do that. And Randolph
wanted her desperately. So desperately he couldn't wait. No, I
had to travel to this barren little town so I could sign her over
to him.'

Granny Rose is right, Rees thought. This woman is jealous of
Sandy, so jealous she can scarcely see anything else.

'How terrible for you that your trip was in vain,' Lydia said, her soft voice masking her disgust.

'Oh, it wasn't,' Mrs Sechrest said. 'I will find her. And when I do, she will be sorry. Very very sorry.'

TWENTY-SEVEN

'What an absolutely dreadful situation,' Lydia said as they left the tavern.

'I hope Miss Sechrest gives up searching soon,' Rees said. 'I don't know how long Granny Rose will shelter Sandy and her baby.'

'I need to talk to Sandy,' Lydia said, turning to look at her husband. 'We need to visit Granny Rose so I can ask Sandy some questions.'

'What?' Rees thought of the long journey into the hills. 'No. It would take too long.'

'We need to know more about Randolph Gilbert and his sister and their background.' She glanced at her husband. 'You don't really think Cole antagonized someone in town, do you?'

'No. He knew something,' Rees said with certainty.

'And so does Mrs Sechrest. There is more to this than the hunt for a runaway slave.'

'What do you think?'

'I don't know yet. But I think Charlotte Sechrest is in love with her stepson.' She glanced at her husband. 'You saw that, didn't you?'

'She is jealous of Sandy, that I know,' Rees said. He helped Lydia into the wagon seat. 'I thought she might be envious of Sandy's beauty.'

'That is true as well,' Lydia agreed, settling herself and turning her face to the sky. The rising sun was bright and almost warm, a welcome change after the previous few days. 'She accused Sandy, a slave, of seducing that young man. I am sure that is very far from what happened. And there was something about her tone of voice . . .'

'By all accounts, she and Gregory Sechrest are of an age,' Rees said.

'How old is the elder Mr Sechrest?' Lydia wondered. 'How is his health? We know the first Mrs Sechrest passed on so he must be forty at least. I would guess in his fifties. The second, and much younger wife, may have planned to marry the son upon the father's death. We need to know that. Mrs Sechrest won't tell us. Her brother and Cole are both dead. That leaves Sandy.' She smiled sweetly at her husband. 'Unless you wish I try to separate Mrs Sechrest's maid from her mistress and question her.'

They both knew that doing so would put the woman in danger; Mrs Sechrest had already demonstrated her impulsive temper. And since the maid had made no effort to run, they could only assume she had family or other commitments in Virginia.

Rees sighed, knowing he was beaten. 'Very well.'

'Tomorrow is Sunday. Most respectable folk will be at church. The tavern is closed for the morning and since it is illegal to sell spirits on Sunday the establishment should be quiet all afternoon. We will visit Granny Rose tomorrow. I will enjoy seeing her again.'

When they passed the cabinetry shop, they saw Tobias and Ruth outside. Although Rees knew he would need to speak to them both again, he did not stop. He and Lydia both waved and continued on, to River Road, and the bridge. As they crossed, Lydia glanced at the small and shabby tavern on the left. 'I wonder,' she said as she looked at it, 'if someone from there might have seen something.'

Rees glanced at the small building. It appeared closed. Since it catered to the men who worked on the river, this ordinary's season would be mostly summer, after the river ice melted and before the water refroze. 'Worth a try,' Rees said, pulling up in front.

Lydia remained seated in the wagon. This was not a tavern like Rouge's, frequented by the entire town and also serving as a coach stop. Only one type of woman would enter these doors and even accompanied by her husband Lydia did not want to go inside. Rees climbed down and went to the door. As he expected, it was locked and barred. He hammered on it just in case the owner was inside. Rees was on his way back to his wagon when the door opened, and a man peered out.

He was a portly fellow with uncombed yellow hair. He grinned at Rees, displaying only a few remaining teeth. 'Desperate for a drink, are you?' he asked.

'No, thank you. I just have a few questions.'

'Questions?' He pushed the door wide and used a rock as a doorstop. 'What kind of questions?'

'You must have heard about the man we pulled from the river,' Rees said.

'Yeah. Some Southerner.'

'I wondered if you heard anything. This would have been Thursday night. Probably,' Rees amended.

'Thursday night you say.' The tavernkeeper made a big show of thinking. 'Yeah, I heard something. What's it worth to you?'

Rees pulled out a handful of coins from his pocket. 'Ten cents.'

'Twenty-five.'

'Rouge will have to pay me back,' Rees muttered as he handed the money over.

'I heard an argument,' the fellow said as he pocketed the coins. 'I didn't pay it much mind. There's always squabbles here.'

'What could you hear?' Rees asked.

'Well, I could tell one was southern. I could hear it in his voice. Probably that man that went into the river.'

'Could you hear what they were saying?' Rees struggled to hold on to his patience.

'Not much. I wasn't really listening. I heard one of them shout "I know you killed him" and then it got real quiet.'

'How did they get here?' Lydia asked, suddenly breaking into the conversation. 'Did you hear wagon wheels? Or a horse?'

'No,' said the man, looking at Lydia in surprise. 'Nothing like that. No wagon wheels for sure.' He paused, thinking back. 'Maybe a horse. I was in the back when I heard them. Like I said, I wasn't paying attention so they was quarreling for awhile before I noticed.'

'You didn't look out the window or see who they were?' Rees asked.

'No. Why would I?'

'Not even when it went suddenly quiet?' Lydia probed.

'I assumed they'd settled their differences and gone home.' He turned to Rees and said sheepishly, 'Now I understand what happened. But at the time . . .'

'Thank you,' Rees said. 'Thank you very much.'

'Lucky you caught me,' the fellow said as he kicked away the rock and started inside. 'By tonight, the tavern'll be closed until next spring.'

'Well, that's it then,' Rees said as he climbed into the wagon. 'Cole either saw or identified Gilbert's murderer. They met here, argued – probably because Cole was trying his hand at blackmail – and he was struck in the head and killed for his pains. Then it would be a simple matter to carry or drag the body to the river and throw him over.'

'Yes,' agreed Lydia, lapsing into a thoughtful silence. They drove the remainder of the short distance. Rees pulled over into almost the exact spot he'd stopped in earlier. 'There's one other thing,' Lydia said, laying her hand on her husband's arm and preventing him from climbing down.

'Yes?' Rees said.

'Do we know where Cole's horse is now?' Lydia asked. When Rees did not reply, she continued. 'If the beast is still in the stable at the tavern, then we know both Cole and his murderer walked here. But, if it is gone from the stable, where is it?'

'You think someone took it?' Rees asked.

'It is possible, isn't it? In fact, I think that is exactly what happened. Cole doesn't seem the kind of man to walk here from the tavern. And the beast wasn't found.'

'That is true,' Rees agreed. 'There were no reports of a rider-less horse wandering around. And the barkeep did say he did not hear wagon wheels.'

'So Cole's murderer either rode or walked here. And he would have had to deal with Cole's horse.'

'That is also true,' Rees said, considering her words. Reluctantly, he added, 'Both Tobias and the blacksmith live within walking distance. And they are not the only ones. There is Gabriel, Washington's helper. He has a young and pretty wife.'

Lydia nodded slowly. 'You believe they are escaped slaves?'

'I'm certain of it. And they live closer to the bridge than Tobias. It would be even easier for Washington or his young friend

Gabriel to walk here.' Although he did not say it, he thought of
the many hammers in the smithy.

Lydia nodded as she slowly climbed down from the wagon.
'But would Cole, a slave taker, blackmail an escaped slave?'

'Probably not,' Rees admitted. 'It is more likely Cole would
try to recapture him – them – and sell them down south.'

'If we find Cole's horse stabled with one of them, then we'll
know,' Lydia said. She looked at her husband with worried eyes.
Rees nodded.

'I'll look around.' He did not say aloud that John Washington,
Tobias, and Gabriel all had a very good reason for wanting both
Randolph Gilbert and Cole dead.

TWENTY-EIGHT

The path to the riverbank had been trodden down by many
feet, both going out and returning, so it was easy to follow.
When Rees and Lydia left the copse of trees behind and
stepped out onto the bank, Lydia said in some surprise, 'What a
beautiful spot.'

Rees looked around. It was beautiful, now, in the sunshine. A
flock of ducks flew overhead, quacking loudly on their way south.
If one did not know about the body, this place seemed tranquil,
quite removed from the problems of the world.

'Where was the body found?' Lydia's question interrupted
Rees's musings.

'Over here.' He guided her to the bank, the exact place he had
stood looking down upon the body, and pointed to the rocky
shore below. 'The murderer attempted to drop Cole into the water.
But the level is low at this time of the year and when he landed,
he was only partially submerged.'

Lydia nodded and spent several seconds staring at the empty
shore below. Then she gazed at the woods around. 'This is quite
private,' she said at last.

'Now it is,' Rees said. 'In the summer the drifters camp here.
It's too cold currently, of course.'

Lydia nodded, her gaze catching on something snagged in the dry branches a little way down the verge. She made her way to it, picking her way through the dead branches and downed limbs lying on the thick pad of dead leaves. 'It's a hat,' she said.

'A hat? But we found Cole's hat. It was just a few feet away from his body,' Rees said.

'Oh, I don't believe this was Cole's hat,' she said, turning. 'This is a beaver top hat. Quite good quality.' As she began to retrace her steps, Rees went forward to meet her. She handed him the hat. Although battered by its time in a shrub, the hat did not look much worn. Clearly, it had been very expensive when new.

'This looks familiar,' Rees said, certain he had seen this item recently.

'It looks like every other beaver top hat,' Lydia said, shaking her head.

'Yes, perhaps,' Rees said, taking it from Lydia. 'But who in town owns such an expensive hat? Even the bankers and lawyers don't usually wear such costly headgear. Yet I know I've seen someone recently wearing a top hat made of beaver.'

'Perhaps it was Randolph Gilbert?' Lydia suggested.

'Maybe,' Rees said doubtfully. He had no memory of ever seeing that southern gentleman before finding the body in the woods. Rees turned the hat over in his hands. 'I wonder . . .' Lydia looked at him questioningly. 'Rouge and I, we never found Randolph Gilbert's hat. I know it was nowhere near his body. Maybe this is *his* hat.'

'But how would it find its way to this side of town?' Lydia asked.

'Perhaps the murderer brought it here,' Rees suggested. Lydia looked at him. The chilly breeze coming off the river blew tendrils of her dark red hair over her face and she impatiently pushed them back.

'What if,' she began, 'the murderer helped himself to Mr Gilbert's fancy hat and was wearing it when he met with Mr Cole?' They looked at one another and nodded in unison.

'Of course,' Rees agreed. 'And during the struggle to drop Cole's body into the river, he lost the hat.'

'That makes perfect sense,' Lydia said. 'It would be difficult

for even the strongest man to toss such a weight into the river.'
Rees smiled at his practical wife. Most women, he thought, would
dissolve into the vapors during this conversation.

'Exactly.' He turned the hat over and looked inside. 'Perhaps we
can stop by the doctor's and ask Ned to measure Gilbert's head.
We will know then if the hat would fit him.' Rees was already
certain this hat belonged to Randolph Gilbert. Measuring it to his
head would be just a final confirmation.

'At least, this beaver hat argues against Tobias,' Lydia said,
sounding much more cheerful. 'And against that Mr Washington
or his helper. If anyone saw a black man wearing a beaver top
hat, he would be stopped and questioned.'

'That is true,' Rees agreed, encouraged by the thought. 'I tell
you, Lydia, I wish I could believe Cole murdered Gilbert. A
falling out between employee and employer. It would be the best
possible outcome.'

'And someone else murdered Cole?' Lydia asked with a
sidelong glance. 'That is unlikely at best.'

'Yes. Maybe someone else entirely who witnessed the killing.
And then tried to blackmail Cole. He refused to pay and so the
blackmailer hit him on the head.' Rees's voice rose with excitement. 'Once he saw Cole was dead, the blackmailer took off for
parts unknown.'

'Are you telling yourself nursery stories now?' Lydia teased
with a smile.

'That tale answers all the questions,' Rees said, laughing as
well.

'Does it?'

'Well, except for the fact that Gilbert was both throttled and
stabbed so there were probably two people there. And why
would Cole bother to hide the body when he could just flee the
town?'

'And why would Cole bring Mrs Sechrest to town?' Lydia put
in. 'He wouldn't have bothered fetching her, would he? In fact,
he could have run away west and disappeared.'

'And, since Cole was from away,' Rees said, nodding in agreement, 'he would not know of this location by the river. But the
man who killed him clearly knew of it.' He stretched out a hand
to help his wife into the wagon seat. But Lydia, pulling aside

her skirts vaulted over the step. She smiled down at him from her perch.

'See? A nursery story. I'm sorry to say it will not answer.'

They went directly to the doctor's surgery and dropped off the hat with Ned. He seemed surprised by the request but promised to measure the headgear to the corpse as soon as he could.

'Do you know if his sister is planning to bring her brother's body south?' Ned asked. 'Or does she wish to bury him here, in Durham?' Rees shook his head. He had never thought to ask although he now remembered Ned talking about this. 'We need to know. And despite the cooler temperatures, we need to know soon. The body is—' He looked at Lydia and stopped abruptly.

'The body is beginning to corrupt,' Rees finished for him. 'I'll ask Mrs Sechrest when I next see her.'

'We probably should have mentioned it this morning, when we spoke with her,' Lydia said as they left the surgery.

'Yes,' Rees agreed. 'I know there are sufficient funds for a burial too, probably with money left over.'

They crossed the road and went down Commerce Street to the tavern. Instead of entering the tavern through the front door, by unspoken agreement they went around the corner to Main Street and into the inn yard. Since this was Saturday, the yard was crowded with farmers' horses and wagons.

Rees caught the ostler as he ran past. 'Which one of the beasts here belongs to Robert Cole?' he asked. And when the fellow stared at him blankly, Rees added, 'The slave taker with Mrs Sechrest.'

The ostler's face cleared. 'Not here. He took it out yesterday and I ain't seen it since.'

Rees and Lydia exchanged glances. Then he took out a coin and handed it to the other man. 'Thank you.'

'So Cole did ride his horse,' Lydia said.

'I'll look at the cabinetry shop and the blacksmith's,' Rees said unhappily.

The tavern was fairly busy. No coach passenger but a number of farmers and their wives who'd come into town to pick up supplies. Neither Rees nor Lydia were eager to return home to the farm. They both knew they had chores waiting and Rees, once he'd completed the daily jobs necessary for every farmer, would have to turn around and go back to town. Saturday nights tended to be busy times for the constable or his assigned deputy. He was not looking forward to it.

In unspoken agreement, Rees and Lydia went inside the tavern and sat down by the fire. Rees found the number of empty seats surprising. Thomas brought tea for Lydia at once. 'I'll put coffee on as soon as I get to the kitchen,' he told Rees. 'Anything to eat?'

'What do you have?' Lydia asked. She was eating for two now and always hungry.

'Therese made both biscuits and scones this morning,' Thomas said. 'We also have cornbread. And, of course, eggs, steak, bacon . . .' He grimaced. 'Now that the news of Rouge's illness has gotten out, we have food to spare. No one wishes to linger, even the people who've had the disease.' He paused.

'People are frightened,' Lydia said in understanding.

'I know,' Thomas said with a nod. He sighed. 'I am making a nice ragout for dinner but that is not done yet. It won't be for another hour or so. Hopefully, we'll have customers to eat it.'

'Just bring us some of the scones and bread,' Rees said. He stood up. 'I'd better visit Rouge, while I am here.'

'His sister is with him now,' Thomas said. Rouge's sister Bernadette was the local midwife; Rees and Lydia knew her well and expected to require her services within a few months. Rees sat back down again.

'How is he doing?'

'Better, I think,' Thomas said uncertainly. 'The blisters are beginning to break and scab over. He says he feels better.' He exchanged a glance with Rees. Neither of them believed that.

'But he is recovering?' Lydia asked.

'It seems so. Dr Ned came over earlier and says that in his professional opinion my cousin is over the worst of it. But Mon Dieu, the scarring! He'll be marked for life.'

'Well, he was not a handsome man anyway,' Rees said. Lydia shook her head at him. 'At least he'll be alive.'

'I hope so,' Thomas said. He turned and disappeared toward the kitchen. He returned almost immediately with a plate. The cornbread nestled next to the scones was still warm.

TWENTY-NINE

Mrs Sechrest proved elusive so, after a quick search, Rees and Lydia left for the farm. He had not really wanted to speak to her anyway and felt relieved that he'd been spared. When he arrived home, he found, to his great relief, that Annie and Jerusha had fed the livestock and Daisy had been released into the field. Rees checked on all of the animals and was quite proud to find everything in order. Because of the efforts of these young women, he now would be able to spend a few hours weaving before returning to town.

In Annie's presence, Jerusha had lost her pinched anxious expression and Rees heard her laughing several times. Although Annie preferred the domestic arts, baking and such, and Jerusha preferred study, the young women worked well together. Perhaps, Rees thought, taking Annie in would be a positive for everyone.

As usual, while weaving, he allowed his thoughts to wander. Often, he pondered the murders. Today, although he began by meditating upon Cole's death and how it might relate to the murder of Randolph Gilbert, his deliberations soon veered away, into reflections on the current epidemic and upon Jerusha and her worries over the school and the children in her care. Lydia had decided to keep the younger children home, and presumably safe, but Jerusha had refused to stay home. She still went to school every day. Then there was Annie and the questions about her future. Rees sighed. There were so many concerns, all at the same time.

He was quite surprised when Lydia spoke to him from the door. 'It is past mid-afternoon,' she said. 'You were planning to return to Durham?'

Rees leaped to his feet, now in a hurry.

Saturday night proved to be less trouble than Friday – most people stayed home – and after another uncomfortable night on the cot, Rees left town for his farm. It was a clear day, but cold.

Butter and honey – from Lydia's bees – came out next. After Lydia had taken a scone, Rees buttered a square of cornbread and dribbled honey over it. Lydia commented on the honey; it was even better this year than last. The bees, in hibernation for the winter, were a thriving colony and she hoped to establish several additional hives next year. Rees nodded to some of the men he knew and Lydia greeted a farmer's wife who was also active in the local chapter of the Abolitionist movement. Neither talked about the murders. Rees allowed the warmth of the fire and the murmur of a nearby conversation to relax him. The past week had flown by in a blur of activity, and tomorrow, although Sunday was supposed to be a day of rest, looked to be as busy. He didn't want to think about the deaths or about the contagion that, even now, threatened the life of the tavern's owner.

He looked around him at the half empty tavern and realized that the everyday bustle of a tavern on a Saturday was missing. Although he found it pleasant sitting here with his wife, he knew he and Lydia were only pretending everything was normal.

He took another piece of cornbread from the plate. While he was slathering butter on it, he looked up and saw Mrs Sechrest by the door. She was watching him, an odd expression on her face. When she saw Rees looking at her, she hastily turned and disappeared, pretending she hadn't seen him.

All of Rees's responsibilities came crashing down upon him. There was still so much to do today. 'We'd better finish up,' he said. 'It will be noon before we reach the farm. I have chores, especially since we will be gone all day tomorrow when we visit Granny Rose.' He sighed. 'And I should see if I can catch up with Mrs Sechrest and tell her what Ned said.'

Lydia sighed as well but she finished the last of her scone and pushed the plate away.

'Be sure and wrap up well,' Rees told his wife. 'It's cold outside and will be colder still in the hills.'

As they started west on the main road, Lydia asked, 'Did Ned measure the beaver hat?'

'He did,' Rees said. 'He came to the tavern last night to tell me the results.'

'Yes?' she said impatiently. 'And?'

Rees threw a glance at her. 'The hat fit perfectly. In Ned's opinion, it belonged to Randolph Gilbert. He even found a few blond hairs in the hat band.' Rees paused and then added, 'He found some dark ones as well.'

'Cole has dark hair,' Lydia pointed out. 'So, Cole took the hat. That is the answer to that puzzle.'

'I suppose,' Rees said. That conclusion made sense but for some reason it didn't sit well with him. 'I just don't understand why, if he wanted a beaver hat so badly, he was willing to murder his friend for it, when he was wearing a hat of rabbit fur.'

'Well, we don't know that Cole killed his friend,' Lydia said. 'Maybe he found the hat.'

Rees shook his head. He still didn't believe it. Maybe, he thought, that hat had nothing to do with Gilbert's death, or Cole's for that matter. But Rees was still left with the question of how an expensive beaver hat favored by the wealthy, and owned by one murder victim, had ended up in a bush not twenty feet from another.

Rees turned the wagon onto North Road. He glanced to the right and the woods that lined this street. At least it was not snowing and he wasn't searching for a missing girl.

'She is doing well,' Lydia said, understanding Rees's glance. 'I spoke to her mother.'

They turned up the rutted dirt track that went up the mountain. Ice glittered from the frozen furrows in the mud. As they ascended, the hardwoods, plentiful at the base of the mountain, decreased in number. Their places were taken by evergreens so that, by the time they reached the plateau, and the store located there, the woods were composed almost entirely of firs. The dark green of the needles gave the illusion of warmer weather and leafy trees.

Rees began to see a thin layer of snow on the ground beneath the trees, a coating that gradually increased to several inches as they climbed higher. Hannibal began to struggle. Rees climbed down and walked beside his horse. Within a few short minutes Rees too was panting, the cold air knifing into his lungs. But he didn't feel the cold any longer. Instead, he was perspiring under his heavy coat.

At last Rees and Lydia reached the summit of this hill. The track leveled out before rising again but at a gentler increase. They paused to rest where the lane that led to Granny Rose's diverged from the main road. Another family had once lived at the end but, since a fire had consumed the cabin, Rees suspected no one dwelt there anymore. That overgrown track certainly appeared unused.

Lydia climbed down as well. Together, she and Rees climbed the last of the slopes. They could already smell the bonfire Granny Rose kept burning all winter. And soon they could see the worm fence that marked off Granny Rose's yard. Rees turned and, grasping Hannibal's bridle, led the horse and the wagon behind him through the gate. The door to the cabin opened and the midwife stepped out onto the porch. The men's boots she wore clumped on the wooden boards.

'Lydia, dear,' she said. 'What a nice surprise. Come inside.'

Rees unhitched Hannibal and put him into the small barn, next to Granny's mule. Somewhat sheltered and with water and a bundle of hay, Hannibal was content.

When Rees entered the small cabin, Granny had taken Lydia to the bed and was palpitating her abdomen through her linen dress. Since Abram was asleep on most of the counterpane, Lydia reclined across the foot. 'I'd say late April,' the midwife said. She put an ear to Lydia's belly. 'No sooner and maybe a week or two later. May is a good month to have a baby.' She smiled at Rees as she helped Lydia rise from the bed. 'Maybe a son, this time.'

'Maybe,' Rees said. He stamped the thin snow from his boots and removed his coat. Sandy had stirred up the fire and the kettle was boiling fiercely. She poured the hot water into the teapot.

'Granny Rose told me you prefer coffee?' Sandy said to Rees.

'I do,' he said. 'Maybe there is some of the coffee I brought left?'

'Of course,' Granny Rose said.

But Lydia shook her head, frowning at her husband. 'That was a gift for you, Granny,' she said.

'I don't mind tea,' Rees said. He did not care for the coffee Granny Rose drank; coffee with chicory, heavy on the chicory.

He could not remove his eyes from Sandy. She was almost unrecognizable. Instead of a bunch of ringlets over her ears, she wore her hair pulled back into a simple bun. She looked older and much more serious. But she was no less beautiful. The severe hairstyle emphasized the delicate bones of her face and her full lips. She would be beautiful even as an old woman.

'You look different,' Rees said. Sandy nodded.

'Granny Rose thought it more appropriate for a midwife in training. Anyway, I don't have time to fuss with curls.'

Granny offered them a bowl of hot stew. 'I was paid with a chicken,' she said, smiling. 'And I know it is a cold ride up the mountain.' Both Rees and Lydia accepted, taking the bowls of hot soup eagerly. But Granny was not prepared to wait until they'd finished eating. With the niceties of hospitality observed, she turned a stern eye upon her visitors.

'I know you did not come all this way to visit me. What do you want?'

'We didn't come to visit you,' Rees began, waving his spoon in the air, 'but to talk to Sandy.'

'It is lovely to have a chance to visit,' Lydia interjected. 'But there was another murder.'

'But I know nothing,' the girl said, turning around in dismay. 'I wasn't even there.'

'We know,' Rees said.

'But we are hoping you can give us some background,' Lydia said. 'You know these people; we do not.'

'Of course,' Sandy said, sounding puzzled. She sat down beside Lydia. 'I'll help any way I can.'

Lydia looked at Rees and he began. 'The second murder victim was a man called Cole. Do you know him?'

Although he asked the question, it was unnecessary. When she heard the name, Sandy reared back in horror. 'The slave taker. Is he there too?'

'He arrived with Mrs Sechrest and has been searching for you,' Rees said.

'He grew up to be a wicked, wicked man,' Sandy said. Then her lips drooped in sorrow. 'I remember him as a nice boy.'

'Mrs Sechrest said Cole was a friend to her brother, Randolph Gilbert,' Lydia said.

'Friend? Only in the way a dog is a friend to its master,' Sandy said.

Since none of this was helpful, Rees said, 'We were hoping you could tell us about him. About his background,' he amended. 'Mrs Sechrest said Cole's father was poor—'

'He was a drunkard,' Sandy said bluntly. 'Did she tell you Cole killed him? I know she didn't. The old man used to get liquored up and beat his wife and those kids silly. One day Robert Cole, we used to call him Bobby.' For a moment her eyes filled with sadness. 'He wasn't a bad boy, not really. Anyway, he took a rake and smacked it over his father's head until he died. He was just fourteen. I don't think anyone blamed him.'

'What happened then?' Lydia asked.

'He changed. Fell in with Gilbert. Became a slave taker. By now, I do declare, he has no heart left in his body.' Sandy's expression was both sad and angry. 'Did Mrs Sechrest tell you Cole made a specialty of hunting slave women? Young ones particularly. And he earned a bounty if she was pretty.'

'She didn't talk about him much at all,' Lydia said, darting a glance at her husband.

'No,' Rees agreed. 'I am trying to understand why someone would kill him.'

'Maybe he tried to recapture some poor girl,' Sandy said. 'Someone who escaped and is hiding here, in the District of Maine.'

'Maybe,' Rees said slowly, his thoughts going to Gabriel and his very pretty wife.

'Do you know what my punishment would be, after Mr Randolph was done with me?' Sandy's voice rose. 'I'd be sent to a fancy house. So, if his quarry killed him, well, I hope no one ever catches her.' Her passion silenced the others for a few seconds.

'Would Cole try to blackmail someone?' Rees asked.

'Probably,' Sandy said. 'If he could get away with it. I think his goal was to become a landowner like Randolph Gilbert.'

'Would he . . .?' Lydia stopped and started again. 'Do you think Cole could murder Mr Gilbert?'

For the first time, Sandy did not reply immediately. Instead, she stared at the log wall and thought. 'No,' she said at last. 'I don't think so. Cole admired Randolph. Wanted to be him. And Mr Gilbert gave Cole money, women, a certain status. Without Randolph Gilbert, Cole lost all of that.' She turned and looked at Rees and Lydia directly. 'I wish I could say he was Randolph Gilbert's murderer, but I can't.'

THIRTY

After a moment of silence, broken only by the crackle of the fire on the hearth, Granny passed around the teapot once again. Rees, who hadn't touched his now lukewarm tea, handed it to Lydia without taking any. So far, he had found Sandy's information unsatisfactory. She had said nothing that they had not already heard or could have guessed.

'I am curious about Mrs Sechrest,' Lydia said at last. 'Why would she travel all this way—'

'She hates me,' Sandy said.

'Perhaps. She told us that elaborate tale about her brother and how desperate he was to capture you,' Lydia said. 'But I still don't understand why she felt it necessary to travel all this way. Her brother had already hired a slave taker, one whose specialty was young women. Why would Charlotte Sechrest abandon her home and her husband to embark on this wild chase?'

Both Sandy and Rees stared at Lydia. Granny chuckled. 'You're thinking you wouldn't leave your husband and your children without a very good reason,' she said, speaking for the first time.

'Exactly,' Lydia said, turning to look at Rees. 'What must her husband think, her tearing off north, after a slave no less.'

He smiled. Lydia had opted to leave her children once, last month, to save her marriage. In her mind, that alone would provide the very good reason.

'Mr William makes no attempt to control her,' Sandy said. 'He is in poor health.'

'How much older is Mr Sechrest to his wife?' Lydia asked.

'He is in his fifties so he is quite old,' Sandy said with the unconscious superiority of the young. 'And Miss Charlotte is only twenty-two.'

'How old is Gregory?'

'Twenty-one, now,' Sandy replied, blushing. Gregory was Abram's father.

'So, he is of an age with Charlotte?' Lydia said.

Sandy nodded. 'I heard rumors that she'd set her cap for him. In fact, everyone warned me. But he wasn't ready to set up his household.' Now her cheeks were scarlet.

Lydia and Rees exchanged a smile. It didn't take much intelligence to understand why Gregory had no interest in the woman who became his stepmother. From all accounts, the young man genuinely cared about Sandy and Abram.

'Does Gregory have siblings?' Lydia asked, returning to her train of thought. 'You've never mentioned any.'

'No,' Sandy said, shaking her head. 'He is the only child. Mr Sechrest was taken ill when Gregory was a baby . . .' Her voice trailed away.

'Do you know what he fell ill with?' Granny Rose asked.

Sandy shook her head. 'That was before I was born,' she said.

'Why is this important?' Rees asked.

'There are certain illnesses that affect a man's seed,' Granny explained.

'I see,' Rees said sympathetically. 'Mr Sechrest no doubt hoped that, by wedding a young woman, he would have more children.' He looked at Lydia, both of them thinking of Sharon and the baby that was coming. 'I'm sorry for him.'

'So, Gregory is the only child, and the heir,' Lydia said.

'That does not mean Abram would inherit,' Rees said. 'The child takes on the same status of his mother.' Rees looked at Sandy. 'Since Sandy was enslaved, Abram too would be considered property. Even if Gregory has no other children, unlikely considering his youth, Abram cannot be his heir.'

Lydia did not reply for a few seconds. She regarded Sandy thoughtfully. 'Did Gregory care enough about you to free you and Abram?'

'He talked about it,' Sandy said. 'Several times. He wanted to do it when he discovered I was pregnant.'

'What happened?'

'He hadn't reached his majority then.' Sandy paused. 'His father would have permitted it, I believe. And Miss Minerva always treated me well so she would probably have agreed, if she still lived. But Mr William was already married to Miss Charlotte and she forbade it.'

Lydia looked at Rees as though he should understand the importance of that information.

'She is jealous,' Rees said. 'We already knew that.'

'She wed the father, no doubt believing that Gregory would grow as fond of her as she was of him. Then, when the patriarch passed away, an event that would happen sooner rather than later, Charlotte and Gregory could marry. Except Gregory's heart was already engaged.' Lydia nodded at Sandy. 'To insure the future Mrs Sechrest wanted, she had to remove Sandy and the baby from the plantation.'

'By giving me to her brother,' Sandy whispered, the blood draining from her cheeks.

Lydia nodded. 'When you left the plantation, you ruined all her plans.'

'Wait a minute,' Rees objected. 'Who is the one telling nursery stories now?'

'Maybe I have exaggerated a trifle,' Lydia admitted with a smile. 'But you yourself identified Mrs Sechrest's motive as jealousy. Moreover, she did not hide her fury with Sandy.'

Rees nodded reluctantly. 'Yes,' he said. 'But still . . .'

'Something very powerful inspired her to leave Virginia, and her poor ill husband, to chase this particular escaped slave,' Lydia continued relentlessly. 'Remember what Miss Charlotte said; that Sandy seduced Gregory and he had to be rescued from his poor decision.' Rees nodded even more reluctantly.

'That certainly sounds plausible,' he admitted.

'Also, Mrs Sechrest sent Gregory away at a pivotal moment. That was when she chose to beat Sandy. Fortunately, we were there and able to rescue Sandy and Abram both.'

Both Sandy and Rees nodded. The journey north to Maine had been terrifying. Rees only wished now he had taken the same precautions as they approached New York that he had followed earlier. They might not be having this conversation about Charlotte Sechrest.

'I am only speculating here,' Lydia continued, 'but I suspect Gregory came home and asked about Sandy and his son.'

'She certainly does not want to return me to him,' Sandy blurted.

'No. We know that. But what if Gregory insisted that you be returned to him?'

'Huh,' Sandy said dubiously. 'He did not come to find me.'

Lydia nodded. That was a fair point. 'But what if he swore he would free you?' she continued. 'What if he even threatened to marry you?'

'That is a great many ifs,' Rees said. 'Besides, I am quite certain marriage between Gregory Sechrest and Sandy would be against the law.'

'Yes. But we are dealing with strong emotions here,' Lydia said. 'So strong they overpower all reason.'

'This sounds plausible to me,' Granny Rose said. 'And even if that young man could not wed Sandy, he could install her in his house as his mistress.'

'And Charlotte Sechrest would still lose Master Gregory. So, determined that Sandy and Abram disappear forever, she travels north to meet her brother. She uses as her excuse for Gregory and his father that she will search for Sandy. If she finds her, and of course Cole was an experienced slave taker, Charlotte will bring her home.'

'And planning all the while not to do so,' Rees said.

'Exactly,' Lydia said, nodding with approval. 'When Sandy and Abram were safely taken away by her brother, Mrs Sechrest would return home. So sorry, so sad, but Sandy and Abram escaped to Canada. They are gone forever.'

The shocked silence lasted several seconds. Rees broke it. 'Is this the way all women think and behave?' he asked, appalled. 'Why, this level of manipulation would put Machiavelli to shame.'

'Most women are not so calculating,' Lydia assured him.

'I would not claim you men are the rational sex, if I were you,' Granny Rose warned Rees acerbically. 'Strong emotions are not unique to the female. If they were, young men would not react to the most minor of perceived insults with a duel.'

Since this was true, Rees could not argue.

'That is exactly what Miss Charlotte would do,' Sandy said, returning to what for her was the most important point. 'Planning the most terrible future for me and for Abram and all the while behaving as though butter wouldn't melt in her mouth.'

'Would Gregory be susceptible to her machinations?' Granny Rose asked.

'Maybe. Probably,' Sandy said. 'His father was entirely taken in. And Gregory is younger and less experienced than Mr William. I thought Miss Charlotte was nice at first too, until I was warned not to trust her. Her slaves knew and they talked. But no one listens to slaves, and women slaves at that.' She sounded quite bitter.

'When you are safe, if you choose to, you may inform Gregory of your location,' Lydia suggested cautiously. Sandy nodded but she did not look as eager as Rees might have expected.

'Perhaps. But I will do nothing, ever, that puts Abram into danger. And Mr Gregory may no longer feel the same. Probably doesn't. We were both very young.'

Rees glanced at Sandy in surprise, startled by that unexpectedly mature response.

'Does all this help you identify the murderer?' Granny Rose asked.

Lydia and Rees exchanged a glance. 'I don't know,' Rees admitted.

'It tells me that both Mr Gilbert and Mr Cole, by their indifference to human life and their actions, inspired their own murders,' Lydia said. 'And they call themselves Christians. It does not bear thinking of.'

THIRTY-ONE

Rees did not raise the subject of the murders again until he and Lydia were on their way down the mountain. Then he said, 'Do you think this long journey helped? Did you get what you wanted?'

Lydia responded with a question of her own. 'Considering what we heard about the characters of both Mr Gilbert and Mr Cole, do you think it possible either one or both saw a young woman they assumed was an escaped slave and tried to capture her?'

Since Rees had suspected right from the beginning that two people were involved in Gilbert's murder, he nodded. 'Very likely,' he said.

'What if that young woman was Ruth?' She turned an anxious glance upon her husband.

'If you're asking whether Tobias would attack the other man to defend her, of course he would. We already know he will do anything to keep Ruth safe,' he said. Once Tobias had escaped enslavement and fled north, he had enlisted the help of both Rees and Lydia, and then risked his life traveling south right back into the lion's den, to rescue her.

'But there are others too,' Lydia said. Like her husband, she did not want to suspect Tobias and Ruth of murder. 'We know Sandy cannot be involved, at least in Cole's death. She was already with Granny Rose. But John Washington is sweet on her. Would he kill Cole to protect her?'

'Probably,' Rees said, considering the blacksmith. He was slender but wiry, and Rees was confident Washington had the strength to overcome both Gilbert and Cole, especially singly. 'He might try to protect her even if he were not sweet on her. Who knows, maybe Cole threatened Washington himself.' He glanced at Lydia. She nodded, her mouth thinning to a narrow line.

'Unspeakable,' she muttered.

'And there's Gabriel,' Rees continued. 'I met his wife; she is young and attractive.' He paused, thinking. He had seen Gabriel swing a sledgehammer over the forge. Such a blow, even with the smaller shaping hammer, could explain the injury to Cole's head. He said as much to Lydia.

'But, if Gabriel brought a hammer, even a small hammer, to the forest, wouldn't Cole have seen it?' Lydia asked. 'Wouldn't he have become suspicious?'

'I would be,' Rees agreed.

'Besides, both Gabriel and Cole are newly arrived. How would they know about the woods and the riverbank?' Lydia persisted. 'Since we are assuming the same party murdered Mr Gilbert as well as Cole, how would Gabriel know about the forest by the weir? It is on the other side of town.'

'John Washington would know,' Rees said. 'Unfortunately.' He liked the fellow.

'Yes. Does he own a wagon?'

Rees cast his mind back to his visit to the blacksmith's. 'I believe so.'

'Perhaps Gabriel murdered both Gilbert and Cole? He could have borrowed the wagon.'

'But the wounds Randolph Gilbert displayed indicated he had been both strangled and then stabbed,' Rees said. 'That argues against one man with a hammer. It looks as though, while one party was strangling Mr Gilbert, the other stabbed him.'

'Perhaps Gabriel went to Washington for help,' Lydia suggested, almost immediately adding, 'no, that doesn't work.'

'Unless either Gilbert or Cole, or both, harassed Gabriel's wife,' Rees said, trying to understand how Gabriel might be guilty. 'She might have stabbed Gilbert to protect her husband. The confrontation could have taken place at the smithy.'

'And they asked Mr Washington for help,' Lydia said, nodding. 'He transported the bodies to the places they were found.'

Rees nodded slowly. That certainly answered all the questions. 'I must speak to both Washington and Gabriel again,' he said.

'I should accompany you,' Lydia said. 'Someone needs to talk to the wife. I doubt either of the men will allow you anywhere near her.'

'That is true,' Rees said, remembering how the two men had stiffened when he wished the woman good evening.

'We will have to leave this for tomorrow,' Lydia said.

'I know,' Rees agreed, adding with some impatience, 'they will be in church today.'

'Where we should be,' Lydia said, casting a stern glance at her husband. Rees, a confirmed skeptic, ignored her comment. 'The community in Zion will also be attending services all day. Otherwise, I would suggest we visit them.' She paused for several seconds. When she spoke again it was in an entirely different tone of voice. 'You and I need to talk.'

Rees disliked those words; it usually meant she was unhappy with him for some reason. 'About what?' he asked, his voice flattening.

'Annie.'

'Annie?' he repeated in surprise. He had not expected that. 'You're worried about Annie?'

'She will soon be expelled from Zion.' As a former Shaker herself, and one who had been expelled from the community, Lydia knew what she was speaking about.

'Did Esther tell you that?'

'No. But I know it. Annie hates living there and escapes every chance she finds. Running away from the Nurse Shop was the final straw. So, I want to be prepared when one of the Elders raises it. We should discuss her future.'

Since Rees had already been considering the problem, he nodded. 'I've been pondering the exact same issue,' he said.

Lydia turned to look at him. 'And?' she asked anxiously.

'She'll come and live with us,' he said. 'Of course she will. What else could she do?'

Lydia exhaled in relief. 'I wasn't sure you would agree.'

'Jerusha is spending her days at the school now and will be of limited help to you.'

'Annie prefers the work that comes with a home anyway,' Lydia said. 'She relishes working in the garden and cooking. Jerusha loves words, loves reading. She does what I ask but she doesn't enjoy it.'

Rees nodded. He knew his daughter was a scholar, some would say a bluestocking. 'Besides,' he said, 'I suspect Annie will be marrying and moving to a home of her own in a not too distant future.'

'Not Thomas,' Lydia said. And when Rees looked at her in surprise, she added, 'I saw the way he looked at her.'

'Why not Thomas?'

'She can do much better.'

'He is a good man,' Rees said, leaping to Thomas's defense.

'He works in a tavern,' Lydia said disparagingly. 'He doesn't even own that business.'

'There is far more to that job than serving drinks,' Rees said.

Now that he had slept at the tavern two nights running, he had a greater appreciation of all the different skills required to keep the business operating. And Rouge did that and served as constable as well. It was surprising. 'Besides, Rouge has no wife nor children. Thomas will own that establishment someday.'

'Does he even know how to read or write?'

'Of course he does. He learned from the nuns in Canada.'

'In French.'

'Thomas can read and write in English as well. He'd be of little use to Rouge otherwise.'

'And he's Catholic.'

'The midwife's daughter moved to Canada and wed a Catholic,' Rees argued.

'She was pregnant. I sincerely hope Annie is not expecting a child when she marries,' Lydia said.

'That was an entirely different situation,' Rees said.

'He's French,' Lydia persisted.

Rees turned to stare at her. 'If you are this protective of Annie, I shudder to think of how terrible you will be with Jerusha. Or Sharon.'

She burst out laughing at the expression on his face and he realized only then that she was teasing him. 'Oh, very well, if he remains interested, I'll consider it,' she said.

'That was not at all funny,' he said.

'Yes, it was.' Lydia smiled, amused again. 'We can talk to Brother Jonathan tomorrow. Then we'll tell Annie. I'm sure she'll be relieved.'

THIRTY-TWO

Assuming that both town and tavern would be quiet on a Sunday night, Rees chose to spend the night at home. Besides his weaving commissions, which supported his household and what he would use as an excuse if asked, he wanted to spend time with his family. He hoped Rouge would soon recover; Rees tried not to think of what would happen if the constable didn't. Fortunately, no one arrived at the door to tell him he was needed.

He spent some time watching Annie before retiring to the weaving room. She had matured from a half-starved waif into a pretty girl. He expected she would soon marry, if not Thomas then some other young man. After the years spent with the Shakers, she knew everything she needed to run a household. And she was so clearly happy among children, sitting on the floor with them and playing games.

The following morning, despite early-morning chores, Rees and Lydia were able to make an early start. Lydia had put out a basket of apples the night before, since the budding teacher left before anyone else. They left the younger children in Annie's care and drove to Zion. The Shakers were early risers as well, finishing the first of the daily assignments before breakfast at six thirty. Rees timed their departure so that he and his wife would reach Zion just after eight a.m. By then, everyone should be done with breakfast.

Rees parked the wagon at the southern end of the village. From here, the herb house was only a ten-minute walk. Clouds blanketed the sky but although the wind was cold and raw, Rees thought it was still too warm for snow. The calendar would soon change to December so a heavy snowfall would not be unusual. Rees could remember blizzards occurring in November.

Esther was not in the still house. When they entered the steamy and pungent interior, another Sister was pounding something in a mortar and pestle. She looked up when they entered. 'I believe you have lost your way,' she said. She was quite thin, with graying hair drawn back under the linen cap. Like many aging women, she appeared to be gradually shrinking into herself. Rees thought her two young assistants were the same ones who he'd seen helping Esther, but he wasn't certain. He had not paid much attention to them.

'We were looking for Sister Esther,' Lydia said.

'She isn't here,' said the older Sister. 'She has a different assignment this week.'

'Do you know what that might be?' Lydia asked.

'No.' The Sister returned to her pounding. Underneath the relentless thumping, Rees heard the woman mutter, 'All of these strangers just arriving here as though we are some kind of freak show.' Lydia glanced at Rees, she'd heard the woman too, and passed through the door.

'We'll ask someone else,' she said.

As they started down the path, they heard the door close behind them. When Rees glanced over his shoulder, he saw the oldest of the helpers running after them. 'Wait,' she called.

'Yes?' Lydia said, turning around.

'I believe Sister Esther is in the kitchen today,' the young woman said. 'They'll be cleaning up from breakfast.'

'Thank you very much,' Rees and Lydia both said in unison. With a shy nod, the young woman returned to her duties.

When the end of the path joined the main street through the village, they turned right instead of left and directed their steps to the kitchen. They passed the herb garden. Most of the plants were gone, and the dirt where they'd grown neatly raked, but there were some blackened stems still shivering in the breeze. The thrifty gardeners would collect the seeds for planting next year. In the four or so years since Rees had first visited Zion, and met the woman who became his wife, the herb gardens had expanded four-fold. Like the vegetable seeds which had proven such a popular commodity, the herbs grown by the Shakers was fast becoming a thriving business.

They could smell the kitchen before they reached it, a heady aroma of bacon and some kind of fresh bread. Rees recalled the hearty meals he'd eaten here, when he and his family had sought refuge within the community, and the water rushed into his mouth. 'I'm hungry,' he said, just as if he hadn't eaten barely two hours ago. Lydia shook her head at him.

This time Lydia went inside alone. Even when they'd stayed here, Rees had never entered the kitchens. She reappeared a few minutes later carrying a napkin wrapped bundle. 'For you,' she said, handing it to him. Inside he found two large slices of freshly baked bread thickly buttered and layered with strawberry preserves. Rees took a large bite.

'Where's Esther?' he asked, chewing as he talked. Usually Lydia would reprove him for talking with his mouth full. This time she did not.

'She is assigned to the kitchen this week,' Lydia said with a worried frown. 'But she isn't there right now. She is at the Infirmary.'

Rees choked and tried to swallow. 'What? Is she ill?'

'No.' Lydia glanced at Rees. 'It's Aaron. He is . . .' She hesitated as though not quite sure of the proper word. 'He is doing poorly. She went to sit by him.'

'I saw him a few days ago. He didn't seem too ill. But Annie told me he wasn't doing well,' Rees said. 'Is it smallpox?'

'I don't know. The Sister didn't say.' Lydia began walking faster. Rees hurried to catch up.

They crossed the village rapidly. When they reached the Nurse Shop, Lydia pulled open the door and went inside without hesitation. Rees followed close on her heels. He wanted to see Aaron himself.

Esther was seated in a chair near to Aaron's bed, but not so close they could inadvertently touch one another. She looked up when she heard the door open and managed a wan smile.

Rees's gaze went immediately to Aaron. Although he looked tired and ill and his skin was grayish, it did not exhibit the pustules common to smallpox. But Rees knew it usually took some time for the characteristic rash to appear.

'You should not be here,' said the Nursing Sister, appearing suddenly at the door.

'We'd like to speak to Sister Esther, if we may,' Lydia said, trying to placate the woman.

'Wait outside please. Conversation will disturb this poor ill man.'

Lydia nodded at Esther and meekly walked to the door. As Esther rose to her feet and followed Lydia, Rees paused by the nurse. 'Has Dr Ned seen Brother Aaron yet?'

'No. We care for our own,' she replied tartly.

'There are cases of smallpox in town,' Rees said.

'Yes, I recall you saying so. If Aaron becomes worse, or if the rash erupts on him, I will consider asking Elder Jonathan to call for the doctor,' said the Nursing Sister. 'Thus far, he has shown no sign of the blisters.'

Rees nodded and withdrew. While it was true Brother Aaron showed no signs of the rash as yet, and the Nursing Sister seemed convinced he did not have smallpox, Rees was not persuaded. It just seemed too coincidental that Brother Aaron could be so ill when there were smallpox cases nearby.

'I know this is not a good time to discuss this,' Lydia was saying to Esther when Rees joined them. 'It certainly is not the most important matter on your mind. But Annie will never make a Shaker.'

'No, indeed,' Esther agreed. 'The poor child wants to obey our rules. It just isn't in her to do so.'

'She hasn't signed the Covenant,' Lydia went on.

'And she won't,' Esther agreed.

'We'd like to take her home. To our home.'

Esther nodded without surprise. 'I do not see a problem. You brought her to us – what was it, two or three years ago? – for her own safety. She prefers living in the World, with you. At the next meeting of the Elders, we can discuss it, but I believe you are well within your rights to take her.' She paused a moment and then added, 'And the children? Are they well?'

'Yes. So far,' Lydia said.

'If Aaron has smallpox,' Rees said, leaning forward, 'and I know the Nursing Sister does not think so, you may catch it from him by sitting by his bed.'

Esther smiled faintly. 'I caught it, long ago, on the plantation where I lived as a child.' Her face crumpled with worry. 'Many people in the slave quarters died from it that year.' Turning, she looked at the Infirmary. 'But he doesn't have the rash.' She sounded as though she were trying to persuade herself that all would be well. She hesitated for a few seconds and then said, 'Is that all?'

'For now,' Lydia said in surprise. It wasn't like Esther to be so rude.

'I should return to Aaron, sit with him while I can.' Esther smiled at Rees and Lydia, almost as though she didn't really see them, and disappeared into the Infirmary once again. Both Rees and Lydia stared after her.

'How very odd,' Lydia said.

'I did not realize she was so fond of Aaron,' Rees said.

'She isn't. She never used to be anyway.' Lydia shook her head.

'Jonathan told me she spoke up for Aaron and asked that he be given another chance.'

'People are always surprising, aren't they?' Lydia said.

THIRTY-THREE

Since the Infirmary was located near the woodworking shop and they had to pass it anyway, Rees stopped to look for Jonathan. He knew Esther would tell the Elder about Annie, but thought it best he mention it first. But Jonathan was not there and the Shaker Brother working on the chairs did not know where he was.

'He should be here soon though,' the man said. He whacked the mallet on the bottom of the chair leg with a satisfying thump and turned to face Rees. 'If you care to wait.'

Rees shook his head and went down the stairs to join his wife.

They walked through the village, attracting a few curious stares. Most of the people who had lived here for more than a year recognized them but newer arrivals, and there were many as the homeless sought shelter for the winter, did not and saw only outsiders. Rees found himself speeding up. For some of these new people, curiosity was tinged with a certain animosity. It made Rees uncomfortable.

When they left Zion, they drove directly to town. As Rees turned Hannibal over to the tavern's ostler, he said to the gelding, 'Don't worry. You'll have a nice rest now, in the nice comfortable stable.'

'We must purchase another horse,' Lydia said, her brow wrinkling. 'Especially now that Jerusha takes the cart every day.'

'I know,' Rees said as he opened the door. 'I've been thinking the same thing. Maybe in spring.' He did not want another animal eating its head off all winter in the barn.

'I don't want to wait that long,' Lydia said as they walked down the hall to Rouge's office. 'We need one now.'

Rees, sighing, nodded. 'Very well. I'll ask around as soon as I have a chance.'

Bernadette, Rouge's sister, was standing in the open door. 'How is he?' Rees asked. Even from here, the smell of sickness and human waste was overpowering. It smelled worse than an animal den.

'I am not sure,' the midwife replied. Rees followed her gaze into the room. Thomas was spooning broth into Rouge's mouth. With a quick glance at Rees and Lydia, Bernadette continued, 'I am afraid to go too near.'

'You haven't had smallpox either?' Rees asked.

She glanced at him. 'Did he tell you that tale of living in the woods away from everyone?' When Rees nodded, she shook her head. 'That was only for a few years before Mother brought us to town. He chose to remain in the woods with our father for another year or so while the rest of us went to school. So, yes, I've had smallpox. I caught it from a new mother.' She paused and then added in a husky voice, 'The baby died. I am afraid to approach too closely. I have mothers ready to deliver. Who knows how the disease travels? I might bring it to a newborn on my clothing.'

Lydia reached out to comfort the midwife.

Rees stepped into the office. The stench brought tears to his eyes. Rouge did not look better. Unkempt at the best of times, his unshaven chin had progressed to a heavy beard. Rees saw a lot of white in those black whiskers. And his face was a mass of pustules, many of them scabbing over. He looked at Rees from bloodshot eyes. Even his eyelids had scabs. 'I feel better,' Rouge said. 'Don't worry. I will soon be back to work as constable.'

'You certainly will,' Rees agreed heartily, his voice sounding too loud in the sickroom. He began to back up. Although he had had the illness, he did not want to spend any more time than necessary in this room.

'How is your investigation into the murder progressing?' Rouge asked, twisting his head to keep Rees in his line of sight.

'Do not think of that now,' Rees scolded as he continued his slow march to the door. 'You need to recover. Focus on that, please.'

Breathing a sigh of relief, he took the last few steps to the door and crossed the threshold.

'He is in the last part of the illness,' Bernadette said. 'Although he still might die . . .' Her voice broke, surprising all of them, including her. Her relationship with her brother had been conflicted for many years. 'I'm sorry.' She struggled to pull herself together. 'Usually, once the scabs begin falling off, the patient recovers. Usually.'

'But he will have scarring,' Lydia said.

The midwife nodded. 'Probably. Some people are fortunate but my brother . . .' Her voice trailed off.

In other situations, Rees would have made a joke. He would have told Rouge he was already so homely a few scars would make no difference. But Rees couldn't muster the enthusiasm for that right now. And although he tried, he could come up with no words of consolation.

Thomas came out and closed the door. 'I'll meet you in the back room,' he said to Rees.

'Be sure to wash your hands,' Bernadette commanded him. He nodded and shot ahead with the dirty bowl and spoon.

The others followed, silent with distress.

By common consent, they assembled at a back table together. Bernadette reached out a hand to touch Rees. 'Thank you for your friendship to my brother. He is difficult. Always has been. But you . . .' Tears began running down her face. Rees stared at her in consternation, unable to think of anything to say.

'My husband is grateful for your brother's friendship as well,' Lydia said. She put her arms around Bernadette and held her as she wept. Finally, the midwife pulled away and raised a handkerchief to her eyes.

'Here is coffee and tea,' Thomas said, putting the pots onto the table. He collapsed in one of the chairs. Rees looked at him sympathetically. Dark smudges ringed Thomas's eyes.

'You look exhausted,' Rees said.

Thomas nodded. 'But my cousin is improving. He's begun eating again. I know he looks terrible but I really believe he will survive.'

Feeling that he needed something, Rees helped himself to coffee. Therese arrived right then with sugar and cream and a plate of cornbread. 'You didn't have to do this for us,' Lydia said. She took a large piece.

'Cooking helps with . . .' Therese flapped her hand in the direction of Rouge's office. 'Besides, it will all be eaten.' Turning to her brother, she said, 'I need help. The coach just arrived, and the passengers are disembarking.'

With a muttered curse, Thomas rose to his feet and followed her.

'I should go as well,' Bernadette said, rising to her feet.

'I am sure your brother will weather this,' Lydia said. Bernadette nodded and disappeared through the back door.

Rees looked at Lydia. 'Although I want to speak to Tobias again, and to John Washington as well as Gabriel and his wife, I am not quite ready to leave.'

'I am not either,' Lydia said with a strained smile. 'Oh Will, what happens if this dreadful disease attacks our children?' They were both only too aware that smallpox was lethal, particularly for infants and young children. Rees reached out to touch her shoulder.

'We've done all we can do,' he said. He prayed with his entire being that Dr Ned was correct about the efficacy of cowpox inoculations.

'I know. It is in God's hands now,' Lydia said. But the fear did not fade from her eyes.

THIRTY-FOUR

When they left the tavern, Rees and Lydia walked west on Main Street. Although the sun was bright, it was not warm, and an icy wind was blowing off the river. Lydia soon put up the hood on her cloak.

Many of the businesses concerned with transportation were located on River Road, not just the blacksmith and livery where horses and donkeys could be rented, but also the wainwright and, right next door, the wheelwright. Rees knew him slightly. He had been called in to repair a broken wheel on a circus wagon the previous spring.

As Rees and Lydia passed by the wagon maker's shop, he looked through the open door and waved. Rees nodded to the proprietor. From him, Rees had purchased not just the wain he used on the farm and the wagon that carried his loom but also the cart Jerusha drove. The wainwright also built small carriages and coaches although the demand in Durham for such vehicles was limited.

Rees could hear the clanging of the smith's hammer from the end of the block, a sound that grew more thunderous as they approached. When they reached the yard, Rees looked around. As he had remembered, a beat-up wagon was pulled up to the back fence. He looked inside. The wooden bed was scarred and charred where hot metal had been dropped inside, but there was nothing that resembled blood. And he did not see a horse.

'What do you want now?' John Washington had come to the open front of the smithy and was staring out, his expression unfriendly.

'I have a few more questions,' Rees said, walking toward him. As he did so, Lydia stepped away from her husband and continued walking, around the smith to the small house at the back. 'But first, I wanted to tell you I saw Sandy. She is safe and doing well.'

Washington's expression softened. 'Where is she?'

'I think she is safer if no one knows,' Rees said. 'Mrs Sechrest is still in town and she is determined to find the girl.'

'And why did you hide Sandy? What is she to you?' Washington asked suspiciously.

'Someone in need of protection,' Rees said. He tried not to feel insulted by Washington's innuendo. 'My *wife* and I' – heavy emphasis on wife – 'rescued her from Virginia. We are not about to let her be taken back into slavery.'

'I heard,' Washington said with a nod.

'My wife is also very active with the antislavery circle,' Rees said.

The other man did not speak for several seconds. Then, as some of the tension left his shoulders, he said, 'You better come inside.'

'Where do you stable your horse?' Rees asked, looking around him.

Washington threw him a surprised glance. 'I don't own a horse. Too costly. If I need one for something, I rent one from the livery.'

'You friendly with him?' Rees asked, referring to the livery owner.

'No. He's expensive too.'

Since Rees thought the same, he nodded. Although he didn't press the issue, he knew Washington could stable a horse at the livery; that was one of the services the proprietor of that business offered. Had Washington stabled Cole's horse there? It would be a simple task to ask at the livery.

Rees followed the blacksmith into the smithy. Sun streamed through the two windows on the western wall, illuminating the counter. But the center remained in shadow and the sparks rising from the fire illuminated the hearth with an orange glow. 'I'd like to speak to Gabriel,' Rees said, turning to look at the man working by the anvil.

Gabriel looked up from the tool he was shaping on the anvil, his eyes widening. 'What do you want to know?' he asked, too wary to be anything but polite.

'Did you ever meet Mr Gilbert?' Rees asked.

'The Southern gentleman?'

'Yes.'

'No. Never met 'im.' Although he did not look directly at Rees, Gabriel sounded definite.

'What about Cole, the slave taker?' Rees asked.

'No.' Gabriel's eyes shifted away.

'I think you did,' Rees said, taking a step forward. 'He threatened you, didn't he? Threatened to take you south.' Washington stepped forward but when Rees glanced at him, he stopped.

'No.'

'I think he threatened you and your family,' Rees continued.

'No.'

'Or did Cole promise he wouldn't take you if you paid him. Was that it?'

'Paid 'im?' Gabriel stared at Rees. 'I got no money.'

'So you met him across the river and hit him in the head with that there hammer of yours and—'

'No, no,' Gabriel shouted, sweat breaking out across his face.

'You hit him in the head,' Rees continued as though Gabriel had not spoken.

'Stop it.' Lydia's voice cut across Rees's accusation. The words died in Rees's mouth and all three men turned to stare. Lydia and another lady had come through the back door. Rees recognized the young and pretty woman as the one he'd seen before: Gabriel's wife. Her hands were twisted in her apron and she was trembling. 'Tell them,' Lydia said to her companion. She gulped and opened her mouth but no words came out. 'Go ahead,' Lydia encouraged her gently.

'He, the slave taker, he saw me in town,' she said.

'You weren't supposed to go out,' Washington said in annoyance.

'And?' Rees prompted. The young woman stared at him with wide eyes.

'Tell them the rest,' Lydia said, her voice warm and soothing.

'He threatened me, said he would take me and my husband back if I didn't . . .' She stopped, tears running down her cheeks. Rees glanced at Gabriel. His mouth was agape in horror.

'Why didn't you tell me?' he asked.

'And what could you do?' she replied. 'I figured I'd have to meet 'im,' she added so softly Rees could barely hear her.

'And did you?' he asked.

She shook her head, a smile breaking through her tears. 'No. I didn't have to. I – we – heard he was dead. I wasn't never so happy in my life.'

'Sandy said something similar,' Lydia said, glancing at her husband.

For the first time, the young woman looked directly at Rees. 'Gabriel didn't know. I swear it.'

God help him, Rees believed her. But when he glanced at John Washington and caught the angry and triumphant expression on his face, Rees realized that although Gabriel might not have been told, Washington knew everything.

'You satisfied?' Washington asked Rees.

'For now.'

Lydia took her husband's elbow and drew him from the smithy. Rees did not speak until they were outside in the street. 'She might not have even confided in Washington,' he said. 'She might not have had to. Mr Washington seems to keep on top of everything. He might have intercepted Cole and dealt with him without Gabriel and his wife even knowing.'

'That would make sense,' Lydia said. 'He would want to protect both Sandy and this young woman.' She paused and added, 'I can't blame him for it either.'

Rees nodded. He still suspected Washington. In fact, more and more, that man appeared guilty.

They walked to the livery so that Rees could question the owner. But he supported Washington's story in every particular. 'No, he doesn't own a horse. Sometimes he comes to borrow one.' He stared at Rees to see if he understood. 'We work out a trade. He shoes the beasts that need it in exchange.'

'Has anyone turned in a stray?' Rees asked.

The livery owner turned a look of disbelief on Rees. 'Of course not. Is a horse missing? Probably halfway to Ohio by now.'

Rees nodded his thanks. He and Lydia began walking to the other end of River Road. 'Mr Washington would be foolish to keep the horse,' Lydia said. 'Something that could be traced back to a murder victim.'

'That is true,' Rees agreed absently. 'And of Tobias too.'

He was beginning to worry about the upcoming conversation with Tobias. They had become good friends after they had collaborated to rescue Ruth from the Great Dismal Swamp. But now, since Rees had begun investigating the death of Randolph Gilbert, and now Robert Cole, the relationship between them had become acrimonious. Rees was dreading this next conversation.

THIRTY-FIVE

The walk to the cabinetry shop was a short one so Rees did not have too much time to fret about his meeting with Tobias. As they approached the house, he veered to the small barn at the back and looked inside. The only horse in the stall was Tobias's old brown mare. She peered at him over the wall and whickered.

'Where can that animal be?' Lydia wondered.

'Maybe it is in Ohio,' Rees said as Tobias opened his door.

'What are you doing back there?' Tobias asked coldly.

'We have a few questions for you and Ruth,' Rees said, evading the question. Tobias gestured to the open door, but he did not speak. Then went inside. Ruth, who was stirring something in a pot over the fire, looked up in surprise.

'More questions,' Tobias said, not troubling to hide his anger.

Ruth nodded. This time neither she nor Tobias offered refreshments or even suggested their visitors sit down.

'We are sorry to intrude,' Lydia said. Rees looked down at her. She was smiling at Ruth but her eyes were full of pain.

'I have no doubt you've heard about the newest death,' Rees said.

'And, of course, you come to us,' Tobias said.

'I'm talking to everyone,' Rees said, struggling not to react to the animosity in his friend's voice.

'We heard a rumor a man had been killed and tossed in the river,' Ruth said softly.

'It is not a rumor,' Rees said. 'His name was Robert Cole. He was a slave taker hired by Randolph Gilbert.'

'I weep no tears for him,' Tobias said, making a sharp dismissive movement with his hand. 'He is no loss. Rees, you know what the slave takers are like. You've been in a slave state.'

'But it is still murder,' Rees said.

'Is it? How do you know? You weren't there.'

'Were you?' Rees asked.

'Of course not. Are you accusing me of the murder?' Tobias's voice rose.

'No,' Rees said. 'I am merely trying to discover the truth of the matter.'

'No, you aren't,' Tobias argued. 'You are looking to assign blame.'

'No, I'm not,' Rees said, his voice rising. He stopped and took a breath. 'The victim deserves justice.'

'Justice!' Tobias spat out the word as though it were a curse. 'What is justice? Neither Randolph Gilbert nor his lackey Cole were innocents. They weren't victims. They preyed on the vulnerable. Their deaths are a form of justice.'

'But it isn't up to each one of us to decide who deserves execution—' Rees began.

'Do you know your Bible, Mr Rees?'

Mr Rees? Tobias was too good a friend to call him 'Mr'. He

realized Tobias was very angry, and much of that anger was directed at him for pursuing this investigation.

'Those that live by the sword, die by the sword. I say these brutes deserved their deaths.' Tobias would have continued but Ruth put her hand on his arm.

'I understand. I do,' Rees said. 'I agree about both Gilbert and Cole. They were not good men. But I do not want to take on the authority to determine who should pay the ultimate price. That is why we have laws. That is why we have juries. The other way, your way, leads to chaos.'

'Would a judge and jury take on a case of a rich white plantation owner who murders his abused slave?' Tobias asked bitterly.

'Well, no,' Rees said, unable to refute the argument.

'Exactly. Where is your justice there? And, if that slave murders his master or, God forbid, even talks back, well, that man would be hanged from the nearest tree. Where is your law then?'

'But without laws, we have anarchy,' Rees said. 'We are not beasts who follow no laws. We strive for justice.' Even though he believed that, it sounded lame even to him.

'In the world of men, justice is a rare commodity. And, before you claim the laws of men as your ultimate good, perhaps you should examine what those laws actually say.' Tobias paused, panting.

Into the sudden awkward silence, Ruth said, 'I never met the man. Either man. But I believe I have seen the slave taker.'

Everyone turned to look at her. 'When? Where? You never told me,' Tobias said, his voice rising with fear.

'I didn't think of it, until just now,' Ruth admitted.

'When was this?' Rees asked. He was still tense and breathing hard.

'Last week? No, the week before. It was Wednesday. I was at the butchers. He had some fine chickens . . .'

'Are you sure the man you saw was Robert Cole?' Lydia asked.

'Young man?' Ruth said. 'Black hair. Gray eyes.' She shivered. 'Cold gray eyes. Dressed in knee breeches, high boots, waistcoat, and a long coat over it. High hat with a brim.'

'Was that hat beaver?' Rees asked. 'Or rabbit?'

Ruth shrugged. 'I don't know. It could have been either.' She

paused and then said slowly, 'It looked to me as though the coat
and waistcoat were too large for him.'

'As though they were hand-me-downs?' Lydia said, darting a
glance at her husband.

'Exactly like that,' Ruth agreed. 'And the clothing was soiled.
You know,' she appealed to Lydia, 'that gray look that cloth gets
when it's gotten dirty and then been washed over and over.'

Lydia nodded. With several small children, she knew exactly
what Ruth meant.

'Did he approach you?' Tobias asked.

'Or say anything to you?' Rees jumped in with a question of
his own.

Ruth shook her head. 'I saw him watching me but then Miss
Sally, the milliner, spoke to me. We went together to have lunch
and that man went right out of my head. He wasn't there when
I came out and I haven't seen him again.'

'That confirms Mrs Sechrest's story, to a degree,' Rees said
to Lydia.

'What do you mean?' Tobias asked suspiciously.

'Cole left town,' Rees replied. 'On instructions from Randolph
Gilbert, he went to Boston to meet Mrs Sechrest and bring her back.
That is why you didn't see him again,' he added, turning to Ruth.

'I suppose I had a lucky escape,' she said in a trembling voice.
Rees nodded. He would check with the milliner but expected her
to fully corroborate Ruth's story.

'You have friends here,' Lydia said at the same moment. 'He
would not have dared abduct you from a busy street in the middle
of the day. But you owe the milliner a thank you. Cole might
otherwise have followed you home.'

'I must buy another hat,' Ruth said, trying to make light of
her experience. 'An expensive hat for Sunday services.'

Tobias looked at Rees accusingly. 'He might have taken Ruth
back south and sold her. What would you have said then? Whoever
murdered that man did us a good turn. And I, for one, will not
judge him a murderer.'

Rees and Lydia took their leave soon after. As they began walking
toward Main Street, Rees said, 'Tobias is angry enough to be the
murderer.'

'That doesn't mean he's guilty,' Lydia said quickly.

'I hope he's not,' Rees agreed.

'And Ruth, well, she told us about seeing Cole openly and honestly,' Lydia said, looking up at him with a frown. Rees smiled at her. Desperate for her friends to be ruled innocent, she was terrified that one or both might be guilty.

'That is so,' Rees said. They both had seen suspects in prior cases who had appeared genuinely honest, genuinely innocent, only to prove guilty as the investigation unfolded.

They walked a short distance in silence. Then Rees spoke. 'I wish I had made a better case for obeying the law, that's all.'

'Tobias is not going to become an outlaw,' Lydia said, darting a glance at her husband. 'He is like you, a steady and reliable fellow. In fact, he follows the rules more carefully than you do.'

'I know but—'

'You are offended because you know you lost the argument with him.'

'It wasn't a case of winning or losing,' Rees muttered.

'Perhaps not. But you yourself have railed about the laws declaring people like Tobias property. Men such as Gilbert not only have a right to own people but also mistreat them.' She smiled at her husband. 'I agree with you, a society is based on laws. But some of those laws, made by men for men and demonstrating all the worst of men, are terrible. You are upset with Tobias because, deep down, you know he is right, and you agree with him.'

THIRTY-SIX

R ees drove Lydia home to the farm and then, although he had not intended to, he stayed for the midday meal. Annie had become an accomplished cook. By the time Rees left to return to town, it was well after three. It was so late he passed Jerusha, returning home from school, when he went out the gate.

She pulled to a stop alongside him. 'Everyone appreciated the apples,' she said. 'Thank you.'

'Good. I am glad no one went hungry,' Rees replied. 'Be sure and thank your mother.'

'I will,' Jerusha promised.

'Any more trouble with those boys?' Rees asked, pulling back on the reins as Hannibal tried to start moving.

'Not today,' she said. 'They did not come to school.' A shadow crossed her face.

'Did something happen?' Rees asked.

'No. Everything is fine,' she said. 'I heard the Whitehead boys were sick, that's all. And as much as they torment me, I worry about them . . .' Her voice trailed away.

'We will talk tomorrow,' he called after her as she drove into the yard. He could see everything was not fine. Was she that worried about the Whitehead boys? He would be sure to question her when he met with her again. But now, he had to leave if he wished to speak to the milliner and confirm Ruth's account.

Dusk was rapidly setting in when he parked his horse and wagon at the tavern. He did not go inside, opting instead to cross Commerce Street to the milliner's shop. He had never been inside – until now. When he looked around at some of the artfully displayed confections, he wondered if his wife had ever visited this shop. Lydia tended toward the practical and plain in her clothing. And where would she wear the hat decorated with ribbons and feathers anyway?

'Mr Rees,' said a high fluting voice.

He turned to face the petite woman behind the counter. She was shorter than Lydia and wore her dark hair in a youthful *à la victime* style. Despite the hair, and the filmy, low-cut gown, however, she appeared closer to Rees's age than to Lydia's. Mutton dressed as lamb, he thought.

'Do I know you?' he asked, trying to keep his thoughts from appearing on his face.

'We've never met,' she replied, adding archly, 'and your wife has never graced my establishment with her presence.'

'Really?' Rees said. Since there seemed no appropriate response, he pivoted to his question about Ruth.

'Oh yes,' the milliner said. 'I remember the day well. She is a good customer and has become a friend. We spent a very enjoyable few hours together. Why?' For the first time, she lost the artificial sweetness to her voice and sounded genuinely concerned. 'Is she in any trouble?'

'None at all,' Rees said. 'In fact, she has you to thank for saving her from trouble.'

'That is wonderful to hear, although I have no idea what I could have done.' She smiled at Rees and continued, her voice once again taking on the almost childlike treble. 'I'm sure I could make a hat exactly to your wife's taste. Please have her visit me.'

'I will,' Rees said politely but untruthfully. He could not imagine Lydia looking upon a hat made of lace as anything but a moral failing.

With a final nod, he withdrew from the shop and returned to the tavern. With the onset of evening, most of the customers had departed, either on the coach or for home. Rees stopped to look in upon Rouge. He seemed much the same although even more of the blisters had scabbed over. He looked like something no longer human, but he professed to feel much better.

'I am eagerly awaiting your return to duty,' Rees said truthfully. 'I don't know how you manage to run the tavern and serve as constable as well.' He recalled now all of the times he'd judged Rouge lazy and added, 'It is a lot to take on.' Rouge mumbled something. Rees thought he was pleased by the compliment but couldn't tell; the suppurating blisters occluded the expression on his face.

Then Rees went in search of Thomas, just in case something had happened. Unfortunately, before he found Thomas, Mrs Sechrest found Rees first. 'Why Mr Rees,' she said, 'you are a busy man. I haven't seen you all day.'

'Yes, I am very busy,' Rees said, taking a step backward.

'I know you are and so I'll come straight to the point. Have you found my brother's murderer?'

'Not yet,' Rees said. Mrs Sechrest sighed and although he knew she wanted him to feel humiliated by his failure, he couldn't repress the spasm of guilt that shuddered through him.

'Well then, as soon as I find my wench, I will regretfully return home. It is clear to me that my poor brother will never find justice.'

Rees winced, hearing an unwelcome echo of his argument with Tobias in her speech. His need to solve the case warred with a sudden and irrational desire to confound her wishes. 'Dr Ned,' he said, clumsily changing the subject, 'asked that you decide the disposition of your brother's body. Will you bury him here or take him home?'

'Inter him here, I suppose,' she said. 'Even though we are almost into December and the weather is cold, I don't believe it is practical to bring the remains home. It would make for a most unpleasant journey. Does the doctor still have the body in the surgery?' Mrs Sechrest asked.

'I believe so,' Rees said. 'And I believe there are funds—'

'Excuse me for interrupting,' Thomas said.

Rees turned with a glad smile. 'Not at all. How can I help you?'

'Dr Ned wanted me to give you a message.'

'A message?'

'He wants you to come to the surgery when you can. He has something to show you.' Thomas paused and then added regretfully, 'He may be gone by now. It is almost suppertime. I'm sorry. I forgot to tell you.'

'Please, don't worry,' Rees said. 'I'll go to the surgery first thing tomorrow morning.'

'I will as well,' Mrs Sechrest said, smiling at Rees. 'The doctor may have more information. Something useful.'

If she meant that to sting, Rees thought, she succeeded.

Rees did not intend to visit Dr Ned with Mrs Sechrest. When he descended the stairs early the following morning – and he could barely wait for Rouge to reclaim his position – he found her waiting for him in the back room. 'I thought, since we both had to visit the surgery, we should accompany one another,' she said sweetly.

Left with no alternative but a rude refusal – and he thought about it – Rees submitted with bad grace. They left the tavern together. Rees had not even had an opportunity to drink his coffee.

They did not speak on the short walk to the doctor's office. Although Dr Smith had not finished his breakfast yet, and was not available, Rees was not surprised to see Ned already in the office.

'You're early,' Ned said.

Rees stepped back so that Mrs Sechrest might speak to Ned first. 'I understand you have my brother's remains,' she said, her voice so sweet it was almost a coo.

'Yes,' he said. 'I thought you might want to bury him in a family plot.' He looked at her sympathetically as she brought out a handkerchief and dabbed at her eyes. Rees could see the young man bending towards Mrs Sechrest protectively and felt like shouting a warning; she is as tough as an old boot under that delicate exterior.

'I would,' she said, 'but my home lies such a distance away. I cannot imagine . . .' Her voice trailed away.

'You could submerge him in rum,' Rees suggested. 'That should keep him preserved until you reach Virginia.' Ned turned a startled glance on Rees.

'You have such a sense of humor, Mr Rees,' Mrs Sechrest said. 'No, I do not believe that will serve. By the time I reach home, the ground will be hard. I think it best if he is buried here.'

Ned, looking shocked, nodded as though he could not think of anything to say. Most people would prefer to bury their relatives together, somewhere close by where they could plant flowers and visit the graves. Rees could have told the young man that there did not seem to be much family feeling here.

'I can probably arrange for one of the local ministers to say a few words,' Rees said, more for Ned's benefit than for the bereaved.

'Why, that is very kind of you,' Mrs Sechrest said, glancing at him in surprise.

'I will take care of the other arrangements,' Ned said, executing a little bow. The gesture seemed very odd in light of his informal shirtsleeves, but Charlotte Sechrest bestowed a generous smile upon him.

'I am so very grateful,' she murmured. 'And now, although I dislike discussing such crass matters as money, I feel I must ask if he had anything in his pockets?'

'Yes—' Ned began but Rees jumped in.

'Everything but the charges for your brother's burial will be remitted to you,' he said. He knew he had to protect Ned from his own chivalrous impulses.

'Thank you,' Mrs Sechrest said. She shot an annoyed glance at Rees and put out a gloved hand to Ned. 'Thank you so much. You have been more than gracious.' *Unlike Mr Rees*; the words were unsaid but that was what she meant.

Ned blushed to the tips of his ears. 'I hope you can make your own way back to the inn,' Rees said to her. 'I have another matter to discuss with the doctor.' She wanted to argue, he could see it in the frown she directed at him, but instead chose to withdraw gracefully.

'What an attractive lady,' Ned said as Charlotte closed the door behind her. Rees grunted. He did not agree. 'Since I will be speaking to the pastor at the Congregationalist Church about the funeral, why don't I ask him to say something. There is no point in both of us doing this.'

'Thank you,' Rees said with relief. The less involvement he had in Mrs Sechrest's affairs, the happier he would be. 'You wanted to show me something?'

'Oh yes. Come along to the shed.'

THIRTY-SEVEN

With no fireplace, the shed was very cold. Colder, Rees thought, than the barn in which he kept his livestock. But that was no doubt fortunate considering the presence of two corpses. Rees tried to breathe through his mouth.

The remains of Randolph Gilbert had been pushed to one side and covered with a thick canvas sheet. Fluids were beginning to leak through the covering. Ned guided Rees to the center of the shed, where Cole's body reposed on the table.

It was probably the first time in Cole's entire life, Rees thought, that he had achieved the principal position – especially when competing with Gilbert.

Ned began to pull back the sheet but stopped suddenly. He was not quick enough to prevent Rees from seeing the cut marks in the chest. Rees turned a startled glance upon Ned. First Gilbert and then Cole. Many people were horrified at the thought of an autopsy. As they saw it, such an act was blasphemy – mutilating God's vessel. Rees did not know how he felt but Ned's fascination seemed morbid and strange. Rees wondered if Ned had let his fascination take him beyond the law. That would explain why he had left Edinburgh for a small town in Maine.

'What did you want to show me?' he asked.

Ned turned Cole's head so the wound on the side was visible. 'The blow fractured the skull,' Ned said. Rees nodded. He'd seen that for himself. 'But that isn't what I wanted to show you. Do you see the blood?'

Rees did not want to look but, steeling himself, he bent forward. Under the black bruise, blood matted the hair and ran down the side of the neck.

'Yes.'

'After a person dies,' Ned said, 'the heart ceases to beat.'

'Yes?' Rees said, puzzled.

'The blood stops flowing, right? I was surprised to see so much of it in Cole's hair and down the collar of his shirt.' Ned looked at Rees, as if expecting him to understand. He took a few moments to deconstruct what Ned had said.

'He was still alive when he went into the river,' Rees breathed.

Ned nodded. 'There was froth on his lips and when I examined him – when I looked further – I found water in his lungs.'

Rees considered this for a few seconds. 'Could one man have done this?'

'Yes. Once the victim was struck on the side of the head, he would have been disoriented at best. I would guess he was probably unconscious. Then he was thrown into the water.'

'So, the murderer is probably very strong,' Rees said.

Ned nodded. 'Yes. Clearly this would have been easier with two men.'

Rees would have wagered his farm that Gabriel was telling the truth when he professed to be unfamiliar with Cole. Now Rees wondered if Gabriel had he been lying? Or was it possible John Washington had managed both murders by himself?

In a daze, Rees nodded his thanks to Ned and found his way outside. He began walking back to the tavern, his thoughts whirling. He stopped so suddenly as a thought struck him that a woman with a basket over her arm almost collided with him.

'So sorry,' Rees said automatically. What if, he wondered, John Washington had asked Tobias to help him? They'd known one another for a few years now and perhaps each found the other trustworthy. Gabriel, after all, was a new addition to town.

He would have to discuss the possibility with Lydia when he went home this afternoon.

But first, breakfast.

After he ate his meal, Rees stopped by Rouge's office to check on him. Therese had removed the bedding – Rees could see it hanging over the fence outside – and was busily scrubbing the floor and all the pots. Rouge had removed himself to his desk. A plate of mush sat at his elbow; he had graduated from broth. He turned and nodded affably at his visitor.

'You must be feeling better,' Rees said. He did not doubt the constable would be scarred as the crusty scabs that covered every inch of visible skin flaked away.

'Still very tired, but yes, I do feel better,' Rouge said. 'I thought I would review some of the invoices.' He managed a lopsided smile. 'I don't dare look in a mirror.'

'Probably best for now,' Rees agreed.

'And the murder? How is the investigation faring?'

'I have several suspects,' Rees said cautiously. 'We can talk tomorrow.'

'Very well,' Rouge agreed. He hesitated and then said without meeting Rees's gaze, 'Thank you. I understand you had some trouble with one of our regulars.'

'You're welcome,' Rees said.

'I'm on the mend now and I'm certain to feel better tomorrow,' Rouge said. 'I'll soon be able to reclaim my responsibilities from you.'

'I'll be glad to surrender them,' Rees said. 'I've done almost nothing of my own work, the work that supports my family, during this time.'

'Now you understand why I am not so eager to hare off with you and investigate every little thing,' Rouge said. 'As God is my witness, the job of constable could take all my time if I permitted it.'

Rees grinned at Rouge. He must be feeling better; he was

snapping back. 'I understand much better,' he agreed. 'I'm glad to see you recovering. This inn is not the same without you.'

Although pleased, Rouge looked embarrassed and flapped his hand to brush away the tribute.

Rees arrived home almost half an hour before dinner. Usually, during the spring, he was desperate to leave the farm and all the work necessary to keep it running. But today, he felt a lift of his spirits as he drove through the gate. Hannibal was also glad to be home. He whinnied and sped up. After walking the horse around for a little while to cool him, Rees spent some time currying him. The ostler at the inn was competent and Hannibal had not been mistreated; but the horse had worked hard this past week and deserved special attention.

After leaving the barn, Rees stepped into the cheerful noise that seemed to characterize his family. Sharon and Joseph were quarreling as Annie set the table. Rees quickly crossed the floor to wrest the wooden horse, that Sharon was slamming Joseph with, from her hands.

'I didn't expect you for dinner,' Lydia said in surprise.

'I promised Jerusha I would see her today,' Rees said as he went to the basin to wash his hands.

'I made cornbread last night for her to bring into school today,' Lydia said.

'I'm sure her students will appreciate that,' Rees said. He sniffed the air appreciatively. 'What are we having for dinner?'

'Codfish cakes,' Lydia said.

'Cod! Where did we get the fish?' Rees asked in surprise. Lydia smiled at Annie who was suddenly very busy arranging and rearranging the silverware. 'Thomas brought it.'

'Did he now?' Rees said, glancing at the young woman. 'And why did he do that?'

'It was a gift for Annie,' Lydia said.

'I daresay we will have a wedding soon,' Rees said. Annie went scarlet.

'Don't tease her,' Lydia reproved her husband in a near-whisper.

'Thomas is a good man,' Rees said, adding with a glance at Annie, 'you could find worse.'

'You're embarrassing her,' Lydia scolded.

'Have you told her yet?' Rees asked his wife.

'Told me what?' Annie asked as Lydia shook her head 'no'.

'Lydia and I spoke to Sister Esther yesterday,' Rees said. 'We have arranged for you to come and live with us for the time being.'

With a shriek of joy, Annie hurled herself into first Rees's arms and then into Lydia's. 'Thank you,' she said emphatically. 'Thank you, thank you, thank you.'

'You spend most of your time here anyway,' Rees said, laughing.

'Although I admire their faith and their simple lives,' Annie said, brushing happy tears from her cheeks, 'I will never make a Shaker. I want my own home and my own family.'

'I imagine we all know that now,' Rees said.

'Of course we are very glad to have you with us,' Lydia said warmly. 'I am certain I will truly appreciate your help after the new baby comes.'

'I am looking forward to it,' Annie said eagerly. 'That is the one thing the Believers cannot teach you; how to care for a baby.'

'Even that can be addressed if you were to stay in Zion,' Lydia said. Some Sisters were chosen to care for the children; apprentices, orphans and adoptees that had made their way to the safety of the Shakers.

'But none of them will be my own,' Annie said, inarguably.

Something popped and spattered into the fire. 'Oh my,' Lydia said. 'Let's put dinner on the table before the fish dries out.' Hurrying to the fireplace, she pulled the pan away from the flames. Potatoes boiled in one pot and when she scooped the contents of the second pot into a dish Rees saw the dark red globes of beets. He loved beets although by spring he would be heartily sick of them.

They sat down at the table. Lydia said grace. Rees picked up his fork and took a bite of the cod cake. Flavored with onion and the bacon fat it had been fried in, it was tender and delicious. 'Will,' Lydia said, watching him eat in dismay, 'there is no need to eat quite so fast.'

'Breakfast was a long time ago,' Rees said, mashing his potatoes with a chunk of butter.

He had just lifted the fork to his mouth when someone knocked at the door. Rees shared a look of consternation with his wife and then he rose from the table to answer it.

Esther stood on the porch. Shivering despite her cloak, she turned an anxious face to Rees. Smudges discolored the café au lait skin beneath her eyes as though she had not slept for several days. 'It's Aaron,' she said, her already reddened eyes welling up with tears. 'The rash has come out. You were correct, Rees. It's the smallpox.'

THIRTY-EIGHT

'Y ou'd better come in,' Rees said. 'Sit down and have some dinner.'

Esther shook her head. 'I'm not hungry.' But she stepped over the lintel and Rees shut the door behind her. He reached out for her cloak. She hesitated, clutching it around her, so he did not insist on taking it.

'At least sit down,' Lydia said. 'I'll bring you a hot drink.'

'Oh, I can't intrude on your dinner,' Esther said. But Rees put another chair next to Annie and Lydia pressed Esther down into it.

'How long has it been since you ate anything?' Rees asked. He and Lydia exchanged a glance and she put a plate and a fork in front of the Shaker Sister. Annie brought over the cup of tea and Esther took a sip, leaning back in the chair as though exhausted.

'Did you walk over?' Lydia asked.

Esther nodded. 'I don't know what possessed me. When I saw the first blisters on his forehead, I took my cloak and left. I just started walking.'

'Do you think many of your number have already recovered from the contagion?' Rees asked, thinking of practical steps.

'Most of the adults perhaps,' Esther said. 'But I don't know about the children.' Tears of fatigue and worry filled her eyes and began running down her cheeks.

'Aaron must be quarantined,' Rees said.

'The children live in a separate building,' Lydia said. 'Aaron will have had no contact with most of them, or with the Sisters who care for them.' She smiled at Esther, trying to calm her.

'I saw him building chairs in the woodworking shop,' Rees said. Usually the boys in the Shaker community learned from the Brothers.

'But he went into the shop very recently,' Esther said. The color was returning to her face. Lydia passed the plate of fish and the bowl of potatoes. Esther took both, almost as though she couldn't help herself. 'He has no roommate.' Rees nodded, remembering that Jonathan had said the same. 'He only worked in the workshop a few days before he fell sick. And when he first returned to the community, he sat with the other new Shakers. The Winter Shakers.'

'I would guess,' Rees said, 'that most of the landless men would have already suffered from this disease and survived. Will any of them be working alongside the boys?'

Esther shook her head. 'They'll be working more closely with the hired men.' She took a bite of her cod cake. 'This is good.' She took another bite.

'After dinner,' Lydia said to Esther, 'Rees can drive you back to Zion.'

'Oh, that's not necessary,' Esther said. 'I can walk.' She finished the last of her cod cake. Lydia quietly slid another onto her plate.

'I need to speak to Jonathan anyway,' Rees said. He had not intended to do so today but he supposed, if he was already conveying Esther home, he might as well. 'Don't worry about Aaron,' he added. 'Constable Rouge also came down with smallpox and he is recovering well. I expect we will soon see him behind the bar.'

He was happy to see Esther manage a smile. 'I will pray for the same for Brother Aaron,' she said.

She finished both cod cakes and the rest of her meal as well. Her cheeks regained some color and she no longer appeared so drained. After dinner, while Lydia and Annie cleared away the food and the plate, Esther played with Sharon and Joseph. From the whooping and the giggling, Rees could see Esther enjoyed it as much as the kids did, maybe more. By the time she was ready to leave, under the combination of good food and sociability, Esther was almost her old self again.

Jerusha arrived home from school as Esther was donning her cloak. Rees hurried out to ask Jerusha to leave the donkey hitched to the cart. Hannibal had been working hard these past few weeks. Rees did not want to take the gelding out again, even though the distance to Zion was short. Let Hannibal enjoy his afternoon in the paddock.

Rees and Esther squeezed into the cart and drove through the gate in silence. Esther did not speak. Since the Shakers prohibited unnecessary speech, Rees assumed she was following the custom. But when he glanced at her a few lengths down the road, he saw that she had been rocked to sleep by the motion of the cart. No doubt, in addition to not eating, Esther had not been sleeping either.

Rees slowed the donkey to a walk. He did not want Esther to fall from the seat. Besides, the slow pace would take a bit longer and she could sleep for that extra time.

As they plodded slowly along, Rees reflected upon Esther's distress. If Esther and Aaron were different people, Rees would assume she was in love with the Brother. In this case, however, he found that hard to believe. The Shakers were celibate and took every effort to keep the sexes separate. Still, the human heart could not always be denied. Lydia, Rees's own wife, while a member of the Shaker community, had fallen in love. She'd married in secret but had been expelled when her pregnancy became obvious. Rees and his family were now living on the farm Lydia had inherited from her first husband.

But Aaron, Rees thought, was such a quarrelsome soul, always argumentative. Rees found the very thought of any woman loving Aaron preposterous. And Esther had been a Shaker for a very long time.

Nonetheless when it came to human emotion, Rees supposed anything was possible.

He woke Esther when they arrived in Zion. She stared at him in dazed confusion. 'My goodness,' she said, swiping her hand across her eyes. 'Where are we? I did not mean to fall asleep.'

'You needed it,' he said. She covered her yawn with a hand and climbed down. Rees watched her make her way toward the kitchen for a few seconds before he parked the cart in front of the barn.

Then he cut across the main street toward the Infirmary.

The Nursing Sister saw him approach. When he neared her, she opened the door and motioned him in. She was normally a combative woman but today her face was crumpled into lines of worry.

Rees moved toward the bed. Aaron had been positioned in a half-seated position against a stack of pillows. He turned his head as Rees moved toward him. The patient did not look as terrible as Rouge. Not yet anyway. So far, the rash had only erupted on his forehead and cheeks. But he was breathing heavily, as though respiration was a struggle. Rees nodded at him and seated himself in the chair by the bed. He didn't know what to say. He and Aaron had never enjoyed even a civil relationship; Aaron was too cantankerous for that. But they'd known one another for several years now and Rees was sorry to see the other man so ill. So, he sat quietly for a little while, hoping his presence gave some comfort.

When Aaron fell asleep, Rees rose from the chair. He was stiff from sitting in one position for so long. He nodded at the Sister and left the Infirmary. As he passed by the workshop, he heard the sound of hammering and went inside. Jonathan looked up. 'I hope you are not coming to gloat,' he said.

'No,' Rees replied.

Jonathan unbent a little. 'We are making plans to keep the children completely separated,' Jonathan said. 'And any of our older family who haven't suffered this disease . . .' He paused and then added, 'Of course, it would be Aaron who caught this dreadful scourge. He was living in town for several months. I have no doubt he was exposed there. And then brought it to us,' he added bitterly.

'It is true the constable also contracted it,' Rees agreed. 'Rouge is on the mend now. And I hope Aaron survives as well.'

Jonathan nodded soberly. 'We are all praying for him,' he said.

Rees nodded. 'Have there been any strangers here, in Zion, other than the people who have joined?' Rees asked. A few years previously, it had been fashionable for people to attend the Shaker services, as though they were some form of entertainment. But the practice had been stopped.

'I haven't heard of any visitors,' Jonathan said. 'I will ask around. Why?' He looked up at Rees. 'Do you think a visitor brought the disease to our community?' Then he answered his own question. 'No, that is not what happened. If that were so, others besides Aaron would have fallen sick.'

Rees did not feel so certain of that. Since epidemics regularly affected the population, he guessed many, even among the insular Shakers, would be immune. 'I will stop over again to check in on Brother Aaron tomorrow or the next day,' he said.

When he arrived home, all of the children were in the yard chasing one another around and screaming. Jerusha instantly detached herself from the group and joined Rees as he climbed down from the cart. 'No homework today?' he asked.

'They've finished some. They can do the rest after supper.' She followed Rees around the yard as he walked the donkey, putting her hand on the animal's silver neck. Rees glanced at her.

'What's the matter?'

'Miss Francine is making plans to close the school.'

'Permanently?' Rees turned to look at his daughter. He knew how much this teaching position meant to her.

'I hope not.' Jerusha managed a lopsided smile. 'After the Whitehead boys got sick, several parents chose to keep their children home. There is hardly anyone there now.'

Rees stopped walking. 'Sick with what? Smallpox?' It felt like his heart was sinking to his boots.

'Maybe. Probably.' Jerusha scratched her arm where Rees had inoculated her with cowpox. 'Miss Francine says it is my decision.' She began stroking the donkey's neck. 'What shall I do?'

'Did you ask your mother?'

'Yes.' Jerusha looked at Rees. 'She said to ask you. What shall I do?'

Rees released the donkey into the paddock with Hannibal and turned to face his daughter. Even in the fading light, he could see how distraught she was. 'We are almost into December,' he said. He could hardly believe it. The presidential election would take place next week and he *still* did not know who he would vote for. 'The school would be closing for Christmas

anyway. Why don't you close now and start again in January?'
Likely, the disease would have run its course by then. He hoped
so anyway.

'That sounds like a wonderful plan,' Jerusha said in relief. But
she did not relax and when Rees started walking toward the
house, she fell into step with him.

'Is there something else?' he asked.

'I want to go to Boston,' she blurted.

'Boston! Why? It is so far from home.' First Simon had opted
to live with Rees's oldest son David in Dugard, Maine. Now
Jerusha was also threatening to leave home. 'Why?'

'I want to learn to be a proper teacher.'

'You mean, like the schoolmaster in town?'

'Yes. No. He mainly teaches Latin and penmanship. I want to
be better than that,' Jerusha said vehemently.

'I suppose your mother suggested you speak to me,' Rees said.

Jerusha nodded. 'She went to school in Boston. A private
school for girls. She thought I . . .' Her voice trailed away and
she stared at him beseechingly. 'It would only be for a year or
two.'

'Let me think about it,' he said at last. He wanted to refuse
her, but he also did not want to crush her dream. 'I will discuss
it with your mother.'

'Thank you,' she whispered. Gathering her skirts in her hand,
she broke into a run, dashing up the steps to the porch in front
of him. Rees smiled. Jerusha was not quite grown up after all.

The farmyard was now in shadow; his children ghosts running
and shouting in the gloom. 'It is time to go inside,' he called to
them. 'It's growing dark.' Led by Judah and Nancy, the children
thundered up the steps and into the house.

THIRTY-NINE

Although Rees spent Tuesday night in his own bed, he had
trouble sleeping. The thought that Jerusha might leave
weighed on him. In the way that dreams have of

combining two worries into one, he imagined that she died from the disease and awoke with tears on his cheeks.

It was almost dawn. He knew he would not be able to go back to sleep and he must arise for the day in a little while anyway. He slid carefully from the bed and went into the weaving room. He looked at the cloth he had been working on. He had woven little since Rouge had fallen ill. He sat down, tested the treadles and the tension of the warp, and began. He'd already forgotten the pattern but, as he wove, it came back to him and he went faster and faster. He stopped only when he ran out of thread on the shuttle.

'I guess Jerusha told you,' Lydia said from the doorway.

Rees jumped, startled, and turned to look at her. 'I didn't know you were there,' he said. 'Yes, she told me last night.'

'I thought she could attend the school I did as a young woman. It is run by a man my father knows, a Mr Caleb Bingham.'

'I don't want her to go,' Rees said. 'She'll be so far away. And what if something happens to her? We won't be there to help.'

Lydia nodded in agreement. 'I know. But I want you to remember one thing. She is barely one year younger than you were when you joined the Continental Army.'

Rees stared at his wife in a befuddled silence. Lydia had spoken only the truth, but he felt like exclaiming, 'Jerusha is only a baby!' Instead he said, 'Why did my parents allow me to enlist?'

'You ran away,' Lydia pointed out dryly. 'You were sixteen then. Jerusha will turn fifteen on her next birthday.' She paused a moment and then added, 'She would not be alone. I could arrange for her to live with family or, better still, an old friend.'

Rees regarded his wife for a long moment. He knew almost nothing about her family; Lydia spoke of them rarely. 'Would she be welcome, do you think?'

'We would ensure she was.' She looked at the expression on Rees's face and said gently, 'We would be losing her soon in any case if she chose to marry. All of the children are growing up, Will.'

When he said nothing, she returned to their bedroom to dress. After a few minutes of paralysis, Rees too rose from his seat and followed his wife. Lydia was right, he knew she was right. But

when he went downstairs after washing and shaving, he picked
up Sharon and hugged her tightly. It would be many years before
she was old enough to leave.

After breakfast, Rees drove to the tavern. Rouge was again
seated in his chair. A dirty plate with the remains of a hearty
breakfast rested on the desk by his elbow. He turned when Rees
tapped at the door frame. 'Come in, come in, Will.'

'How are you feeling today?'

'Much better.'

Rees examined the constable's face. Many more of the
scabs had fallen off, leaving depigmented scars behind. But
with pink in his cheeks and a smile on his face, he no longer
looked ill.

'Tell me what is happening with the murder investigation,'
Rouge said. 'That Mrs Sechrest has been in here almost daily
with demands for action.'

'Well, I am sorry to say I haven't yet identified the murderer,'
Rees said. 'I suspect there were two people involved because Mr
Gilbert was both strangled and stabbed.' Rouge nodded. He knew
that already.

'What about the slave taker, that Robert Cole?' he asked.

Rees hesitated. He knew of Rouge's predilection for running
off half-cocked from previous investigations and was afraid to
offer too much information. 'I believe the murderer is local,' he
said finally. 'Cole's body was found on the riverbank, near the
other tavern.'

'Hmm,' said Rouge contemptuously. 'That establishment can
scarcely be called a tavern. More like a stall with a roof for the
beery men.' Since Rees had seen more than a few drunkards in
Rouge's tavern, he thought Rouge a little arrogant for dismissing
the other bar. 'Mostly the lumbermen and the river folk stop
there. And of course any of the drifters camping on the riverbank.'
Rouge paused and then said suspiciously, 'You haven't told me
how Robert Cole was murdered.'

Damn, Rees thought. He had been hoping Rouge wouldn't
ask. 'He drowned,' Rees said evasively.

'And how did that happen to come about?' Rouge asked even
more suspiciously.

'He was hit in the head,' Rees said.

'Hit with what?' Now Rouge was staring at Rees with narrowed eyes.

'I don't know,' Rees said. That at least was true. 'Maybe a hammer.'

'A hammer. Well, well. Mrs Sechrest told me both her brother and Cole came to town searching for a young woman. A young woman that exactly matches the girl you brought back from Virginia last month,' Rouge said, fixing his black-eyed gaze firmly on Rees.

'Yes?' Rees said, his heart sinking.

'Where is that young woman now?' Rouge asked.

'I don't know who you mean,' Rees said with a shake of his head. He was very glad he had removed Sandy from town. Rouge would never think of looking for her in the mountains.

'What if one or both tried to recapture that young woman?' Rouge demanded. 'They have the right. She is Mrs Sechrest's property. That is the law.' Rees said nothing. He was struggling to align his passion for justice with a law he had come to believe was immoral. 'Then,' Rouge continued, 'her man defended her. While he was protecting the girl, he killed those two men.' He paused.

'And?' Rees asked cautiously. He didn't quite understand where Rouge was heading but he was very sure he was not going to like it.

'Well, when I looked at it like that, I knew who the murderers were.'

'You did?'

'Of course. Only ones it could be. John Washington's helper Gabriel and that pretty young wife of his.'

At first Rees felt weak with relief. Rouge hadn't set his sights on Tobias and Ruth. But then, as he fully understood what Rouge had said, Rees erupted. 'It's not him,' Rees said. 'Not them, I mean. Gabriel is almost certainly innocent.'

'I thought you said you haven't identified the murderer.' Rouge grinned at Rees as though he'd caught him in a lie.

'I haven't. But I am certain Gabriel had nothing to do with the killings. He's the only one I *am* certain of.'

'He told you he was innocent, did he?' Rouge asked.

'Well, not in so many words,' Rees admitted. He recalled the horrified expression on Gabriel's face when his wife admitted she'd been approached by Cole. 'But I am absolutely convinced Gabriel is innocent.' He almost disclosed his suspicions about John Washington but suppressed the impulse. He was afraid Rouge, eager to prove himself after his illness, would not only not release Gabriel and his wife but would also accuse Washington of the crime.

'Gabriel and his wife are escaped slaves. You realized that as well, I am sure. And Gabriel, besides being a big strong man and well able to overpower either Gilbert or Cole, is also a blacksmith.'

Rees acknowledged Rouge's train of thought with a nod. His thoughts had once followed the very same pattern. He was embarrassed by it now.

'Fortunately, once I understood all of that, I had them removed to the jail.'

For a moment Rees just stared at the other man. Then he started shouting.

FORTY

Thomas appeared at the door almost immediately. 'What is happening here?' he asked, his gaze darting from one man to the other.

'He's shouting at me and making me tired,' Rouge said.

'He put an innocent man and his wife in the jail,' Rees said, his voice still very loud.

'They are escaped slaves,' Rouge pointed out, raising his hand to his face and rubbing his forehead wearily, 'so they are not innocent. At least, not in the eyes of the law. Mrs Sechrest – or the slave takers – have a right to recover their property.'

Rees stared at Rouge. 'What is wrong with you? They are people, not parcels.'

'The law says otherwise,' Rouge said. 'Listen, Rees, they are safe for now—'

The rage that exploded in Rees's head caught him by surprise.

He took several steps forward and who knows what he would have done if Thomas had not caught him by the arm and pulled him back. 'Come outside now,' he said, tugging Rees to the door.

'They are safe from everyone while we continue the investigation,' Rouge called after him. 'But no, you had to come in here, all loud and belligerent, and start shouting. If you'd done your job, this wouldn't be necessary.'

'Did you hear him? He's willing to give those poor folks to that woman,' Rees said to Thomas. 'What kind of brute is he?'

Thomas jerked Rees through the door and shut it. 'He didn't say that.'

'Then why would he put Gabriel in jail?'

'He felt he had to do something. Mrs Sechrest wore him down.' Thomas paused for a few seconds before he continued. 'Not everyone is as confident as you are. In fact, your self-confidence is intimidating to some.'

'What does that have to do with anything?' Rees asked.

'One of the customers this morning said maybe you should become constable permanently. My cousin was . . . upset.'

'I don't want his position,' Rees said. 'I never have. I took over as a favor. For him.'

Thomas offered Rees a lopsided grin. 'I know. And he knows too. But you did such a good job he now feels threatened. Give him a little while. He'll calm down.'

'By then, Gabriel and his wife may have been re-enslaved,' Rees said. He was still shaking. While he understood Thomas was most likely correct, the constable would calm down, Rees also knew that significant damage could be done by then. Mrs Sechrest could be very persuasive. Regretting the consequences when it was too late to change them would not help. 'I've got to go,' he said, brushing past Thomas. Rees had to intervene, and quickly too, before anything worse happened to Gabriel and his wife.

He paused outside the tavern and took several deep breaths. As he calmed down, he began to shake. Perhaps he had been a trifle hard on Rouge, but he was so afraid Mrs Sechrest would abduct some poor soul and take them south.

Movement at the church across Commerce Street caught his attention. It was Mrs Sechrest, dressed all in black, climbing the steps into the Congregation Church. Ned, wearing a fine suit, waited for her at the top. An empty wagon, decked out with black ribbons, stood in the street. Rees shook his head in admiration; Ned had arranged the funeral for Randolph Gilbert in double-quick time.

With Mrs Sechrest occupied, Rees could safely put his plan in motion.

With a mix of running and fast walking, Rees hurried to Tobias's cabinetry shop. Flushed and panting, he burst through the shop door. Tobias jumped and dropped the wood he was shaping. 'What the—?'

'Rouge just arrested Gabriel and his wife and put them in the jail,' Rees blurted.

'He did what?'

'Yes.' Rees paced around a work bench. 'I am quite sure Gabriel is innocent of the murders.' He spun around to face Tobias. 'I fear Mrs Sechrest will persuade Rouge to allow her to take Gabriel and his wife to Virginia since she has not been able to find Sandy.'

Tobias very carefully put down the rag in his hand. 'What do you want me to do?'

'We need to alert all of the abolitionists,' Rees said. 'I want them to gather in front of the jail and prevent Mrs Sechrest from taking Gabriel.'

'I don't know all of them,' Tobias said.

'Lydia knows several of the wives from the anti-slavery sewing circle,' Rees said. 'I'm sure she will be willing to speak with them as well. And perhaps, once we have the beginnings of a group, others will join.' He paused and regarded Tobias in a tense silence.

'Of course we will help,' Ruth said from the bottom of the stairs. 'I know some of those women as well.'

'But Ruth—' Tobias began.

She shook her head at him. 'We could be in that jail, facing enslavement, instead of Gabriel,' she said.

'Exactly,' Rees said. He promised himself they would never know that he had suspected them of murder, still did in fact, and that they could be the ones who ended up in jail.

'It is our duty to help,' Ruth added.

'Very well,' Tobias said. 'We will do what we can.' He looked at Rees. 'I hope you remember that I did warn you to drop the investigation.'

'You did,' Rees said. He was still wrestling with the ethical questions posed by Tobias. What would Rees do when he found the murderer? Murder was a crime in every society, a crime that horrified decent people. But it may have been something else in the case of the murders of Gilbert and Cole. Rees was in a quandary. 'I still want to know,' he said. 'After all, if I'd done nothing, the constable might still have settled on Gabriel and his wife. Or upon you two. I don't think he sees the nuances of this case,' he added under his breath.

'We'll begin now,' Ruth said.

'What will you do?' Tobias asked Rees.

'Talk to John Washington,' Rees replied.

'You come to turn me over to the slave takers?' John Washington demanded when Rees walked into the smithy. He held the small cats head hammer in his hand and as he spoke, he brandished it.

Rees lifted both hands in defense. 'That was none of my doing,' he said. 'The constable is feeling better and he thinks I am not moving fast enough in identifying the murderer.' He could have said more; he was still furious, but decided it was more important to resolve the problem of the jailing of Gabriel and his wife.

'Then why are you here?' Washington did not lower the hammer.

'I need your help.'

'What?' Washington stared at Rees. 'Doing what?'

'I am gathering all the anti-slavery folks to meet in front of the jail.'

'What are you talking about?'

'I want them to provide a distraction while I chop a hole in the back wall so Gabriel and his wife can escape.'

Washington eyed Rees for several seconds. 'You're serious? You're going to chop a hole in the jail?'

'Yes. So, I may need to borrow that hammer as well.'

'In the middle of the day?'

Rees heaved a sigh. 'I need to do it as soon as possible.

Otherwise that Mrs Sechrest may attempt to remove those prisoners. Anyway, I don't think we'll be ready much before one or one thirty, if that soon. It will take several hours to gather everyone.'

'What will prevent her from taking Gabriel now? Before you have everyone assembled?'

'She's otherwise engaged just at the moment and will be for another hour or so. That's where you are important. You and Tobias and everyone you know should congregate in front of the jail now. By the time she is finished burying her brother, I hope there will be so many people she won't be able to reach them.'

'And what's to stop her from trying to capture me?' Washington asked dryly.

'I hope enough people who oppose slavery, or who just plain know you and want to defend you, will be there,' Rees said. When Washington did not speak, Rees added, 'Tobias and Ruth are collecting those they know.'

Washington sighed. 'Very well. I'll do what I can. And one other thing.'

'Yes?'

'This hammer is too small.' He held it up. Rees looked at it. One side was an odd shape, the other a small metal circle. 'You're going to need a sledgehammer.' He nodded at the wall where several were hanging from hooks. 'We'll take one of those to break open the jail wall.'

'We?' Rees asked in surprise.

'Of course. You'll be taking one of my sledgehammers. Stands to reason I'll be helping break down the wall.' He smiled mirthlessly. 'I know the constable. He'll suspect me anyway.'

Rees nodded. Rouge might, especially if his interactions with Washington were argumentative. 'Very well. I'll meet you here about one. Assuming,' he added, 'that there is a large group in front of the jail.'

Washington nodded and Rees turned and left. He still had to drive home and speak to Lydia. She had not been as active in the Durham anti-slavery sewing circle as she might have wished but she had attended some of the meetings and would know who to call upon.

Then Rees planned to ask Jonathan for the Shakers' assistance.

Since they believed every person was a child of God and deserving of good treatment as such, they strongly opposed slavery. They were also pacifists but, if they did not have to fight but only assemble, maybe the Elders would agree to lending some of their members to join the group in front of the jail.

Mrs Sechrest would try everything she could to take possession of Gabriel and his family. And Rouge, out of sheer contrariness, might allow it. Rees couldn't risk it.

FORTY-ONE

Lydia and Rees left the farm at the same time; she to visit the farmwives who were also members of the abolition group and he to stop at Zion before traveling back to town. Once he reached the village, he went directly to the woodshop. He hoped Jonathan was inside working and he was. The Elder looked up in surprise.

'Rees. Have you already visited the Infirmary?'

'No,' Rees said, feeling a spasm of guilt. 'I will. But I don't have time right now.'

'What do you need?' Jonathan asked in a resigned tone.

'Constable Rouge has begun recovering from smallpox,' Rees said. 'Now that he is feeling better, he . . .' Rees stuttered to a stop as he searched for the proper word. Jonathan grimaced. He and Rouge had butted heads several times and although the Shaker Brother would claim he disliked no one, Rouge probably came the closest. 'Well, because I have not yet identified the murderer, he has arrested the blacksmith's helper and his wife. They are escaped slaves and are under threat from a slave owner who will return them south.'

'And you have a plan to stop it,' Jonathan guessed.

'I do,' Rees said. 'I am hoping you can help.'

Jonathan did not speak but reluctance to become involved was expressed in every line of his tense body.

'We are forming a group to stand in front of the jail and prevent Rouge and Mrs Sechrest from taking possession of the two people imprisoned in it.' Rees thought it best to refrain from mentioning his own illegal plan.

'Who is "we"?' Jonathan asked.

'Some of our community. The local abolition chapter,' Rees said.

'We are pacifists . . .' Jonathan began.

'I know,' Rees said. 'The purpose isn't to engage in a battle. It is to form a human shield.' He paused and then added, 'Lydia will be there as well.' He almost continued his efforts to persuade Jonathan but suppressed his impulse. He thought – he hoped – that the Elder would reach the conclusion that the Shakers should help as a moral imperative on his own.

Finally, Jonathan nodded. 'I must discuss it with the other Elders. If they agree and' – he directed a cool smile at Rees – 'you already know you have one vote – Esther – then we will join you in town.'

'I hope there is already a large group at the jail,' Rees said. He thought Jonathan might ask why, if there was already a large group, would Rees need the Shakers. But he didn't. Instead, he nodded and bent to his work. Understanding the conversation had concluded, at least as far as Jonathan was concerned, Rees left.

Although he drove into town as rapidly as he could, he could tell from the sky that it was past noon. When he drove down Main Street, he could hear voices to his right, in the direction of the jail and felt a shiver of relief. There were people there; he hoped that meant Gabriel and his wife were still safe within the walls of the jail. Some of the shouting sounded angry, though. What did that mean? Were arguments taking place between Mrs Sechrest and those providing protection to the prisoners?

Rees couldn't guess. He urged Hannibal into a faster trot.

'You're late,' Washington said when Rees rushed into the smithy. He had parked horse and wagon in the smith's yard. 'Better get them out of sight.'

Rees unhitched Hannibal and brought him through the big double doors. While he put the gelding in the bay, Washington threw a canvas tarpaulin over the wagon. Rees took the heaviest sledgehammer he could find down from the wall and hurried outside. The two men closed the doors.

'There are a lot of people at the jail,' Washington said.

'That's good, isn't it?' Rees asked.

Washington laughed bitterly. 'Yes and no. There are still some folks that think we black people should be slaves, even here in Maine.'

Rees thought of the angry shouting he'd overheard as he'd come through town. 'We better hurry,' he said grimly.

As they approached the crowd in front of the jail, Rees saw that there were more people than he would have believed, both men and women. He saw Ruth standing at the back. And more people were coming; as he watched, a wagon of Shaker Brothers discharged its passengers in front of the jail.

A line of men had positioned themselves in front of the jail door, Tobias among them.

But not all of the crowd were there to protect the prisoners. Mrs Sechrest, still wearing her black gown, stood at the back, playing her part as a delicate woman with fluttering handkerchief. She was encouraging the man in front of her, a farmer, by the look of the axe he carried, to do something. Rees wasn't quite sure what; he couldn't hear her above the clamor of the other voices. But the farmer shouted at the men who stood shoulder to shoulder in front of the jail and held up his axe.

'We'd better hurry,' Washington said. 'The mood is getting ugly.'

Rees nodded and cut around to the back of the small structure. A small copse of leafless trees and the dried canes of dead underbrush blocked their way. No one could hear them, though, over the shouting out front. Rees and Washington fought their way to the featureless back wall of the jail.

'We better make every stroke count,' Rees said.

'They'll hear us soon enough,' Washington agreed. He took the sledgehammer from Rees's hands and swung it. Rees could see the muscles in the other man's arms bunch, even through the thick fabric of his jacket. One stroke, two strokes. Somebody out front fired off a gun. Rees jumped, imagining they were coming for him and Washington. But no, now he heard Rouge's voice. Rees guessed the constable had fired over the heads of the crowd, warning them. Rees spared a thought for Lydia. He hoped she, and Ruth too, had found a place of safety.

Washington handed the tool to Rees. The bricks of the wall
had begun to crack and, in some places, the mortar was splin-
tering. Rees lifted the sledgehammer and aimed for the center
of the weakest spot. This time the heavy instrument went through.
Rees hit that spot twice more, and then, sweating like a horse,
he lowered the hammer. Washington began pulling away the
broken bricks. The hole was not overly large. Rees feared Gabriel
might be too big to push through it.

'Hurry,' Washington hissed through the opening. 'Come on.'

The young woman came first, squeezing easily through the
cavity. While Washington pushed her behind him, Rees pulled
another section of brick down. A sharp edge cut his hand and
blood mixed with brick dust.

'Get out of the way,' Gabriel said. Washington grasped Rees's
shoulder and moved him aside. Gabriel started through the hole,
pushing with all his weight, until he rammed his shoulders
through. With a pattering like hail, more of the mortar and a few
loose pieces of brick rained down on the ground.

Maybe the men standing arm in arm at the front might have
known something was going on but they did not react. The crowd
in front of them most certainly did not know. The sound of the
sledgehammer against the brick had been lost in the din:
the gunshots and the shouting, at the front.

Gabriel, coated in mortar dust, stared at Rees in surprise.
'Thank you,' he said.

'Don't worry about that now,' Washington told the other man.
'You and your wife come with me.'

'Where are you taking them?' Rees asked.

'I don't know for sure. And it's best you don't know,'
Washington said to Rees. 'I'll see you later. Just make sure you
put my sledgehammer in the smithy.'

Rees nodded. He watched the people walk quickly away,
toward the field where market was held. Once they crested
the hill and disappeared down the other side, he picked up the
sledgehammer and went around the corner of the jail.

FORTY-TWO

He tried to keep the sledgehammer close to his leg and as unobtrusive as possible as he joined the people in front. He paused on the edge of the crowd and surveyed the throng. There were many more anti-slavery than pro. Tobias and his companions formed a solid line in front of the jail door. A few men occupied the open space in front of them. The larger number of people were behind them, watching the stand-off. Mrs Sechrest, applying a handkerchief to dry eyes, called encouragement to the men menacing the jail. The farmer, burly and still faintly tanned from the summer sun, brandished his axe, but the line of people in front of the jail did not break.

Rees caught Tobias's eye and offered a faint nod. Then his gaze swept over the mass of people squeezed into the lane. A group of Shaker Brothers, including Jonathan, were watching the melee at the front with a mixture of disapproval and fascination. This was probably the most entertainment they'd witnessed for some time. Although a few women stood at the front, most of them had withdrawn to the back, almost to the dilapidated porch attached to the midwife's home. Rees spotted Ruth and then, a little behind her shoulder, Lydia. She shifted her position and lifted her head to look around. Rees caught her eye. He pointed at himself and then at her, trying to indicate he would come for her. He thought he could push through the crowd to the fence that separated the inn yard from the street. He had scaled it before, from the other side, but he thought he could make it.

Since the crowd was somewhat thinner on this side, he was able to thread his way through the people to the fence. He tossed the sledgehammer over and then jumped up to put his hands on the edge. He wasn't sure the fence would hold his weight, but he managed to swing his legs over and drop to the other side. The decaying wood left several splinters in his hands. He tried to grab the bigger splinters with his teeth and pull them out as he ran.

On a normal day, he would enter the tavern through the back

door, thread his way through the establishment, and exit through
the front door. This time, with the sledgehammer that had just
freed two prisoners from the jail, he went through the yard instead
and walked around the tavern. He broke into a rapid trot as he
hurried to the next corner. As he ran past the midwife's house,
Lydia and Ruth appeared at the corner.

'Did Gabriel and—' Ruth began. Lydia put a warning hand
on Ruth's arm and her mouth shut instantly.

'Everything is fine,' Rees said. 'So far.'

'John Washington is a good man,' Ruth said. But the worried
pleat between her brows did not smooth out.

'Rees.'

Rees turned and saw Ned crossing from the doctor's surgery.
'What's happening? Dr Smith and I saw people gathering. And
now there is shouting.' He glanced at the sledgehammer in Rees's
hand but did not ask.

'The blacksmith's helper and his wife were jailed,' Rees said.

'Gabriel?'

'Yes. Do you know him?' Rees asked in surprise.

Ned nodded. 'Blacksmithing is a dangerous business. I treated
him for a bad burn. Why was he put in jail?'

'He and his wife were accused of the murder of Randolph
Gilbert and Robert Cole,' Rees replied.

'Murder!' Ned exclaimed.

'He's innocent,' Ruth said. 'The truth is he and his wife were
put in jail because they are escaped slaves.'

'They are easy targets,' Lydia said. 'It is disgraceful.'

'Why does the constable believe Gabriel is guilty?' Ned asked
Rees.

'I'm not sure he believes it exactly,' Rees said. He wanted to
add that Rouge chose to think they might be guilty because he
was a stubborn bastard who wouldn't listen to reason. Instead
he said, 'Cole was hit by a hammer. Rouge assumed Gabriel, as
a blacksmith with access to hammers, was the most likely culprit.'

'But Cole wasn't hit by a metal hammer,' Ned said.

'He wasn't?' Rees stared at him.

'No. A metal hammer would have done more damage. Instead
of fracturing the bone, a metal hammer would have splintered
it. At least. Depending on the force behind the blow. Besides,

the head of the tool that struck him was much larger than a hammer head. You saw the bruise. I estimate the size of the tool that hit him was at least three inches across. Maybe more.' Ned shook his head. 'So, if Rouge is assigning the blame to Gabriel on the basis of a hammer, he is wrong. And I will tell him so.'

'Good,' Rees said approvingly. He was happy to see that someone else agreed with his conclusions. He didn't think Rouge would listen, certainly he wouldn't right now, but it couldn't do any harm for Rouge to hear this from someone else.

'We'd better go,' Lydia said. 'I am tiring.'

Rees looked at her. He didn't think she was, but Ruth looked limp. 'When is the baby due?' Ned asked her.

'January.'

'Congratulations.' Nodding at both women, Ned headed toward the crowd in front of the jail.

Neither Rees nor the two women spoke until they were well past the tavern. They saw few people about; the combination of the cold weather and the activity at the jail had lessened the traffic on Main Street. As they approached the corner, Rees said, 'I hope Tobias is not injured.'

Ruth acknowledged that with a nod but said, 'He will account it a small price to pay to save those two lives.'

'But will the constable take it into his head to accuse someone else now?' Lydia asked. 'Will he now jail Mr Washington?' She glanced at Ruth with an anxious expression and then at her husband.

Rees knew she worried that the constable would pursue Tobias and Ruth.

'I don't know,' Rees said. Rouge wanted to demonstrate his superiority as an investigator. He wasn't incompetent but Rees knew from the past that Rouge tended to take shortcuts. He usually chose the easy way, and as often as not that way did not lead to the guilty party. 'I must work harder . . .'

They saw Ruth into the cabinetry shop and then continued on to the blacksmith's. To Rees's surprise, the large double doors stood open. The tarpaulin had been removed from the wagon and Washington was busily hammering a shoe on Hannibal's right foreleg.

'What are you doing here?' Rees asked in astonishment.

'Don't you think the constable will immediately suspect me?'

Washington asked. 'I handed off the parcel to someone else and came back here. That way, all the shop proprietors can honestly swear that they saw me working while the ado was happening at the jail.'

'Here's the sledgehammer,' Rees said. He carried it into the smithy and hung it on the wall.

Both Lydia and Washington followed him. 'Will they be all right?' Lydia asked Washington in a whisper. There was no need to say who 'they' were.

'I think so. My friend will bring them into Canada. We've done it before and it's always gone all right.'

'Thank you,' Rees said to Washington, holding out his hand.

Washington eyed Rees's nicked and bloody hand a moment before taking it. 'Thank you, Mr Rees. The battle against the forces of evil is eternal. Know you were on the side of the light this time.'

'Thank you,' Rees said, somewhat awkwardly. He wasn't a religious man and always found such talk uncomfortable. He took Lydia's elbow and they went to the wagon. Washington bustled out to help hitch the horse and stood waving as Rees and Lydia climbed to the seats. Rees turned the wagon around and pulled out onto River Road.

As Hannibal shifted into a trot, Washington shouted at Rees, 'Don't forget, you owe me for that there shoe.' Chuckling, he walked back into the smithy.

FORTY-THREE

They turned off River Road and went east, toward Tobias's cabinetry shop. Another turn, and they headed toward Main Street. Rees wondered if the crowd still congregated in front of the jail.

'Is there anyone you suspect of the murders?' Lydia asked, breaking into his thoughts.

Rees turned to look at her. 'Tobias and Ruth,' he said aloud. 'John Washington. And I don't want any of them to prove guilty.'

'We have to do something,' Lydia said.

'Not sure what,' Rees said.

'If we don't discover the guilty person, the constable will just continue casting about for someone, anyone, he can declare guilty.'

Rees nodded. He feared Rouge might do exactly that. It wouldn't take him very long to settle on Tobias and Ruth. 'I wish I'd listened to Tobias and dropped the entire investigation,' Rees said gloomily.

'You couldn't do that,' Lydia said. 'It is not in your nature to give up like that. Besides, we both know the constable would do exactly as he did now: choose someone and declare them guilty without even a shred of proof.'

Since that was the truth, Rees could only nod in agreement.

'I have an idea,' Lydia said. 'Why don't you work out a time-line of everything that has happened? Maybe you'll see some clue you missed. At the very least, it should clarify your thinking.'

Rees smiled at her. 'That's brilliant. I will do as you suggest.' He frowned. 'But I still don't know if I will want to inform Rouge.'

'You may have to decide that at that moment,' Lydia said.

As they turned right on Main Street, Rees said, 'I'm starving.'

Lydia smiled. 'I'm hungry too,' she said. 'It is past dinner time. Well past.'

Under normal circumstances, Rees would suggest stopping at Rouge's tavern but, considering the events of the last few hours, he doubted they would find a welcome. Even if the constable never guessed Rees was behind the jail break, he would remember their quarrel. Rees, himself, did not think he would forgive Rouge for some of the things he'd said, at least not for a long time to come.

When they drove past Rouge's establishment, they could still hear the clamor emanating from the area in front of the jail. Rees was surprised that no one had discovered the escape as yet. But then, maybe the men protecting the door knew Gabriel and his wife had escaped and were trying to give them as much time as possible to get away.

Rees wanted to be far away as well when Rouge discovered his prisoners were missing. He cracked the whip and Hannibal surged into a canter.

'I left the cart at Dr Smith's,' Lydia said.

'Oh, yes,' Rees said. He'd forgotten that Lydia had driven

herself today. He turned down Commerce Street, heading directly to the surgery. Even from here, the noise from the street outside the jail was almost deafening. He listened. It sounded, from what he could hear of the shouting, that the various participants had resorted to speechifying. Well, as long as they were talking, they weren't hitting one another with their weapons. Naively, he had not expected to see a pro-slavery force in Maine but realized now that, although there were far fewer of them, they existed here as well.

He waited while Lydia collected her cart and donkey. Rees allowed her to take to the road first and fell into the lane behind her. Since the donkey could not travel as quickly as Hannibal, this was a far slower trip than Rees would have liked to see.

With all of the children home, and Annie here as well, the house seemed crowded. Rees retreated to the weaving room upstairs. He sat down and as he picked up the shuttle he thought back to the beginning of this case. Rouge, already sick although no one knew it, had ridden over to ask for Rees's help. Together, they had followed Jonathan over the weir and through the November woods to recover the body of Randolph Gilbert. Then what had happened? Rees had been forced to walk back to fetch his wagon so they could bring the body into town. At the same time, Rees had tied Rouge's horse to the back of the wagon. The constable had refused to walk any further on his blistered feet.

Rees wondered if Rouge would ask for his help ever again, now that they had argued so fiercely. And Rouge was to blame, for suddenly charging off half-cocked, interfering in Rees's investigation like the loose cannon he was.

Rees spent several minutes arguing with Rouge in his head. Finally dragging his thoughts back to the murder inquiry, Rees realized he'd heard or seen something in the last few days that was niggling at him. He couldn't remember what it was, though, or why it was important. Although he pondered all that had happened, nothing popped into his mind.

'It is almost supper time,' Jerusha said, appearing at the door. 'Mother says you should finish here and come downstairs.'

'Very well,' Rees said. He'd spent almost three hours in his weaving room and although he'd made significant progress on the cloth, he'd come to no conclusions about the murderer at all. Feeling that he'd wasted the afternoon, Rees went down to supper. At least no one had come from town to accuse him of aiding Gabriel and his wife's escape.

That evening, after the kitchen had been cleaned and the youngest children were in bed, Rees sat down again, this time with Lydia. 'How far did you get this afternoon?' she asked.

'Not very far at all,' Rees admitted. He didn't want to confess he'd been woolgathering.

Lydia sat down beside him and looked at him encouragingly. 'Let's begin again, shall we,' she said.

'This investigation began a week ago this past Monday,' Rees said.

'No, this all began earlier than that,' Lydia said. 'Remember, Ruth said she saw Cole the previous Wednesday. He and his employer, Randolph Gilbert, were already here.'

'Right,' Rees said. 'And Rouge said he engaged in a card game with Gilbert Wednesday, Thursday, and Friday nights.' Lydia nodded.

'Mr Cole had probably already left, to go south to Boston and meet Charlotte Sechrest, by then.'

'He probably left Thursday morning,' Rees agreed.

Lydia nodded and, rising to her feet, she extracted a piece of Jerusha's limited and valuable paper. 'I suggest we write this down.' Lydia took a sharpened pencil and brought both to the table. In her elegant penmanship, she wrote the information in tiny script at the top of the page. 'What happened next?'

'Um. I saw the body at the surgery. Then we talked to Tobias and Ruth.'

'And to Sandy,' Lydia reminded her husband. 'Sandy knew who Randolph Gilbert was.'

'That's right,' Rees agreed. 'And the next day Charlotte Sechrest arrived.' As Lydia wrote that down, Rees added, 'We can't forget that Gilbert had already contracted smallpox.'

'Yes, that's right,' Lydia said. 'Rouge caught the disease from him.'

'And then I removed Sandy from town to take refuge with Granny Rose,' Rees continued.

'Wait,' Lydia said. 'You left something out. You met and spoke with Mr Washington also.'

'Yes,' Rees agreed, thinking back. 'I believe I spoke with him the same day Mrs Sechrest arrived.'

'Yes. We spoke to her as well and she did not believe you when you claimed you didn't know Sandy.'

'Right. She and her slave takers came to the farm to look for Sandy and Abram,' Rees agreed.

'I will never forgive her for terrifying my children,' Lydia said with a frown.

'Was it the next day or the one after that we found Robert Cole's body?' Rees asked.

'That was Friday, I believe,' Lydia said.

'Then, on Sunday, we visited Sandy and Granny Rose,' Lydia continued.

'Somewhere in there, I went to Zion to warn Jonathan and the Elders that Rouge had come down with smallpox,' Rees said.

'But Esther didn't come to tell us that Brother Aaron had the rash until yesterday,' Lydia said. 'That was Tuesday.'

'That's right,' Rees agreed, staring at the closely written lines. Although most of his activities the last ten days were represented in the list, he knew several things were missing. He'd seen and heard several bits of information that were important. He had the answer, he knew he had it. But he couldn't bring it to the front of his mind.

Lydia looked at him questioningly. Rees shook his head. 'Maybe it will come to you tonight, when you sleep on it,' she said.

FORTY-FOUR

Rees spent an uncomfortable night, tossing and turning, his slumber interrupted by strange dreams. He awoke, miserably certain he knew the identity of the murderer. Lydia turned over to look at him.

'You're awake,' he said.

'Most of the night, listening to you flail around,' she replied. She studied his expression. 'You've identified the murderer,' she breathed.

'I'm not sure,' he said. 'I don't want to be sure.' He turned a sorrowful look on her.

She stared into his face for several seconds. 'You think it is Tobias and Ruth,' she said. 'Oh no. And with a baby on the way.'

'I know,' he said.

'Why do you think so?' She stared at him and he knew she wanted him to be wrong.

'First, their motive. I think Randolph Gilbert tried to abduct Ruth. As did Robert Cole, a few days later. And Tobias, of course, defended her.'

Lydia remained silent for a moment. 'And how did he do that?'

'Dr Ned said Cole was hit with something wooden. You were there.' He paused and looked at Lydia pointedly. When she did not respond, he went on. 'Tobias is a cabinet maker, but he also makes other pieces of wooden furniture. He uses several sizes of wooden mallets.'

'Surely there are other craftsmen who use mallets,' Lydia objected.

'Possibly. But who else that is connected to Randolph Gilbert and his slave taker?' Rees demanded. Silenced by that question, Lydia could only stare at her husband.

'But there could be someone else,' she said at last. 'Ruth admitted seeing Cole but not Mr Gilbert. And Tobias has sworn over and over that he had nothing to do with the murders.'

'I know,' Rees said with a nod. He tried to smile at her. 'I don't want to believe they are guilty of murder either.'

'Wait. If Tobias had hit Cole with a mallet, wouldn't the head be stained with blood? Or some other mark?' Lydia asked.

Rees considered that. 'Yes,' he said. 'I believe it would. Especially since Cole was hit with significant force. I'll have to visit Tobias and examine every one of his mallets. If I find blood . . .' His voice trailed off.

'I'll go with you,' Lydia said. 'Ruth will require some comfort.'

They rose and dressed and went downstairs. While Lydia stirred up the fire, Rees went out to tend to his livestock. By the time he finished and returned inside, the children were awake. Lydia was making pancakes for breakfast. Although she was trying to behave as she normally would, she snapped at Sharon for spilling her milk and Rees realized his wife was very upset. He went to console his youngest, but Annie was there before him.

Rees sat beside Jerusha. She was scratching at the rash left by the cowpox. At least the inoculation seemed successful so far in combating the other, more lethal contagion. At least none of his children had come down with it. 'Have many children in school contracted smallpox?' he asked, just to make conversation.

'I'm not sure. The disease is spreading but a lot of people took their children out of school early. In the beginning, there was only one older boy. Samuel Whitehead.'

'You said.'

Jerusha looked at her father. 'Apparently he was with his father in town when he was playing cards with that Mr Gilbert. He got sick about the same time as the constable.'

Rees nodded. That made sense. The illness seemed to follow a definite pattern of infection.

'The contagion spread from him. Some of the younger children . . . I can only hope all of my students survive,' Jerusha added, grimacing with worry.

'The constable survived and has returned to his usual difficult self,' Rees said, putting his hand over his daughter's. He elected not to tell her of the scarring. At least Rouge was not a woman and it did not matter so much if he was even more unattractive than he had been previously.

'What about the Widow Francine?' Lydia asked as she slid a plate stacked with pancakes in front of each one. Both Rees and Jerusha liberally poured syrup over them.

'She told me she contracted the disease as a baby,' Jerusha said once she'd chewed and swallowed. 'She is not afraid for herself.'

'Enough about that terrible illness,' Lydia said. 'At least let us not discuss it while we are eating.'

The remainder of the meal passed in silence.

It was just past eight when Rees and Lydia left for town. Busy with their own thoughts, neither one spoke. When they pulled into the drive at the cabinetry shop, Lydia leaned across and touched Rees's wrist. 'It will be all right,' she said. Rees just looked at her. He knew she was trying to reassure him; he also knew how unrealistic the hope this would go well was.

While Lydia went to the front door, Rees went down the stairs to the shop. He paused outside and took in a deep breath. Then he opened the door and went inside. Tobias looked up.

'Are you here to congratulate me on my efforts yesterday?'

'We did well, didn't we?' Rees agreed, relieved by the topic. 'What happened after I left?'

'Besides the brawls in the street, you mean?' Tobias shook his head. 'By then, most of the women had left. And, since I knew Gabriel was gone, I suggested we leave as well. I don't know when the constable discovered his prisoners had escaped. Or even if he did discover it.'

'The longer he takes, the better for everyone concerned,' Rees said. He paused. Tobias stared at him questioningly. Finally, Rees spoke. 'Did Dr Ned speak to you?'

'No. He wouldn't have been able to reach me through the crowd anyway. Why?'

Now Rees had to take the next step. 'Because he told me, and he said he was going to inform Constable Rouge as well, that Cole was bludgeoned with a wooden tool. I am postulating a mallet.'

Tobias stared at Rees for a long moment. 'I see,' he said at last. 'And you instantly assumed it was my mallet. I should have guessed you didn't come here simply to speak to me. You really seem eager to put me in that jail.'

'That's not it,' Rees said quickly. 'I am attempting to protect you. You must know that Rouge will keep searching for someone else to accuse of the murder.'

'Oh no? I told you from the very beginning you should drop the search for the investigation and claim you couldn't find the murderer,' Tobias said.

'I'm trying to identify the murderer before Rouge hangs an innocent man,' Rees said, his voice rising with annoyance.

'So, lie to him. Tell him Cole murdered his employer and was then murdered in turn by a drifter who has gone far away.'

'But these are murders!' Rees exclaimed. 'Someone in this town took the lives of not one, but two human beings. That person did not have the right.'

'I agree,' Tobias said as Ruth and Lydia came down the stairs.

'We heard the two of you shouting from the kitchen,' Lydia said, raising her eyebrows at her husband.

'The Bible is very clear on the subject of murder,' Tobias continued, barely acknowledging the presence of the two women. 'Thou shalt not kill. But we don't know what these men did to cause their own deaths.'

'We don't know. That is right,' Rees said. He took a breath. What could he say to Tobias that would fully explain why Rees had to continue this investigation, especially when he didn't understand it completely himself. 'I don't do this to protect the guilty,' he said finally, haltingly. 'I am not searching for the murderer of these two men to find justice for them. Not entirely anyway. I am doing it to protect those who are innocent of the crime but who may be accused anyway. As long as the constable believes the murderer is in this town, and is also being urged forward by Mrs Sechrest, he will look for someone to declare the guilty man. You know that is true.' He paused and when Tobias did not immediately speak, he added, 'You said it yourself. The law and justice are frequently two different things. But the safety of the innocent – that is always important.' He stopped, realizing he was panting with the intensity of his emotion.

'So, you are saying I must trust you,' Tobias said. 'Trust that you will follow the moral and ethical course, not necessarily the legal one.'

'I guess I am,' Rees said.

For a moment the two men stared at one another. Finally, Tobias pointed to his workbenches and the wall with hanging tools.

'Look at them then.'

Lydia reached out, to deliver a consoling pat to Ruth. She flinched and Lydia dropped her hand.

With a grim expression, Tobias took his wife's arm. They moved a few steps away, although they remained close enough to watch.

FORTY-FIVE

Rees exchanged a glance with Lydia. Her eyes were moist with unshed tears; she and Ruth had been good friends. He squeezed her arm and went first to the mallets hanging next to the chisels, clamps, various knives, braces and other tools. Several of the mallets Rees dismissed immediately; the heads were either too large or too small. But there were three or four, one lying on the workbench where Tobias had dropped it, with heads that Rees thought matched the bruise on Cole's temple. Although the tools were old, the handles were worn smooth with use and the heads lightly scarred, the wood was white. Rees stared at the white wood for a few seconds and then held the tools out to Lydia. She glanced at them and nodded as a wide smile crossed her face.

Rees inspected them more closely. Sanding the heads would remove the top layer of wood. He wasn't sure how deeply a blood-stain would soak into the wood, nor how many times a mallet would have to be planed to remove the stain. But these heads still exhibited nicks and scars from impact onto the bottoms of chair legs as well as other surfaces so they had not been sanded recently.

'You know there are other craftsmen who use wooden mallets,' Tobias said belligerently.

Rees knew that to be true. But had Cole been struck by someone unrelated to this investigation? Maybe by the drifter Tobias had mentioned? That seemed extraordinarily convenient. The wain-wright and the cartwright both used wooden mallets and their shops were located on River Road. But what was their reason?

'Tell me,' Lydia said to Tobias, breaking into the silence, 'have you ever owned a beaver top hat?'

Her question surprised a snort from Tobias. 'What would I do with a top hat of any kind, beaver or otherwise? Besides, if I had ever the temerity to wear one, one of those farmers we saw yesterday would likely snatch it off my head and give me a thrashing besides.'

Rees recalled the red-shirted, and red-faced, farmer holding the axe yesterday and nodded regretfully.

'Are you satisfied now?' Tobias asked.

'Yes,' Rees said even though he was not satisfied. He could not confirm any of those he'd suspected as the murderer. No one fit perfectly. 'I may not succeed in identifying the murderer,' Rees thought, not realizing he'd spoken aloud until Tobias spoke.

'You would have saved yourself a lot of time and energy if you had listened to me in the beginning,' he said. Rees bit back a flash of annoyance.

'My husband always tries to accomplish the right action, no matter how difficult the struggle,' Lydia said, her even voice no less reproving for its calmness. 'Nothing good would ever be achieved if everyone quit at the first sign of trouble.'

For several seconds the two couples stared at one another. Then, with an almost painful politeness, Rees and Lydia withdrew.

'I am sorry to lose such friendships,' Lydia said.

'Their ire may not last forever,' Rees said comfortingly.

Lydia threw him a look. 'I think it might. They expected us to believe them. To be loyal to the friendship. To trust them completely.'

Rees did not speak for several seconds. 'I trust very few that much,' he said, surprised to recognize that about himself. 'Almost no one in fact.' He glanced down at Lydia so she knew she was foremost among that limited number. 'After all, although the possibility Tobias and Lydia are guilty is slim, it still might be true. People operate from all different kinds of motives and in this case, to protect Ruth and their unborn child, I can see even Tobias committing murder. I might,' he added after a long pause.

Lydia nodded, unable to disagree. 'What do we do now?' she asked, stepping up to the mounting stone. Rees offered her his hand to help her into the wagon seat.

'I'm not sure.' Rees climbed up beside her. 'Maybe we should re-visit Mr Whitehead.'

'But you spoke with him first, about Mr Gilbert,' Lydia said, 'and he had no useful information.'

'I know,' Rees agreed. 'I am hoping he thought of something else, something he forgot to tell me before.'

Lydia did not argue but he knew by her quick doubtful glance that she thought he was grasping at straws. By God, he thought so himself.

When Rees pulled the wagon out of the cabinet maker's drive, he went south instead of north to Main. This street very quickly turned into a muddy lane with fields on either side. They drove for a bit over half an hour before turning right and driving through the gate of the Whitehead farm. Although the soil here was as rocky as elsewhere, the Whitehead farm backed up to the river so they always had access to water. Rees saw that the fields appeared even more uncared for than they had before.

They drove into the farmyard, the chickens squawking as they fluttered from the wagon wheels. Rees looked around in surprise. No one was about. And there was an indefinable air of neglect, almost abandonment, about the farm.

'Where is everyone?' Lydia asked.

At that moment, Solomon Whitehead staggered onto the porch. 'Go away,' he croaked. 'We are sick here.'

Lydia gasped. Rees, who had seen Rouge several times recently, was less shocked. Still, the face peering at them from the shadow of the porch was horrifying: a mass of sores.

'Mr Whitehead?' Rees said tentatively.

'Didn't you hear me? We're sick. Samuel, my son, has already died.' His battered face crumpled and he began to weep great racking sobs.

'I'm sorry,' Rees said, knowing it was inadequate. He dreaded telling Jerusha.

'First, I fell sick, then the son who went to town with me. Soon after, the rest of my children.' He was crying so hard Rees could barely understand what he was saying. 'All my babies. All sick.'

Although Rees had prepared several questions, he realized as he watched the other man sob that he couldn't ask them. He just couldn't interrogate this man who was broken by grief. 'All right,' Rees said. 'We're leaving. Is there anything you need? Food, maybe? Meat?'

Mr Whitehead shook his head. Turning, he made his way back into his house and slammed the door behind him.

'Dear God,' Lydia murmured, her voice trembling with shock and pity.

Rees clucked to Hannibal and slowly turned his wagon around.
'Where are we going?' Lydia asked.

'Home.' He could think of nothing else to do. No further plans
or strategies presented themselves and right now he didn't care
about the murder anyway. All he wanted to do now was go
home and see his children and assure himself of their continued
health and safety.

FORTY-SIX

That evening, after the kitchen table had been scrubbed,
Lydia brought out the timeline she and Rees had prepared.
'What are you doing with that?' Rees asked, moving
to her side.

'I'm just wondering if we left out certain particulars that will
help identify the murderer,' Lydia said. 'I think we can both
agree it is not Tobias.' She regarded her husband defiantly.

'What particulars do you mean?' Rees looked at the paper in
her hand.

'I'm not sure exactly.' She stared at the list. 'What if
we considered the past two weeks in a different way.' As she
spoke, Lydia rotated her hands around in a circle. 'What if we
were tracking Mr Cole instead of Mr Gilbert? Or, instead of
trying to identify the murderer by his movements, we followed
the outbreak of the disease? That trail would begin at the same
point: the arrival of Randolph Gilbert in town.'

'But not everyone becomes ill,' Rees objected. 'I'm not
sure the last would help at all. Many people in town contracted
the disease without ever meeting Mr Randolph.'

'That's true,' Lydia agreed, dropping her hands. 'I just thought,
maybe a different way of interpreting the information we have . . .'
Her voice trailed off and she dropped the paper on the table.

Rees picked up the sheet and examined Lydia's neat inventory.
Despite staring at the timeline for several seconds, he saw nothing
new and finally, frustrated, he too abandoned it.

*   *   *

When Lydia came downstairs to stir up the fire, Rees was already awake and in the kitchen. He had arisen early to examine the timeline once again. 'What are you doing?' she asked, staring at him. Rees looked down at his nightshirt and then back up at her. 'What happened?' she whispered, staring at his expression.

'I awoke during the night. I had an idea, you know? You were right, Lydia. I had to look at this in a different way.' He shook his head unhappily.

'You know who the murderer is?' She moved forward to put her hand on his arm.

'No. Well, I have a suspicion . . . I am not entirely certain yet. I hope,' he added fervently, 'that I am wrong.'

'Who is it?'

'I don't want to tell anyone, even you, until I'm absolutely sure,' Rees said. 'I need to confirm some facts before I accuse anyone.'

'Well, wherever you are going, I am joining you,' Lydia said as she tied on her apron. 'Now I have to know as well.'

Rees nodded and, dropping the paper on the table, he brushed by her on his way upstairs to dress. When he looked back over his shoulder, he saw that Lydia had gone to the table and picked up the list. This was exactly the same timeline she had written. He had added nothing to it. Shaking her head in bewilderment, Lydia put it back down again.

After chores and breakfast, Rees hitched Hannibal to the wagon and climbed into his seat. Lydia climbed up beside him and they started out. 'You aren't happy, are you?' she asked.

'How can you tell?'

'You are chewing your lip. You do that when you aren't happy.' When Rees did not reply, she asked, 'Is it Tobias? After all, Tobias might have thrown a bloodstained mallet away.'

Rees did not answer her. And, instead of driving west to town, he turned left at the turn off towards Zion.

'Where are you going?' Lydia asked, turning an astonished glance on him.

'I have to look in on Brother Aaron,' Rees explained.

'Now?' she asked. 'I thought you were in a hurry. There is a murderer out there.'

'I know,' he said. 'But Brother Aaron is quite ill. I meant to stop yesterday and then I didn't. We don't know if he'll survive this contagion . . .'

They pulled up in front of the barn and crossed the village toward the Infirmary. As they passed the workshop Rees turned to stare at it. Brother Jonathan was making something with the lathe; he could hear the muffled whir through the door.

'Do you think we should ask Brother Jonathan to join us?' Lydia asked. Rees shook his head and walked quickly across the grass. The Nursing Sister met them at the Infirmary door.

'How is he?' Rees asked her.

'Not well,' she said, her face creased with worry. When she turned back to Rees and Lydia, she added, 'Please don't stay long.'

Rees and Lydia nodded.

There were a few other patients and Rees glanced at them in concern. None of them were children but at least two were young men. The Nursing Sister nodded at Rees. 'These were men Brother Aaron had contact with so we fear they may have caught smallpox from him,' she said.

'They don't have the rash,' Lydia said.

'Not yet anyway,' said the Nursing Sister. 'The illness follows a pattern. They are tired now. The rash may come out in another few days.'

'Has Dr Ned seen them yet?' Rees asked. 'He might be able to tell by examining their mouths.'

'No. But I will call him in,' she promised with a nod.

Rees and Lydia continued on to the final bed, pushed to the back wall.

Brother Aaron was still propped up on a stack of pillows but, even from a distance, Rees could hear the other man's labored breathing. 'Oh my God,' Rees muttered, staring at the ill Shaker. The eruption covered his entire face, including his eyes, and went down his neck right to the sheet that was tucked around his shoulders. Although Rees had already suffered from and recovered from this sickness many years ago, he remained at the foot of the bed. He threw a glance of admiration at the Nursing Sister. He did not believe he could devote himself to caring for Brother Aaron; Rees felt sick to his stomach just looking at him.

'I've been expecting you,' Brother Aaron said. He spoke slowly, forcing out each word.

'I'm sorry I didn't visit yesterday,' Rees said.

Aaron puffed out a strained laugh. 'I know you. Like a burr. You don't ever give up.' Briefly, he sounded almost like his old self.

'No,' Rees agreed. Seeing this curmudgeonly fellow laid low hurt. Although the relationship between the two men had always been conflicted and antagonistic, Rees knew how Aaron was and expected him to be that way. This ashen skeletal shell was not the man Rees knew.

'You follow the truth,' Aaron gasped out. 'I respect that. Even if it is inconvenient.'

Rees moved around the foot of the bed. Leaning over, he whispered so that none of the other patients in this room could hear him. 'Tell me about the deaths of Randolph Gilbert and Robert Cole.'

FORTY-SEVEN

After a few seconds of shocked silence, Lydia gasped. 'What?'

'Figured it out, have you?' Aaron managed a breathy chuckle. 'I knew you would.'

'It was you?' Lydia asked in shock. 'Why?'

'That Gilbert fellow came here, looking for the girl.' He looked at Rees. 'I wouldn't call Esther a girl, would you? We'd argued. I left in a temper. When I went back to plead with her, that Gilbert was there.'

'Please start at the beginning,' Rees said. Mr Gilbert had been looking for Sandy but Aaron had not known that. He'd thought it was Esther. 'When did you first see Randolph Gilbert?'

'He came to Zion on a Saturday. I saw him roaming around, told him he wasn't welcome here.'

'Did he refuse to leave?' Rees asked.

'Of course. Thought he owned the world, that one,' Aaron said with his usual asperity. 'He told me he was looking for a girl that had been rescued from the South. He thought she might be hidden here.' He looked at Rees, who nodded. He'd hidden several people within the community and some of them had brought trouble.

'But you had not been accepted back into the community yet,' Lydia said.

'That is true,' Brother Aaron said. 'I wanted to re-join. I was living in town then, working odd jobs.'

'So, I did see you there, wearing Gilbert's beaver top hat,' Rees interjected, glad to clarify one of the puzzles.

Aaron nodded. 'I took that hat . . . and God most certainly punished me for vanity and for the theft of that fine headgear.'

'Of course He did not,' Lydia said, attempting to comfort. 'It was a small sin and He would understand.'

Aaron shook his head at her and went on. 'Anyway, I wasn't sure Brother Jonathan would allow me back. I am not so obedient.'

Since this was only too true, Rees nodded in agreement. 'But he isn't the only one who decides,' he pointed out.

'That is true. I'd asked Sister Esther to support my request. More than once.'

Rees and Lydia exchanged a glance.

'And did she support you?' Rees asked.

'Not at first. That day, that Saturday, I visited her in the still house to ask her to approach Jonathan for me. She refused, once again. We had . . . words. I was angry. I stormed out. But when I calmed down, I went back to plead with her. When I entered the still house he was there. That Southerner. He had Sister Esther by the shoulders. He was trying to drag her out. I guess he planned to carry her back south and sell her once again.' He stopped to catch his breath.

'You intervened?' Rees asked.

Brother Aaron nodded. 'I tried to pull him away.' Now Rees understood why Esther had been so moved by Aaron's illness. She was grateful. 'He threatened me with the law. Told me he'd have the constable arrest me.' Aaron uttered another breathy laugh. 'As though I care about that incompetent Frenchman.' Rees nodded. Although he had not met Randolph Gilbert, he could guess from all the accounts that Gilbert had behaved arrogantly, so certain no one would dare deny him.

'I didn't mean to kill him,' Aaron said. 'I tried to pull him away. Before I knew it, I had my hands around his neck and was trying to strangle him. He-he escaped. He was trying to catch Sister Esther. She ran away. He ran after her. I picked up one of the knives that the Sisters use to cut the herbs and I stabbed him.' He coughed raggedly. 'I am not sorry. I would do it again.'

'You were trying to protect Sister Esther,' Lydia said. But she sounded shaky, disbelieving and horrified both.

'Yes. The one you have been searching for is me, Rees. I did it all. There was no one else.' He began coughing again.

'And Cole?' Rees asked.

'Who?'

'The slave taker.'

'Oh, him.' Aaron took in several breaths. 'I am not sure how he knew I was involved. Maybe he saw me wearing the hat?'

That sounded possible, but thin, to Rees. 'He tracked you down?' he continued.

'Yes. He saw me walking to Zion from town last Wednesday or Thursday, I'm no longer sure exactly. I had an appointment to meet with the Elders.'

'That must have been the day Charlotte Sechrest and the slave takers came to the farm,' Lydia said, looking at her husband.

'What did he want?' Rees asked.

Aaron looked at him, breathing hard. Rees waited. Finally Aaron spoke. 'He told me he wanted the girl. If I gave her to him, he wouldn't tell anyone I'd murdered Mr Gilbert.'

'The girl?' Lydia asked, glancing at Rees. 'And he never said her name?'

'No. But I knew he meant Sister Esther. I supposed that Gilbert had told him about her.'

'So you arranged to meet him?' Rees murmured.

Aaron nodded. 'I told him I'd see him at the river. I'd stayed there, during the summer. I knew no one would be there when it was cold. It would be private.'

'You took the mallet from the workshop?' Lydia asked, sounding faintly judgmental. Carrying a weapon spoke to premeditation; Aaron had planned to, at best, disable Cole.

'Mallet?' Aaron sounded befuddled. He pulled himself together. 'Yes, I took the mallet.'

'Did Cole ride his horse to your meeting?' Rees asked.

'He had it there so he must have,' Aaron said.

'Where is the animal now?'

'In the paddock here.'

'It is time to leave,' the Nursing Sister said, appearing behind Rees.

'I just have another question or two,' Rees protested.

'No. I allowed you more time than I should have. Out now.'

'I will return again,' Rees promised, turning a glance upon the man in the bed.

'I am certain of that,' Aaron said, his grin barely a shadow of its former self. Rees felt a stab of pain in his chest.

'Come, now,' the Nursing Sister said.

Reluctantly, Rees and Lydia followed her from the Infirmary. When they stepped outside, Rees inhaled several lungfuls of the fresh clean air. He had not realized how close and fetid the air inside the Nurse Shop was until then.

'I am very worried about him,' the Sister said. 'Usually, those afflicted with smallpox do not have trouble breathing. Unless it is some complication I have never seen, I am very afraid he has contracted some other disease as well. The combination of two illnesses may be too much for even someone as strong as Brother Aaron to survive.'

'Thank you for allowing us to see him,' Lydia said.

'Your visit seems to have done him good,' the Nursing Sister said, sounding surprised.

As Rees and Lydia walked away, she turned to her husband. 'How did you know?'

'That it was Aaron? You suggested examining the trajectory of the disease. When I did, the timeline suddenly became clear. Randolph brought smallpox to our town. Rouge and Solomon Whitehead contracted it and exhibited the symptoms first. Whitehead exposed his children to the contagion. But where did Aaron catch it? He fell sick within a few days of Rouge so he had to have met Gilbert. When I realized that, I knew he was involved somehow.' He paused and then added, 'I did not expect a confession.'

'This means everything is resolved,' Lydia said. 'And Ruth and Tobias are now free of suspicion.'

'Yes,' Rees said doubtfully. He didn't trust this tidy resolution;

several of his questions remained unanswered. Lydia threw a quick look at him.

'What's wrong?'

'Nothing,' Rees said untruthfully. 'I just want to confirm Brother Aaron's story with Sister Esther.'

'Of course,' Lydia said, sounding puzzled. 'If you think it necessary. And there she is now, coming out of the kitchen.'

Rees and Lydia changed course, veering parallel to the road to intercept the Shaker Sister. Seeing them approaching, Esther paused and waited for them. 'I was planning to visit Brother Aaron for a few moments before the midday services,' she said.

'We were just there,' Lydia said. 'Brother Aaron told us what happened.'

'What happened,' Esther repeated, her voice cracking.

'He told us that Randolph Gilbert attacked you,' Rees said.

Esther's face went through a variety of expressions: shock, shame and fear. 'That is true,' she admitted. 'Randolph Gilbert threatened to take me south and re-sell me. He took hold of me. I don't know what would have happened without Brother Aaron. We'd quarreled and he'd stormed out of the still house. You know how choleric he can be. But he returned. And saved me,' she added in a whisper.

'He told us,' Rees said, looking around. They would not have this bit of privacy for very much longer. Other community members were appearing around them, leaving their places of work to go to the Meetinghouse. Many of them stared disapprovingly at the three people conversing on the path, and one of them an Elder who should know better than to engage in unnecessary speech.

'He did? Did he tell you he defended me?' Esther's eyes filled. 'I owe him my freedom.'

'Why didn't you confide in us?' Lydia asked, sounding hurt.

'He asked me not to,' Esther said. She straightened up and threw back her shoulders. 'I know I should have. But it is not too late to make a clean breast of the entire affair.'

'There is no need,' Lydia said, smiling warmly at the other woman. 'We know the whole sorry tale now. You would be shamed and humiliated for no reason.'

Sister Esther nodded once. Rees and Lydia moved aside so

she could join her brethren as they streamed by. Lowering her
eyes, Esther joined them.

'What are you going to tell the constable?' Lydia said as they
cut through the throng to the wagon on the other side.

'I don't know,' Rees said shortly. He'd identified the murderer
so why wasn't he happier?

FORTY-EIGHT

B
efore they reached the wagon, Rees stopped and turned
around. 'What are you doing?' Lydia asked in surprise.
'I'm not finished,' Rees said. With his height, he was
able to look over the heads of most of the people there. When
he spotted Esther, he started walking back for her.

'Wait.' Lydia hurried after him. 'Where are you going?'

Rees did not reply. He had homed in on Esther and was heading
directly toward her with such an intense focus he was almost
unaware of those in front of him. And the Shakers, seeing this
red-haired juggernaut bear down upon them, parted before him.

When Sister Esther saw him coming, she stopped short and
stared at him, her frozen expression one of fear and resignation,
like a mouse watching a snake grow ever closer.

'Will,' Lydia called after him. He did not stop until he stood
directly in front of Esther.

'Do you have another question?' Esther asked. She swallowed,
the movement of her throat clearly visible.

'Not a question,' Rees said in a gentle tone. 'Brother Aaron
did not tell the entire tale, did he?'

Esther stared at him for several seconds and then, finally, shook
her head. 'No, he did not. He would protect me, right to the last.'

'What is going on?' Lydia demanded, joining the other two.
They paid her no attention.

'Let's have the truth now,' Rees said. 'The entire truth.'

Esther glanced around her. Most of her fellow Believers had
disappeared into the Meeting House but she still stepped away
from the road, back on the path leading to the herb gardens.

'The first part of Aaron's story was true, yes?' Rees said. 'You were in the still house when Randolph Gilbert came by?'

'Yes,' Esther said with a nod. 'My assistants had left. Aaron asked them to leave when he first approached me, and they had not returned so I was alone.'

'Gilbert entered and threatened you, exactly as Aaron described,' Rees said.

Esther nodded. 'When Brother Aaron returned, Mr Gilbert was attempting to pull me from the herb shop.' She raised tear-filled eyes to Rees's. 'I was so frightened. It was as if the last twenty years hadn't happened. I was a barefoot girl again, standing in front of my master, waiting for him to strike me.'

'But Aaron intervened. When Gilbert fought back, Aaron put his hands around Gilbert's neck.'

'Yes. But Brother Aaron did not stab Mr Gilbert. I did,' she said so quietly Rees could almost not hear her. Rees heard Lydia gasp behind him. 'Aaron was trying, oh so hard, to subdue the other man but Gilbert was younger and stronger. I picked up the knife I'd been using for the herbs and stabbed him in the back. I didn't mean to kill him, I swear.' She took in a deep sobbing breath. 'I just wanted him to stop punching Aaron. Mr Gilbert dropped like a rock.' Her voice broke and for a moment she could not continue. 'There was so much blood. I tried and tried scrubbing it up through the rest of the week but I couldn't get it out.' She wiped the back of her hand across her wet eyes. Rees nodded, recalling the large stain.

'You and Aaron took the body into the woods and hid it there?' he said.

She grimaced and bowed her head. 'Brother Aaron fetched a cart and layered the bottom with straw to soak up the blood. It was so difficult. Aaron carried the body part of the way. He had to burn his clothing after, buy all new.' She heaved a sigh. 'We scattered the straw and brought back the cart. When he asked me to intercede with Jonathan, of course I said yes. I had to then. I owed him a debt I could never repay.'

Rees did not reply. If Aaron hadn't taken Gilbert's hat and if Rees hadn't seen him wearing it, he might never have guessed.

'I took a human life,' Esther said with a sob.

Lydia may have been shocked, but she stepped around Rees

to put her hand on Esther's shoulder. 'God will understand,' she
said. 'You were not only protecting yourself, you were protecting
Aaron.' Esther tried to nod.

'Then there is the death of Robert Cole,' Rees said. Esther
nodded. 'What happened?'

'I did not know the slave taker was attempting to blackmail
Brother Aaron,' Esther said. 'Not until later. Aaron had been
accepted back into the Family. He'd lived in the Dwelling House
for only a few days. Less than a week. That night, long after
dark, I saw him leave and start walking to town. He was wearing
that silly top hat.' Rees nodded in understanding. Once Aaron
had been accepted into the Shakers, he would not be allowed to
keep it. Wearing it one last time was his way of saying farewell
to the World. 'So I followed him,' Esther continued. 'I knew he
was up to something. And Aaron, for all of his bluster, is still
naïve about the ways of the World.'

'You were both walking?' Rees asked. Esther nodded. Rees
did not know why he should be surprised; she had walked all
the way from Georgia to Maine. Of course, that had been some
twenty years ago.

'I went on the lane. It is shorter so I assumed I could keep up
without him realizing I was following him. He never even looked
around.' Esther still sounded surprised by that.

'Did you take the mallet?' Rees asked.

'Yes. I'm not sure what I intended to do with it.' As Esther
spoke, Rees heard Lydia's sudden intake of breath. 'But I did
not think he could defeat a younger man. Aaron was already
sick, although we didn't know it, and he was feverish and
tired.'

'You pursued him all the way across the bridge?' Lydia asked.

Esther nodded. 'I lost him in town. Fortunately, I saw him
turn on River Road. I hurried, but by the time I crossed the bridge
they were fighting. Aaron was on the ground and that slave hunter
was attempting to pull his pistol from his pocket. I ran forward
and swung the mallet and hit Cole as hard as I could. I killed
him too.' Tears began rolling down her cheeks.

'He wasn't dead,' Rees said. 'Your blow only stunned him.'

Esther looked at Rees disbelievingly. 'But I heard . . . Aaron
told me that Mr Cole was dead.' Another sob shook her.

'He wasn't then,' Rees said. 'He was still alive. What happened after that?'

'We dragged Cole through the woods and Brother Aaron pushed him into the river.' Her voice began to tremble once again.

'And the horse?' Rees asked. 'Cole's horse?'

'I made Brother Aaron ride it back. He was so weak by then he could barely stay in the saddle. I took the reins and walked the horse back to Zion.'

'And released it into the paddock with the Shaker animals,' Rees said.

Esther nodded. 'We . . . didn't . . . know Mr Cole was s-still . . . alive.' She wept into her hands.

Rees thought that it was probably just as well they were unaware. If they had saved Cole, and he lived to tell the tale, Aaron would have been executed for murder and Esther would have been taken south as an escaped slave. The law, after all, was on the side of the slave owners.

'It was self-defense,' Rees said now.

'Maybe,' Esther said in a whisper. 'But I will never forget I took not one, but two lives.'

'Both in defense of another human,' Lydia said vehemently. 'Don't you forget that either! What would have happened to Aaron without you?'

'What would have happened to me without him?' Esther shook her head. 'He is difficult. Opinionated, wrathful, unwilling to listen or be obedient to the Elders—'

'But, when it counted, he was on the right side of the angels,' Rees said. He paused and then added slowly, 'I was a soldier. Killing another, even in defense of God and country, is not something one ever forgets. But the memory, and the sheer horror of the experience, does fade. For me, it has made me appreciate all the more what life offers.' He turned to look at Lydia. She smiled, her eyes filling. Turning back to Esther, Rees added, 'You will find a way to accept what you've done. You must.'

Esther smiled sadly. 'I will not have very long to accept it, once the constable knows.'

'I am not going to tell him,' Rees said.

'You're not going to tell him?' Both women spoke simultaneously.

Rees shook his head. He turned to look at his wife. 'This will be the one investigation I can't solve.'

'As Tobias suggested,' Lydia murmured.

Rees nodded. 'It will not be easy,' he said. He knew Rouge would remind him until the end of his days that he'd failed. Rouge would take great delight in embarrassing and shaming Rees. But he also knew he couldn't even hint that he knew the truth. Doing so would endanger others. In this case, Rees would have to muzzle his pride. 'No one else, but we three—'

'Four, including Brother Aaron,' Esther interjected.

'No one else but we four can know the truth,' Rees said. 'It will be between our consciences and God.'

FORTY-NINE

'What *will* you tell Constable Rouge?' Lydia asked as they left Zion.

'I don't know,' Rees said, directing a worried glance at his wife. They were on their way into town now, and he was keeping Hannibal at a walk. 'I must say something. But I can't accuse anyone else; Rouge will arrest them. And if I simply claim myself unable to solve the mystery of the murderer's identity, Rouge will launch his own investigation and who knows who he will come up with.'

Another farmer's wagon rattled past, the occupants turning to stare at Rees and Lydia in surprise. Hannibal made an attempt to jump into a trot, but Rees held him back. 'I don't like to lie,' he said. In reality, he was a poor liar and tended to blurt out what he thought were home truths instead of manufacturing a plausible falsehood.

'I know,' Lydia said. 'The truth is usually best. But life is messy.' She paused and then added slowly, 'I am not certain the constable would listen to Esther and understand she and Aaron were protecting each other.'

Rees nodded, his thoughts a muddle as he tried to imagine a way of telling the truth without putting anyone in harm's way.

The journey to town passed all too quickly, despite their slow pace. They pulled into the tavern yard without Rees coming to any conclusion. His heart began to pound as he and Lydia stepped through the door and went inside. He and Rouge had parted acrimoniously and Rees did not know how the constable might greet him.

Rouge had returned to his place behind the bar. He still looked frightening. Most of the scabs left by the rash had fallen off, but not all, and the scarring was pronounced. But, when he looked at Rees, Rouge's black eyes took on their accustomed sparkle. 'Come to apologize?' he asked.

'Apologize?' Rees repeated in surprise.

'Of course. You know I was correct all along.'

'You were?' Rees wondered if he sounded as foolish to Rouge as he did to himself.

'Of course. You must have heard?' The constable's mouth twisted. 'I know you have. That fellow Gabriel and his wife escaped from the jail.'

'They did?'

'Someone cut a hole in the back while that folderol was going on in the street outside. Of course, you wouldn't know anything about that.' He stared hard at Rees. 'The two prisoners escaped through the gap and disappeared. They're probably in Toronto by now.'

'When did you discover they were missing?' Rees asked, trying to sound innocent.

'Not for another few hours. I couldn't get through the crowd in the street.'

'Really? There were that many people?'

'Don't play the guiltless with me,' Rouge said. 'I saw Shakers there.' He gestured at Rees and Lydia, inviting them to approach more closely to the bar so he could lower his voice. 'I know you were involved. Those folks from Zion would not have even known about the disturbance unless someone told them. And who else would bring them the news but you?'

Rees and Lydia carefully did not look at each other.

'Besides, Dr Ned told me the wound on Cole came from a wooden mallet, not an iron hammer. And he said he'd seen you in town and told you that while the brawl was happening.'

When Rees could think of nothing to say, Lydia spoke up. 'I was visiting my friend—'

'Yes. Mistress Ruth, whose husband just happens to work as a carpenter and has many wooden mallets.'

Rees went lightheaded. He knew it could not be possible for every drop of blood to drain from his body, but that was the sensation he experienced. From Lydia's ashen cheeks, he guessed she felt the same.

'But his tools were unmarked,' Rees said.

'Yes, I spoke to him,' Rouge said. 'Tobias said you'd looked at his tools and decided he was innocent.'

'He is innocent,' Rees blurted.

'So, you discovered the guilty party,' Rouge said. 'Who is it?'

Rees stared into the constable's avid eyes for several seconds and found he could not betray Aaron or Esther. He had to speak. 'You were correct,' he said at last. 'I did come to apologize.'

'And you should,' Rouge said. 'You were wrong.'

'I realized, after much consideration, that you had imprisoned the guilty parties.' At least Gabriel and the family were far away, and safe.

'Gabriel?'

'Yes.'

'No doubt he borrowed a mallet,' Lydia put in, speaking rapidly.

'So,' Rouge said, savoring every word, 'I was right, and you were wrong.'

Rees looked down at the floor. He heard the faint rustle of Lydia's clothing as she turned and directed an anxious glance at him. 'Yes,' Rees said although he felt as though the word was strangling him.

'Say it again,' Rouge said. 'I want to hear you repeat it.'

'You were right and I was wrong.' Rees forced out the words.

'Gabriel would have been safe there, in jail, you know,' Rouge said. Rees looked up to meet Rouge's knowing gaze. 'I would not have handed them over to Mrs Sechrest.'

Rees realized with an uncomfortable start that he had under-estimated the other man. 'Yes,' he said apologetically. 'I see that now.'

'And the men who battered a hole in the back of the jail should be arrested.'

'What?' Rees stared at Rouge in alarm. He guffawed loudly. 'I will be requesting donations to construct a new jail, one much sturdier than the last one.' His clever eyes fixed on Rees. 'I expect all the fine upstanding citizens to give generously.'

'Of course,' Rees said. Since he knew he was guilty of chopping a hole through the jail wall, he felt responsible for supporting the repairs. 'I will be happy to donate. Any citizen who believes in law and order will help fund the new jail,' he added mendaciously.

Rouge grinned but his expression abruptly shifted. 'Mrs Sechrest,' he said.

Both Rees and Lydia turned to look at the young woman who had just descended the stairs. 'Mr and Mrs Rees,' she said in a cool voice. 'Have you any news on my brother's murder?'

'I believe I told you—' Rouge began.

'The constable and I are in agreement,' Rees replied at the exact same moment. He and Rouge exchanged grins.

'Both your brother and Cole were killed by the same individual,' Rees said truthfully.

'The murderer was captured and put in jail, along with his wife,' Rouge said.

'Yes, and then someone rescued them from the jail,' Mrs Sechrest said accusingly.

'This town has a very active chapter of the abolitionists,' Rees said smoothly.

'I have no doubt, no doubt at all, that all of you are leading figures in that illegitimate group,' Mrs Sechrest said. Her soft southern drawl did not disguise her anger. 'I suppose Sandy has fled to Canada as well. With the help of the local abolitionists.' She uttered the final word as though it was an obscenity.

'It is neither moral nor just to own another person,' Lydia said, speaking for the first time. 'And you would know that if you were a true Christian.'

For a moment, Rees thought Charlotte Sechrest would spring across the short amount of space separating them and slap Lydia.

Lydia must have thought so as well. She clenched her fists and straightened up, daring the other woman to make the attempt. Although calm by nature, Lydia maintained a number of strongly held views. And, despite her faith, she did not always subscribe to turning another cheek. Rees wagered his wife would win this encounter, even if it became a physical altercation.

Mrs Sechrest realized she could not bully Lydia and stepped back. 'I will be most happy to leave this primitive outpost of civilization,' she said. 'And especially glad to say farewell to this district's rude and unlawful inhabitants.'

'We are even happier to see your back,' Rees said honestly.

With a contemptuous sniff, Mrs Sechrest turned her back on them and minced toward the front door. Her carriage waited outside in the street. No one spoke until they heard the door slam.

The tension immediately subsided. 'Where's Thomas?' Rees asked, looking around.

'You don't know?' Rouge asked. Both Rees and Lydia shook their heads. 'He is visiting that girl you have staying with you.'

'Annie?' Rees asked.

'I think that's her name.' Rouge eyed Rees. 'It looks as though we will become family within a not too distant future.'

'That doesn't mean we have to get along.' It was the only thing Rees could think of to say.

AUTHOR'S NOTE

Abolition and the Underground Railroad:
By the end of the American Revolution all of the Northern states had abolished slavery or made provision to do so. (The United States abolished the slave trade in 1808.) However, fugitives could and were returned to the Southern states per the Fugitive Slave Act (see below). The first act of 1793 was strengthened in the 1850 revision. One of the elements most annoying to Northerners was the three-fifths rule that counted every five slaves as three people and therefore gave the slave states much more representation in Congress. Although there were abolitionists prior to 1850, the revised law caused a tremendous increase in people who identified as anti-slavery.

The term Underground Railroad did not come into common use until the construction of actual railroads became widespread. An abolitionist newspaper published a cartoon in 1844 that pictured a rail car packed with fugitives heading for Canada. Use of 'conductor' and other railroad terms came into broader use after the 1850 law.

Fugitive Slave Act:
I did not exaggerate the effect of the Fugitive Slave Law of 1793. Not only were escaped people subject to recapture, anyone who obstructed the slave takers were considered in violation of the law. Moreover, any child born to an enslaved mother was also considered to be enslaved. The prevailing custom was one drop of black blood meant that person was considered black, no matter how light-skinned. And the slave takers frequently took any person of color, born free or not, for sale in the South. Occasionally, white children were stolen as well.

Rees and Lydia were disobeying the law and could have been heavily fined or jailed.

The full text of the Act is available from the Library of Congress (and online) in the *Annals of Congress of the 2nd Congress,*

2nd Session, during which the proceedings and debates took place from November 5, 1792 to March 2, 1793.

The appropriate sections are 3 and 4.

This law was further strengthened in 1850 at the request of the slave states.

Smallpox:

The initial symptoms were similar to the flu, Covid-19 and many other viral diseases: fever, muscle pain, fatigue and headache. Before the distinctive rash erupted, small reddish spots appeared on mucous membranes of the mouth, tongue, and throat. The characteristic skin rash formed within two days after the reddish spots on the mucous membranes. The rash was formed of pustules with a dot (that became filled with fluid) in the center. These spots scabbed over and then the scabs fell off, usually resulting in scarring.

The origin of smallpox is unknown although the theory says the virus developed in certain African rodents 60,000 or so years ago. The earliest evidence of human illness dates to the third century BCE with Egyptian mummies. It is a lethal disease with a fatality rate for the ordinary kind of about thirty percent. Higher among babies. One figure I read was one in twelve died from the disease. The Malignant and Hemorrhagic forms are over ninety percent fatal. Occurring in outbreaks, it killed hundreds of thousands, including at least six monarchs in Europe. In the twentieth century it is estimated to have killed 300 million alone. As recently as 1967, fifteen million cases occurred worldwide.

By the eighteenth century, attempts to create immunity had already begun. Variolation, a process by which matter from an active case of smallpox was transferred to a healthy person, was already being practiced.

Although the disease tended to be less severe and less fatal, some people still died.

Edward Jenner is popularly believed to have discovered that milkmaids who had contracted cowpox, a much less serious disease, did not come down with smallpox. In the legend, he was inspired by a milkmaid but there is evidence he was influenced by a friend, John Fewster, who had already begun experimenting with cowpox. Vaccinations with cowpox had already been attempted by a Dorset farmer, Benjamin Jesty, who had inoculated his family in 1774. (I am indebted to *BBC History Magazine*, Vol 21, no 5, p.17. for this information.)

Jenner began a trial and proved that inoculation with cowpox prevented smallpox.

Later, the vaccine was made of the killed virus. In Great Britain, Russia and the United States vaccination was practiced. It was not universal. My father contracted smallpox as a toddler and lived to tell the tale. I am old enough to remember my own smallpox vaccination and still bear the scar on my upper arm.

A concerted global effort to eradicate smallpox succeeded with the last naturally occurring case in 1977. (The last death was in 1978. A researcher contracted the disease from a research sample.) WHO officially certified the eradication of smallpox in 1980.

Presidential Election of 1800:
In the beginning of the new country, the United States of the America, there were no political parties. Presidential elections were established so that the man (and it always was a wealthy, white man) with the most votes won the presidency. The individual with the second-most number of votes became the vice president. For the first two elections, George Washington won easily after running, essentially, unopposed.

In 1796, however, the deficiencies of this plan became obvious. John Quincy Adams won the most votes; Thomas Jefferson the second most. So, Adams was elected president and Jefferson became his vice president. The views of these two men were diametrically opposed. Besides that, they could not stand one another. In the election of 1800, the problem was solved when each man chose a party. John Quincy Adams ran as a Federalist, akin to the Republican party of today. Jefferson ran as a Republican, a party similar to the Democrats. The quotes I include in the story are accurate; those quotes and the partisan vitriol were widely reported in the contemporary newspapers of the time.

Shakers:
The United Society of Believers in Christ's Second Appearing (more commonly known as the Shakers) was founded by a

woman, Ann Lee, in England in 1747. It was, in a way, the evangelical arm of the Quakers. (The name Shakers comes from 'Shaking Quakers'.) The sect arrived in New York in 1774.

A celibate faith, they espoused egalitarian ideals and women enjoyed equal status with men, serving in governance and spiritual roles. Like the Quakers, the Shakers were pacifists and abolitionists.

The Shakers did develop a large and successful herb business. In the millennia before antibiotics and other medicines, mankind relied on herbaceous plants. The English colonists brought their own herbal lore with them and learned of other, New World plants, from the Native Americans.

At first, the Shakers planted medicinal plants to treat their own people, but as outside demand grew, so did the herb gardens. The Shakers did not sell only to people nearby, the herb business was truly international, with pounds of various herbs shipped overseas. In today's money, the business would be valued at more than ten million dollars per year.

Dr Ned Burke:
The medical school in Edinburgh was the center of medical, and specifically anatomical study, in the early nineteenth century. Obtaining cadavers was difficult. Scottish law required that the corpses used for research should come from those who died in prison, from suicide or were foundlings or orphans. The demand led to a shortfall.

This led to a string of murders in 1828. I named Dr Ned after one of the murderers, William Burke, who with his partner William Hare, murdered sixteen people and sold the corpses.

Policing:
The first modern professional police force was established in 1829 in London; the Metropolitan Police Force. Prior to that, policing, which began as a system of voluntary constables and watchmen, was a patchwork of voluntary and paid security. The idea of a professional police force was just beginning to be considered in Rees's lifetime. In 1737, King George II began paying some London and Middlesex watchmen with tax money and in 1749 Henry Fielding organized the Bow Street Runners,

a somewhat professional group financed by rewards. That system was ripe for abuse and scandals tainted the Runners.

In the United States, the Marshals Service was established in 1789. Philadelphia established the first city police force in 1752; Richmond, Virginia followed suit in 1807 and Boston in 1838. Modern policing in the United States did not really develop until the mid-nineteenth century and was based on the 1829 law in Great Britain.